Tantara

Catherine Taylor
www.catherinetaylorbooks.com,
Middletown, Ohio, 45042, United States

Cover by thecoverartisan.com

For my children: James, Jessica, Victoria and Michael

Table of Contents

CHAPTER ONE

"Dad's here, just like he said he would be," Andrew yelled to his sister, who stood toward the end of the hall of the sprawling brick suburban ranch.

"What do you mean Dad is here? No one bothered to inform me!" his mother responded in exasperation. Cathren stood draped in her worn robe, her morning hair uncombed.

Her nerve endings yearned for the morning shot of French pressed coffee. She'd felt the need for caffeine the moment her eyes had opened, well before dawn, which she took to be a bad omen for the coming day. The unwelcome ex-husband who just arrived on her doorstep confirmed her dread. She hated that gut feeling on rare occasions informing her that staying in bed would be the preferred option, the only way to see her safely through the day. Today it was not possible. She had pulled her middle-aged runner's frame upright this morning, forcing her to ponder the unknown, rocky landscape ahead.

"Mom, you know Dad always goes into work late the first day of school so he can see us off," Andrew muttered while stuffing his backpack with snacks.

"Just chill, will ya'? Mom, really! Andrew called Dad last night to see if he planned to stop in this morning." Marisa exited the bathroom, spewing a fog of hairspray and choking every living creature in the household, cat included.

"Please! It is the first day of school. Besides, he's already here. Mom!" Marisa screamed as she turned her attention to her brother. "Look at Andrew! You said those snacks were for both of us and they are to last the entire school week. Look, he's stuffed all of them in his backpack. Hand half of those over or I'll make your life miserable the rest of the week. You A1 brat!" Marisa smacked her bother on the back of the head, sending him into a screaming fit.

"Great! Andrew, you only need one or two snacks for lunch today. Put the rest back on the kitchen counter. And you guys need to tell me the next time you invite anyone! Marisa, touch your brother again like that and you will be grounded for an entire week, and you know I mean it," Cathren scolded, trying to gain control of her morning and to remember not to let Nate get the better of her as she usually would.

Andrew ran to the entry, opening the door for his father, sending the morning into further disaster.

"Mommmm! It's not like he's a stranger!" Marisa's voice quivered with tears. She threw her hands in the air while heading toward one of the doors in the hall. She carefully orchestrated her teenage door slamming technique she had recently developed for when life suddenly fell apart, which was apparently nearly a dozen times daily.

"How's my boy? Come over here and give your Dad a big hug," Nate asked Andrew, while stepping over the threshold. Andrew threw himself into this father's arms. "My, don't you look like a grown man today. You are all of it, my son. Where's my princess?" Nate asked, turning his head toward the end of the house where Marisa would normally be minutes before leaving for school.

"She just headed toward the bathroom so she can paint a ton of make-up all over her face for her new boyfriend!" Andrew shouted.

Andrew knew she was within earshot and was clearly content that his comment would dig under her skin. It was the rightful revenge a sister deserved after she squealed about the extra snacks he tried to abscond with.

Nate tried to avoid turning his eyes toward Cathren, but he was unable to keep from doing so. She was just a magnet for his being. His emotions still shook at the sight of her. He struggled with the same emotions each time she entered a room he found himself in. He had dealt with it for the more than twenty-five years he had known and loved her. Still, in her middle-age years she could still give the drop-dead look that would only drive him closer to her sensuous aura. Nate, those many years ago, knew that one single look from her would send him enveloped with closeness in one moment most women could not endow during an entire lifetime of tries. There had been fierce competition for her and at the time felt he could never win her, but he had to try. For him she had it all. She perfected that look in their college years when he first placed her in his sight at that hangout in one of the old haunts in Oxford, Ohio. He'd stood in that upstairs bar, surrounded in a sea of peanut shells that covered the floor; when eighteen-year-olds could legally drink all the three-two percent beer they could handle, where it flowed freely out the doors onto the streets and throughout the campus.

For Nate, to remember standing there so many years ago as he stood here now, killed him inside. He knew positively she still had it all and he had ruined their life together. Her worn chenille robe still outlined her as well as he remembered it doing when he still lived in this house. And there she was with that annoying cup of coffee she toted around till noon each day. He could not help it. He still loved her so.

She shot him that familiar, dreaded glance. Bulleting it from her eyes, she quickly cut him off at the knees, and his heart dropped to the floor. She let him realize she was not pleased at his intrusion and presence. He, the stranger, was not welcome. Nate had hoped otherwise. He knew she would offer him a cup of coffee in her next sentence to show how civil she could be when put to the task, to cover her hostility for the sake of the children.

On that fateful night of years past, Cathren had let her eyes drift to the direction of the bar staircase where Nate first appeared in her life. She knew then he would be hers. Nate had staggered comically through the two inch deep peanut shells the bar owner let accumulate on the floor, back to his pitcher of three-two beer at the booth near hers. The lingering three-two buzz from prior pitchers left him unable to refrain from dropping long stares toward the booth where she and her friends sat. She knew that very moment the number of children they would have and the beginning of their wedding guest list. During that Oxford evening, she planned their life together, but not before she chose to ignore and torture him through the coming spring.

By then, he knew her class schedule and would pass her casually on the wooded campus, gathering the nerve to say more than hello to her, which often caused him to be late for classes. She instinctively let him hang by her baited hook through the summer months without letting him know her vacation plans, or the plans for their lives together, for that matter. She ensured his suffering till he could find her when classes resumed that fall. That was when she knew it was safe to give him the time of day, and it was assured the dagger she sent through his veins would be so fully penetrated he would never recover from the wounds. Despite all that had passed between them, though they were now apart, she knew she still owned him.

"Fresh coffee in the kitchen. Help yourself while I finish packing Andrew's lunch," Cathren told him in a nonchalant manner.

"I can see the bus turning onto the street two blocks from ours. It will be here in a couple minutes," Andrew yelled, peering out the front window. "Jimmy is already standing outside waiting for the bus."

"Here's your lunch, Andrew. Marisa! You are going to miss the bus if you don't get out here," Cathren told them. Marisa ran from the hall to grab her backpack, gave her father a kiss on the cheek, smiled, then flew out the door behind Andrew.

"Bye, be careful at school today," her father called. "Remember, I love you always, guys."

"Is there any way you could be here when we get home tonight?" Marisa yelled to him.

"We will see, pumpkin," he told her. Cathren rolled her eyes, and Nate saw them roll.

Marisa climbed the bus steps and promptly sat with her best friend. Andrew found his friends.

"Do you mind if I finish that cup of coffee?" Nate asked, trying not to let his voice shake at his request.

"Not in the least," she lied, muttering through her fake smile. She did not want her ex drinking his morning coffee in their former home. She decided to be diplomatic for the children, though they had already left for school. There was really no reason to be civil now, but why continue the bad start of a day and let the kids feel the vibes in the evening, she thought.

"I won't take long. I know you are busy with the shop." Nate nervously smiled back, reminding her of one of the reasons she did not want him alone in her house. That smile, apologetic for the pain he had caused, still managed to annoy her, along with the fear of a meltdown that could cause her to fall back into their marriage mode. They both knew the possibility of this despite her lingering anger toward him.

She forced another fake smile at his comment.

Nate picked up his cup, continuing to drink his coffee only as an excuse to keep his foot back in the door to tell her what was on his mind. "I couldn't sleep after the blackout last evening. I was worried about you and the children."

"I haven't heard the news this morning. Was it the result of another bombing?" Cathren asked Nate.

"A bomb was thrown into a substation again and the electricity was out most of the night. Luckily, this bomb didn't do quite the damage the last one did. Repair crews were able to get the substation up and running before the morning rush hour. Just a few patients had to be rushed to another hospital because of the outage. It sure beats the last time when hundreds of patients had to be moved to Cincinnati. Then there was the two-week wait before the electricity came back to that area. Several of the patients died before they could get medical help in another city. Such a shame. That still really bothers me," he told her.

"I don't understand why someone would do such a thing that would cost lives of innocent people," Cathren told him. "Considering that sort of loss to other families, I shouldn't complain having to throw away all my frozen and refrigerated foods after the last blackout. I am prepared for the next long power outage."

"There wasn't as much fighting in the streets this time. The authorities seem to think this bombing wasn't planned well by the gangs. It seems the biggest street battles take place during the blackouts because the outage is usually a message for gangs to start the usual turf wars," Nate told her. "Listen, Cat, you don't have to keep that shop open if you don't want to. I worry about you on the streets with the way things are going. What would the kids do if something happened to you? There is the farm. You could stay at your grandfather's farm in Kentucky that you now own." Nate could tell by Cathren's tightening lips he had irritated her. He was pushing again. He lowered his tone and the pressure when he saw her delicate frame tense beneath her robe.

"We've been through this a dozen times already. You know how I feel," Cathren harped. "Let's just skip the subject. Shall we?"

"I know, and I'm sorry for bringing it up again. I really don't want to argue. I am sorry if it sounds that way. I just worry so much. The offer will always stand for me to help get you there. Okay? I do mean well. I do care. Listen. It's getting late. I better leave before I upset you further."

Nate's jaw clenched. Frustrated and embarrassed, he walked into the kitchen and his

12

shaking hand placed his cup in the sink and then he approached Cathren before she had time to react. Smoothly, he brought his hands to her shoulders, pulling her to him, kissing her. Cathren's robe shuffled loose from her shoulders, falling to the cleavage of her breasts, reminding Nate how much he still loved her and how much he missed her body against his. An unpremeditated move prompted his hands to glide softly down from her shoulders to her arms.

"I didn't mean to make you uncomfortable. I'll always love you, Cat, and I would do anything to change the past. I'm sorry. You've been so good through all this. You are a wonderful mother. The best any child could have. We managed to get Seth into a great college in a small town situated away from large cities, all for his safety, but you are still coping here. I'll do what I can to help you get out of here if things get too bad."

Cathren's eyes rose to meet his, so close his warm breath tickled her neck before his lips brushed against hers. The light touch of their bodies became firm. Her robe slid further from her shoulders.

She had nearly forgotten the tenderness his hands could emit. It was the tenderness that summarily sent a shocking need for him throughout her body. His lips fully covered hers; eliciting memories of how many ways he could please her, reminding her that he could always satisfy her. She slid her hands under his jacket and around his waist, and then upward to his shoulders so she could feel the strength of him. She could barely breathe for the wanting of him. The need caused her consciousness to focus into oneness of the two. She grew weakened by his invisible stronghold while he engulfed her senses and spun them into a fierce desire. She did not remember unbuttoning his shirt. It came so naturally for her to do so. She felt the flesh of his chest against her breasts and knew she could willingly drown in her lust for him. His hands smoothed to underneath her breasts. He gently held them, caressing their softness and brushing his lips against them. He lifted his eyes to hers, and for a gentle moment it was just the two of them together again, as it was meant to be. Her eyes swooned in his. He could die at the thought of all the love he held for her. Then her eyes blinked, and he read them. She remembered why they were no longer together. He knew the moment was over.

Cathren pulled from him. "Listen, Nate. I think you have to leave. I didn't mean for this to happen. Just go, please."

He came from behind and placed his arms around her.

"I mean it, Nate. I am sorry. I can't help but see her with you when…" She left the sentence unfinished. She mustered confidence. "Please go. Please go now!"

"Cat, I just don't know what to say. I know you want me, and I want you. I just thought we were getting past all this. Can't we just get past this thing?"

"I can't do this. I can't deal with her trying to take my life and you letting her. And I can't forget your enjoying it, with her!" she said, turning to him. "Just leave, please."

"I will. No problem. We'll talk later. Can I stop by this evening? I really promise not to let this happen this evening. I am sorry. I have a surprise for Andrew and Marisa. Will they be here around seven o'clock?" Nate asked as he turned to exit through the garage door from the kitchen, a habit he had not been able to break even though he no longer lived there. Cathren directed him to the front door with her index finger.

"They will be doing their homework," Cathren answered without emotion.

"If you would rather not have me stop by this evening, I won't," Nate held his face down shamefully at the rift he caused.

"Okay with me. Andrew and Marisa will want to talk about the first day of school with you. I want what is best for them," Cathren told him, wishing he would leave because their conversation would only grow more stressful the longer it continued.

"Thanks, Cat. I didn't mean to push you just now. Sorry." Nate told her, turning to make a quick exit.

"I know," she told him. "Old habits die hard."

"Old habits?" He laughed, then waved bye while opening the door. He shut it softly as if not to finalize their visit together with an irritating slam, as he had done many times during the last rocky moments of their marriage. She watched his SUV pull onto the street to leave her. She yearned for him to come back to her so she could feel the warmth of his flesh against her again.

Cathren shuffled to the front door and pounded as hard as her fists would allow.

"Oh damn, I need sex. Life minus sex when you need it is pure hell, just pure hell. I am just going to start this day over again by soaking in a tub full of hot, steamy water to relieve this tension. Help me. I need sex." She drew the water, then leisurely slid into the tub, forcing her stress to lift from around her listless body and rise with the steam to the vaulted ceiling of her bath. Her breasts touched the surface of the water. Cathren was pleased that her breasts were full-shaped into middle age. She had worked hard to keep her body well-toned through her years, and such diligence and commitment to her program with her former personal trainer had paid off. It was just one of many luxuries that bit the dust upon her and Nate's divorce.

She rested her head on the back of the tub to try and soak away the morning. When she was near a slumber, the unconscious splash of her right hand in bath waters shook her into reality. She contemplated the work she would accomplish with the children back in school. The formal schooling they received now was part-time at the church just blocks away. The rest of their schooling was at home, as the public schools were no longer safe to send children to, though many still did attend them. The combination part-time private schooling and homeschooling allowed the best of both for the children. When the streets were not safe, a supplemental program with their teachers' conferencing online via computer kept the children up to date with their studies. Teachers could teach from their homes when the streets were not safe.

Since the divorce, Cathren had worked hard to make ends meet. The small antique shop in a quaint little town just a few miles from her home had provided a means of survival over the past year. Her shop consisted mostly of weekend shoppers browsing through the historical district of small specialty shops and restaurants. Cathren spent most weekdays preparing for weekenders looking to buy at her shop of antiques, home decorating items and essentials.

On summer weekdays, Cathren had to drag Andrew with her to purchase supplies and merchandise. It took bribes for him to cooperate with her daily work routine of driving around the city. Standing in line for pick-ups and sending deliveries wasn't a young man's idea of a summer vacation, but it was necessary for the survival of the family.

The shop would never make the family well-to-do, but it added to the child support, and Cathren managed enough income to pay her bills. The shop had also helped her maintain her sanity through the dark days engulfed by the loneliness of the divorce. She grew better when she finally accepted the end of her marriage and the humiliation of having a middle-aged husband who had nursed a teenage-type crush on the new twenty-seven-year-old associate at the office. Now she could only laugh in the face of her former pain when she remembered how Nate would make any excuse to leave their home and Cathren's company, practically tripping over himself to fly out the door to be with his newfound love.

In the beginning, Cathren was devastated to know her husband could barely wait to leave to be with someone else. At the time, Cathren had been willing to do anything to save her doomed marriage, but all attempts were futile. Nate's entire being had been so absorbed by his lover that it left no room for communication between him and Cathren. Nate's friends saw his future and tried to reason with him, telling him the heated moment of the affair would pass and he would be left without a home, a wife, or his children. They all failed to burst the dream bubble that surrounded him, to warn him of what indeed would happen. It had taken a great deal of counseling between Cathren and Nate to maintain civility for the sake of the children. Nate ended the relationship when he found out he wasn't the only one having an affair with his girlfriend. Seemed she enjoyed the company of other married well established men, too. Cathren got the last laugh, but it had been a sad one for her and the children.

Nate had found reality too late to save his marriage, but decided he would, nevertheless, remain faithful from then on to Cathren in hopes that someday she would see he was truly remorseful about the damage he caused. It was obvious he was trying to repair their relationship as best as possible, considering the circumstances he created between them. He would not have lunch alone with a member of the opposite sex that could give an impression of any sort that anything more than mere friendship could be at hand in the eyes of the public. Cathren respected his commitment, but she was still empty from the betrayal. Besides her sexual attraction for Nate, other feelings were either dead or deeply hidden within herself, unable to be tapped to rebuild their life and love for one another again.

Cathren styled her lengthy hair, dressed in business casual pants, slipped on her loafers, and finished another cup of coffee before leaving for a meeting with a supplier. She now tried to plan several months in advance for delivery of stock so she would not be caught without merchandise again, as she had during the street trouble all through California last spring.

At one point during that particular crisis, gangs cut off the main highways so well that fresh fruit, vegetables, and consumer goods could not leave that state for an entire month for grocers in her region to sell to their customers. It was the same for the dry goods she needed for her shop. The backlog left Cathren without enough merchandise for the business needed to pay bills on time. She vowed that would not happen again.

The crisis also had a ripple effect across the nation, causing other disturbances, but finally the gangs were forced to retreat and life tried to get back to normal. When the calamity ended, deliveries returned to normal. The economy tried to recover. No one expected a situation like that to occur again. All state governors and the President agreed to work together to keep a state of affairs like that from happening again. The government promised to keep the highways open, but Cathren was doubtful. Placing her shop in a better position for the future was important to her survival.

She grabbed her jacket from the closet, picked up her van keys, and opened the garage door. She forgot the hand gun that she was just getting used to carrying and went back into the house to retrieve it. She knew it was illegal for her to carry a concealed weapon without a permit but figured, so what? There were just too many robberies, beatings, rapes, and killings in the city each day. Cathren wasn't about to become a victim without a good fight. She, like millions of other women across the nation, took lessons on the proper way to handle a firearm, and she carried her own protection when she left her home. Law or no law, she had learned to protect herself. Screw the self-righteous who felt no one should own a handgun. She had once been one of those people, but had done a quick turnaround. She vowed to protect herself and her family if need be. She had seen so many killing sprees and robberies across the country that could have been stopped if someone would have had a handgun. The empty, cold steel made her nervous but comfortable in the same notion. She needed the gun for her protection.

Cathren now would not consider being without a gun by her side, no less than her family would have several generations ago as they floated down the Ohio River on canoes and flatboats. To Cathren, and many others, these times were no less dangerous, particularly since there were so many underground gun factories selling to the criminal element, leaving innocent citizens without defense. The good intentions of the recent anti-gun laws on the books had done nothing but disarm honest, law-abiding citizens and create a rampant criminal element that now ravaged the nation from coast-to-coast.

The ringing phone startled Cathren as she checked to make sure the chamber was empty before loading her piece. "Cat? This is Nate."

In a monotone voice Cathren answered, "Yes," wishing she had checked the caller ID and not picked up.

"Would it be possible for us to meet for lunch around one today?" he asked her.

"I have too many errands to run. I don't think I can fit that in." Cathren smiled in a way that said "touché" as she answered Nate's question.

"I really would like to take some time to talk in a neutral setting, if that would be all right with you. I promise not to make you feel uncomfortable. We need to talk." He sounded desperate.

"Make it one-thirty at Patricia's Coffee House on the east side of town. I'll be in that area. It will have to be a short lunch. I have an appointment not long after that. Okay?" Cathren asked.

"Cat? I want you to know I have come to accept that I can only hope we can become good friends again. I know it is too much to ask to try and pull our marriage together. I know there wasn't anything more important to you than our family, and I destroyed that." Nate told her. "I accept your feelings and I will never try to push you into a deeper relationship again. I was so wrong to cross boundaries this morning. I'll keep clear of that because I do not wish to jeopardize what civility you manage toward me now. I am thankful for your letting me have a part in the children's lives as much as you have. I don't deserve the consideration or time you have let me spend with them in our home, rather your home. You were able to see to their interests through all my foolishness. My regrets are the deepest of any that can be felt and my deep sorrow is a reminder each minute of the day."

"Thanks. I wouldn't use the children as a weapon against you. At this point, I just try to remember the good times and let go of the bitterness for my own well-being. Listen, I do have to go now or I will not be able to make it for lunch. Bye," she said, hanging up the phone before he had a chance to say good-bye. Cathren felt a pang of guilt at having cut the conversation short but she did not need to be dragged down by Nate for a second time during the morning hours.

CHAPTER TWO

"Damn it! I'm fifteen minutes late. This traffic is terrible. Great! That restaurant parking lot is packed," Cathren muttered to herself as she pulled her van into a parking space at the far end of the lot. She managed to wedge the van in a space much too small, and she was so close to the cars on either side of her that the drivers would surely be irritated when trying to back out of their parking places. She locked the van and hurried into the restaurant without thinking to touch up her makeup or do a quick fix for her hair.

"I'm supposed to meet a Nate Billiter for lunch. I'm a few minutes late, could you show me our table, please?" Cathren asked the host.

"Mr. Billiter did make reservations but he has not arrived yet. Would you like to be seated?"

"Yes, thank you," Cathren returned. "Could you have my waiter bring coffee to the table while I am waiting for Mr. Billiter?"

Forty-five minutes and three cups of coffee later, she was feeling like a fool for being stood up by Nate. Cathren grew irate, but then she thought she was too hard on him and too quick to judge. It was not like him to not show for an appointment.

"I am really sorry for holding your table for so long," Cathren told the waiter and decided to leave, paying the bill and leaving good gratuity to compensate for the tip money the waiter lost during the busy lunch hours of the day.

"This is for the coffee. Keep the change. Is there a pay phone here I could use? My cell phone is on the blink." The waiter pointed to the phone in the corner near the entrance of the restaurant. Cathren dialed Nate's office to sarcastically thank him for letting her sit alone for so long. Nate's secretary frantically answered the phone.

"Canter and Associates. How may I help you?"

"Sharon, this is Cathren. I'm at a restaurant on the other side of town. Nate was supposed to meet me, but he didn't show. I need to let him know that I am leaving the restaurant because I have another appointment in half an hour. I am not pleased at his forgetting our lunch date!"

"Cathren! I've been trying to get a hold of you. No one knew where you were. I've been trying your cell phone to no avail for the last forty-five minutes."

"I left it in the van yesterday, so it is uncharged. I am trying to not use it much until it is fully charged again. Why were you trying to call me? Is it the children?" Cathren sounded frantic at the thought that something could be wrong with the children.

"No! It is Nate. He's had a horrible accident and you need to get to the hospital. The hospital staff called here and wanted me to notify next of kin and I'm not getting anywhere. Nate told them to call his wife. He was unable to talk on a phone. Something must be terribly wrong."

"Sharon, I'm on my way now. I'll get back to you when I find out what the problem is. Is anyone from the office at the hospital?" Cathren asked.

"Stew left as soon as we heard about Nate. I patched the call through to Stew, but he dropped the office phone after a few seconds of talking to the other party and ran out the door. No one could find out what happened. Stew isn't answering his cell phone. Oh, Cathren, I am so worried," Sharon cried. Sharon and Cathren had become friends through the years of her working relationship with Nate. The two always had great respect for one another. Sharon had asked Nate repeatedly to abandon his past behavior that destroyed his marriage, teetering constantly on the edge of being an employee under Nate on one hand and a friend giving unwanted advice on the other. Nate and Cathren were family to Sharon, and Sharon virtually an aunt to their children.

"I am going to call the hospital now. In the meantime, keep me posted if you hear anything. I will keep my cell phone on and near me," Cathren told her.

Cathren dialed the hospital, trying to get information about Nate, but the blackout the night before had left many injuries from street fighting, so hospital lines were busy.

Trying to find parking near the hospital was nearly as difficult as trying to get through by phone. She called to cancel her other appointment. The parking garage was full, as were the surrounding street-side parking sites, leaving her to park several blocks from the hospital building. Crowds of casually dressed onlookers, along with professionally-clothed reporting crews from area radio and television stations, loitered on surrounding sidewalks. It was nearly the run of a gauntlet to enter the hospital.

Smells of an overcrowded hospital during war addressed each visitor upon entrance into a place where many were born and where many would probably die today. The halls were filled with the injured trying to find where they should be for treatment. Cathren shuddered before she was directed to where she could get information about Nate.

She felt sorry for the person at the desk. His eyes showed he was tired of giving bad news throughout the morning. He informed her that time was of the essence. Being escorted to another door confirmed what she had been told. An attendant hurried her through the opening toward the area of the operating room. Cathren suddenly turned to the corner of the room where she caught sight of Nate's best friend. Stew sat crying alone in a corner. Cathren had never seen Stew in tears through the years of their friendship. Stew turned his eyes upward toward the motion of someone nearing him. He crumbled at the sight of Cathren. She could do nothing but run the few final steps to his side.

"Cathren, you're here. Nate, oh my God, Nate," Stew cried aloud.

"What is going on?" she asked.

"Nate just left the office to meet you for lunch. He said he needed to pick up something for the kids on the way to meet you. He bought them a new computer yesterday and wanted to tell you first. He was so excited and happy when he left, but I could also tell something was really bothering him. He seemed uneasy. He was going to stop at the bank to withdraw some cash to buy computer games. Nate was getting cash because he didn't want to risk the store computers being down when he made purchases, and he wanted to buy the games before this evening. Guess they must have been watching to see who came out of the bank," cried Stew.

"What are you talking about? What do you mean watching?" she asked.

Stew's face turned crimson. He thought Cathren already knew. His stomach grew hard, and his sickened state found him falling back into the chair directly behind him. His hysteria caused his words to drag themselves out between muffled sobs. Stew had to repeat much of what he tried to convey to Cathren so she could understand him.

"The men." He paused. "They were sitting in a car near the bank where Nate parked. Nate just happened to be in the wrong place at the wrong time. As soon as he approached his car, the three men came from behind and held a gun to his side," Stew shivered and rubbed his face continuing. "Nate was still conscious after the shooting. He told the police the thieves said they would not harm him if he cooperated. They demanded the cash he just withdrew from the bank. He removed his billfold from his pocket and handed it over. One of them grabbed the billfold and all three men ran to the getaway vehicle. Nate told police he felt safe at this point, but as the thieves pulled from the curb one of them pulled out a gun and proceeded to shoot four bullets into Nate's chest as they drove past him.

"Some pedestrians remembered the model of the vehicle and reported the license number, but the car was stolen early this morning. The authorities have no idea where to search for the assailants. This type of thing is happening so many times each day that police say those thieves will never be found and tried," Stew cried. Common knowledge said there was not enough time for police departments to meet the needs of everyone. Cities had budgets to stay within and, due to the economy, police funding was slashed along with everything else. This was how things were, and with no end in sight.

Nate's surgeon walked into the waiting room and introduced himself to Cathren. All words spoken seemed to echo and bounce inside without her fully understanding the impact of the information relayed to her. Numbness settled in her arms and spread rapidly through her chest, making it difficult for her to breathe. Cathren's esophagus tried to close, and her body turned numb at hearing what Stew informed her, anesthetizing itself from the damage this unwelcome news was causing.

"The operating rooms have been busy all day and there is one room nearly ready for Nate's surgery," the surgeon informed them. "Nate was still conscious when they brought him in and we were able to speak with him. He knows how serious this is and he realizes his chances are slim. Earlier he requested to see his wife, which I granted, considering the circumstances. Please make it short. We don't have much time left. His chances of survival are not great, for if they were I would have you wait to speak with him after the surgery. Each second counts. I do apologize if I sound harsh and crass. Please keep your prayers going for us, no matter how this day may end. We need all of them."

An assistant led Cathren and Stew to Nate's side. Cathren embraced Nate's hand and kissed him as he lay semi-conscious on the bed.

"Nate, it is Cathren. Can you hear me? If you can, give my fingers a little squeeze," Cathren commanded him. Miraculously, she felt a small squeeze. She responded, "Nate, Stew is here beside me."

"Hey, buddy. I plan to stick around this place until you are up and out of here. So, to save

27

the nurses a lot of grief, you better get through this and get well fast," Stew said, trying to joke as they always did. "I'll leave you two alone now. See you after surgery, Nate. Take care, buddy," Stew told him.

Tears covered Stew's face. He could no longer keep from sobbing, which forced him to abandon Cathren at Nate's bedside.

Cathren's spirit was much stronger than his. Stew, the tall, muscular man women still drooled over, a supposed tower of strength in the business world, was no match for the faith in God and inner strength that dwelled in Cathren's soul. Stew knew she would be good for Nate at this time. She could always be strong through the worst life could offer, he knew. Then he was out of there.

The operating room staff began wheeling Nate away from Cathren. She kept pace with his bed, pressing her lips to his, still holding his hand. Knowing this could be her last moment with him, Cathren pulled up words that had been left buried deeply in her heart.

"I still love you," she told him, and she kissed his lips. "Please make it through this. We need you."

The medical staff urgently maneuvered the apparatus on which Nate lay from the trembling woman he could never bring himself to divorce from his heart. A single tear clung onto Nate's cheek as he was taken away from the woman he had always loved.

CHAPTER THREE

Cathren sat drained of any emotion, unable to hear a word the pastor of her church was delivering for the memory of Nate and the comfort of his loved ones that cold, rainy morning. The surgeon's story of Nate's plight still pounded through her, running again and again through her heart and soul until she was certain madness had taken her to its quarters for the rest of eternity. Phrases like "Lungs filled with blood" and "damage to the heart resulting from the gunshot wound" along with "a miracle he didn't die right there on the street" echoed through her skull.

All this mixed with the sight of Stew running through and out of the hospital, screaming into the afternoon traffic during his own insanity.

Stew had suffered terribly before lapsing into the despairing hopelessness that pushed him into a near fatal move. He had dared any number of vehicles to run him down the moment his sense of self survival was lost in grief. A stranger pulled him off the street onto the sidewalk before an accident could occur, but still the events monopolized and paralyzed his life. Life without his dearest friend was unthinkable to him. The unjustness of the incomprehensible past days racked each ounce of his physical body and soul to the point of no return. Each glance Stew made in the direction of Nate's fatherless children caused the pain of a sharp knife carving on his tumultuous soul. Stew sat empty and lifeless, bled thoroughly of any desire for an existence. He just wanted to die.

Nate's parents caught the first flight from their home in Florida but were not able to tell their son good-bye before he left them. They could only leave this Ohio nightmare and fly back to where they came from so they could pretend the episode never happened and try and convince themselves that they had merely had the same bad dream between them.

Friends drove to the university to break the news to Nate's oldest son, Seth. Already distraught about his sad relationship with his father since the separation of his parents, having the future stolen that was needed to repair their father-son relationship made Seth resentful. Seth's friend and confidant, Susan, came with Seth and stayed with the Billiter family for days to help Seth and his siblings cope with their loss, becoming the pillar of strength where Cathren could not go.

Cathren peered into Andrew's bedroom.

"Andrew, I haven't seen Marisa since we left the service this morning. I thought she went to her room for a nap. Do you know where she is?" She asked.

"She said she was going to Bonnie's house to watch a movie. Bonnie's mom and dad went to visit a relative over the weekend," a despondent Andrew told his mother.

She responded, "Thanks." She softly turned back toward the kitchen.

"Did you find Marisa?" Seth asked.

"Andrew told me she went to Bonnie's to watch a movie. I think she really just wanted to get away from all this for a while. I hope she is all right. It has been hours since I talked with her. I suppose Bonnie will call if Marisa has a rough time of it. I will find the number and call them anyway," Cathren told him.

"Since it is just a short walk around the corner, I'll check to see how she is. Susan, would you like to go along for a walk?" Seth asked.

"No. I think I'll stay here and be company for Andrew," Susan told him. Susan had passed Andrew's room just minutes before and heard the whimpering. After the shooting, he could be seen running to Cathren's arms because he was unable to comprehend why someone would gun down his daddy for a billfold with little money. Andrew's nightmares began the day Nate was murdered, leaving Cathren feeling more helpless. Andrew tried putting up a brave manly front for his mother but was miserable at it. Now he seemed to turn to Susan for friendship. His playmates had not an inkling of the pain he endured.

Seth, relieved to escape the mourning household for the few minutes it would take to find his sister, found the homes in his neighborhood unusually quiet, as if in mourning, too. A blanket silenced the families that dwelt within, woven of the loss of a friend along with the fear of being next to succumb to such circumstances and the unspoken thankfulness that it was someone else's family, not their own. All bore the grief on their street.

Early fall clouds preparing to usher in colder weather addressed the afternoon, and a chilly drizzle accompanied Seth to Marisa's friend's three-story, Tudor home around the corner. Fallen leaves covered the stone path to the doorbell that would announce his arrival.

"Oh my god, it is Marisa's big brother," Seth heard from the high-pitched teenaged squeal that vibrated through the home's exterior wall. Seth

31

had been proud of Marisa's courage for her family the past days. Seth knew Marisa never let go of her hopes of reuniting her family since her parents' divorce. He knew her dreams were broken and she was disheartened from the crushing weight she now carried.

It had been frustrating for Cathren that Marisa was always conniving to get her father back home for the least of reasons, but now Cathren was glad Marisa had been so persistent and headstrong in her determination. For this reason, they had been able to spend a good deal of time with Nate before he was gone.

Seth stood patiently at least three minutes before Bonnie and friends of Marisa slowly opened the doorway to ask him why he was there.

"I came to check on Marisa. Is she around?"

"Sure. She is watching a movie. Bye," one of the girls informed him, then tried to shut the door. Seth caught it before it latched shut. It didn't take much to figure out these adolescents were up to something.

"I just want to see her, to know she is all right," Seth told them as he held the door open far enough to catch a whiff of why the girls were trying so hard to rid him from their presence. Seth had just walked to the door of a house full of drunken teenage girls. "You girls having a bit of a party?"

They answered only giggles.

"Do you mind if I come in for a bit?" he asked.

"He's really cute, Marisa's brother," he heard whispered among them. He smiled to himself. "Let's let him in. This could turn into real fun." Seth shook his head, remembering sneaking into the stash of alcohol his friends' parents thought they kept well-locked during his teenage years. The door pulled open to the fifteen or so giggling adolescent females.

Coolly, Seth leaned against the door and gave his best "I am more mature than you" grin to gain the confidence of the young females in order find his sister.

"Looks like you girls are having a pretty good time. How are things back in the old neighborhood, anyway?"

More alcohol-enhanced giggles filled the entrance hall.

"Got a beer to spare?" Seth asked. Six of the girls stumbled to the direction of the wet bar, leaving the rest to semi-guard the doorway briefly before letting him in. One of the girls locked the door behind him once he was able to slide inside. All of them smiled as if they just caught the only male left on earth. Seth understood Marisa was probably soused somewhere in the Tudor and it would be best to play along and find her while he pretended to be social and answered questions about campus life and such.

Knowing the layout of every house in the neighborhood helped him with the scavenger hunt for his sister. He drifted from the living room that housed Bonnie's parent's antique furniture to the dining area and the kitchen, where stacks of dirty dishes and spoiled food lay on the counters. Conner, the family sheepdog asleep under the dinette, was too full from the feast found on the floor the past several days to wake up and alarm the household of Seth's presence. Seth meandered to the room housing the large, up-to-date television where the latest rock idols splashed across the screen before the empty couch and chairs placed strategically around it. One by one, Marisa's friends slid into the television room, some a ripe fifteen that could pass for twenty-one and no doubt did occasionally at a local bar or two with their fake IDs.

The girls exchanged glances, trying to decide whether they had just let an enemy or an ally pass through the front door. Seth understood the caution that floated around the room. He sat, pretending to watch the screen before him. The girls stood calmed, then went about their conversations about love, makeup, and fashion. A few minutes passed before Seth felt confident enough to ask where the nearest bathroom was, though he already knew the answer to his question. One of the visiting girls told him.

He rose from his seat and steered himself in the direction given. He found the door slightly ajar, but he was unable to open it freely. He peered through the crack in the door and found that a foot stopped him from opening the door. He squeezed his arm through the opening and moved the foot forward to see who was passed out on the floor. He was used to the sight and smell of vomit, a usual occurrence in dorm life, but the face of his sister groaning, unable to move her head from the puddle of puke she had made for herself, alarmed Seth. By now the attention of the young women turned to the bathroom. They were alarmed.

"Somebody get a couple rolls of paper towels. Looks like Marisa drank a bit more than she thought she could handle," Seth said calmly. Yes, he was angry with Marisa's friends for not watching her closely, but he did not dare show it. His air expressed the nonchalance of a university student in the dorm bathroom after a Saturday night.

"Bonnie. When are your parents due home?" Seth asked.

"About midnight."

"Well, let's see here," Seth mused. "It will probably take about that much time to clean this place up and make it presentable for your mom. You girls stick around and help me sober up Marisa so our mom doesn't find out she got drunk, and help Bonnie clean the house. You don't want your mom to walk in with the place trashed. I'll help clean, too." The comment made him an ally.

Having too much alcohol in their systems, the girls had not given the least thought to Bonnie's parents' arrival home. They looked at each other in total dumbstruck, drunken agreement. They were all in this together and would all go down together if their parents caught wind of their little party, especially since Marisa's condition scared them into reality.

"Listen," Seth told them. "I need to call home and tell them I'm going to hang out and finish watching this movie with Marisa." Half a dozen hands with the same color nail polish pointed in the direction of the nearest phone.

"Thanks," Seth told them. Susan answered, and Seth informed her of the predicament and asked Susan not to tell Cathren.

Bonnie found the sweeper and made sure it went its way through the rest of the house via the push of turn-taking teens. Dirty dishes were gathered off tables, from under beds, out of bathrooms, and off the patio. The house filled with working chatter. Dishes sat in the kitchen sink, soaking while awaiting their turn in the dishwasher. According to the girls with kitchen duty, the dishwasher ran much slower than the ones in their own homes. They did not realize it was just their own impatience and alarm at how soon Bonnie's parents would be home. Bonnie tried her hardest to arrange the liquor bottles in the cabinet as her parents had left them—that is, after she watered them to their former levels.

Fresh coffee had been brewed by two girls who had never so much attempted to brew a pot of coffee before. It was all they could think to do to sober their friends, especially Marisa. Several helped Marisa into a shower to wash the vomit from her hair and body. They dressed her as well as any group of drunken teens could dress a friend, then presented her to her brother, who took over the care of Marisa. Two hours later, the teen girls stood proud at the restored house and relieved at Marisa's somewhat canceled hangover. Their admiration for Seth grew without bounds at his heroism of taking charge and directing them through the lesson of the "cleaning up before the folks get back to the homestead" act, a lesson always passed from one generation of teens to the next.

Marisa's friends wrapped a woolen shawl around her shoulders as Seth helped her out the front door. The girls were saved.

CHAPTER FOUR

Stew's headache woke him with a vengeance. His head reeled from too much alcohol, and his stomach churned with an unbearable wrenching that caused him to lunge too late into the master bath. Stew's alcohol-induced stupor that managed to linger for a couple weeks required friends to hover around him twenty-four seven. Graveside good-byes added to the burden rather than giving the expected closure that sometimes comes after such a tragedy. The relief of moving on after the burial of Nate lacked with Stew. The funeral service ended, but it did not bring Stew closure. He could not be the support he wanted to be for Nate's surviving family and friends. Stew was unable to help console Nate's family. The consoling he intended from him to Cathren and her children was too much to bear.

Stew could only manage sobriety several weeks past the tragedy when he finally made arrangements for delivery of the new computer Nate had purchased for his children. Stew's sobriety took hold on the afternoon he knocked on the front door of Cathren's home with a computer desk for Marisa and Andrew's new computer along with games Nate had intended to buy. Stew bought them for the children, just as Nate planned the day he was taken from his family. Nate's children carried him through each unbearable day. They needed Stew but mostly he needed them.

Stew's appearance caused a shock for Cathren when he arrived for visits with her family, the visits that helped him hold onto reality. The stark contrast between Stew now and Stew when Nate introduced her to him during their campus days made Cathren cry at times. In years past, Stew's six-foot-three frame, warm blue eyes, and blond, shoulder-length hair towered over the crowds on campus, accenting his sinewy physique. His athletic scholarships, along with strong academics in business school, helped him gain the respect of Cathren. Stew had never lacked the attraction from the opposite sex that drew the envy of many of his close male friends. But none won the true love and adoration of Stew's heart. Stew had until now been able to maintain his boyish appearance and behavior. Stew's loss forced the appearance of a middle-aged man in the midst of fighting a serious illness. Only his unconscious will to survive carried him as the tragic death continued crushing his body, and his heart.

Stew could not handle grief. He could only be a free bird, flying to where the warm winds would take him, whether it be adventures of love or scaling a mountainside in Switzerland. Freedom-loving Stew had only been captured, according to him "caged," once in a whirlwind marriage that produced a beautiful infant daughter and a nasty divorce. After the split, Stew's former Mrs. packed her belongings and moved to Texas near her family with daughter in tow. With finalized divorce papers in hand, Stew immediately resumed his single lifestyle, surrounded by adoring friends and becoming a not-so-good long-distance father. The absence of Stew's daughter in his life helped him relate with Nate's children, a feeling until now he had not known existed. Stew, for the first time, really felt like a father. His emptiness drove him to become the father they lost and the father he could not be for his own child. In his grief, little by little, he was growing into a father figure. He matured.

Stew grew more concerned of Cathren's mental status. He found that even the strongest could have their breaking point. Nate's faceless murderers continually haunted Cathren. She obsessed, wanting to know if his murderers thought of the suffering they caused her children. Did they have children, as Nate did? Did they do this for a living each and every day? Who did they kill today for a few bucks? Who were their other victims? Cathren wanted to find their other victims, but her own grief kept her from doing so. Were other families suffering as Nate's family suffered because of the same criminals?

"Oh Heavenly Father, help me," prayed Cathren each time she left her home. "Am I going insane? Each time I go out, I do not expect to return alive. I watch each person I see on the street as if they may attack as soon as I leave my vehicle. I suspect everyone of being responsible for Nate's cruel death." Her pistol never left her side. It comforted her, hanging on its shoulder strap when she left her home, waiting cold in its holster to defend at her prompting. It seemed the only survivors of these attacks of late were ones who were able to defend themselves on the streets. Others throughout the nation became reclusive, especially the elderly, as society decayed further. Many rarely left their homes, depending on the internet for food and other basic needs to be brought to their doorstep. Cathren would like to have done the same, but it would be too costly in her situation. Each day her prayers continued as she drove through city streets in an effort to make a living. Trying to keep the shop open became harder as the economy declined.

Cathren occasionally went to local bookstores, often purchasing newspapers from across the nation, and logged onto the internet sites to see if it was like this everywhere. It was. Everyone thought the close of the long, hot summer would bring an end to the violence in the streets. It didn't. Cathren, along with her world, slowly began falling apart as fast as the nation's economy. Emotions raw, she could no longer be strong enough for her children.

Was it not enough that inflation had degraded the dollar to the point of making it impossible to make ends meet? Fuel costs made deliveries of goods to the grocer skyrocket, who in turn passed the expense on to consumers, who saw food prices sometimes quadruple within a week, particularly when gang fighting caused many highways surrounding larger metropolitan areas to close. Job losses, for whatever reasons, plagued the news each day. For each announced job loss, several others were doomed, and crime increased. Many complained that increased government spending on an ever-growing bureaucracy and social programs only resulted in heavy tax increases that stifled business growth and the average family's ability to survive. The stock market continued to jolt the economy in a downward spiral daily.

An unusually wet fall caused flooding across the nation and preceded record-breaking cold temperatures for the introduction of winter. Thousands of local families literally lived in one room of their homes to stay warm. Families could not afford heating costs. And then there were the blackouts, when there was no electricity for days and the nights were cold and damp.

Civil unrest in the United States and military disturbances in the Middle East created a ripple that went around the world. Oil prices, that had once dropped to below eighteen dollars a barrel years earlier, now soared to several hundred dollars per barrel, creating more havoc on the American economic front. This spurred renewed growth in the domestic search for oil and natural gas, along with research for alternative energy sources, but no one could get the jumpstart needed to take care of the energy crisis at hand. Many a patriot blasted past administrations for dragging their feet over America's lack of energy independence. They blamed politicians for being persuaded by special interest groups to squash research and development of alternative energy sources and drilling where oil could be found on the North American continent. Fingers pointed in every direction to lay blame for societal conditions that prevailed. Yet massive financial aid to critical areas deemed as "hot spots" didn't seem to help in the least.

Though Stew continued his visits at Cathren's with regularity through the months, he remained lost without the company of his swinging crowd, which no longer cared to be around a non-partying Stew. Stew started a review of the priorities he had for his life. His blue eyes still grayed over with mourning for Nate as Stew searched his own soul for closure. The wild and crazy group he ran with for so many years now seemed a far distance from the new Stew. He was confronted with the fact that life was short and too precious to waste. The reborn Stew became a serious, soul-searching man.

Cathren felt sorry for him in his grief, but she was witnessing a stronger, sensitive man evolving out of the old party animal she had at many times felt disgust towards. He was no longer just Nate's friend; he now was hers.

Days crept slowly toward the holiday season. For most, gift giving was out of the question, and children were lucky to have one item under their tree. Few families traveled out of town for holiday visits as money grew increasingly scarce and crime too plentiful. The holiday spirits of many local children, as with Cathren's and her friends', were lifted as they created their own, old-fashioned Christmas celebrations.

Each evening for an entire week prior to Christmas Eve neighbors sang Christmas carols, strolling close to their homes. The few inches of snow that kept the ground covered and invitations to hot chocolate and cookies along the way ensured a lot of volunteers for each evening of caroling. Cathren's neighborhood truly mastered the meaning of the Christmas season as each helped everyone in the neighborhood to think more of their blessings and less of the conditions across the country. Cathren and her neighbors mustered the courage to meet the holidays head-on with thankfulness for the birth of their savior. The season ended with a New Year's Eve prayer for better times.

The New Year announced oil prices that continued to soar. Most vehicles sat unused unless a trip or errand was a complete necessity. Fuel could be found, but no one could afford it, and if you could, you didn't flaunt it.

On weekends, Cathren's neighbors gathered, played cards, and ate popcorn. Kool-Aid was the beverage of choice, revived by baby boomers, and no one complained much. Without the usual pile of plastic toys left over from Christmas, the neighborhood children became creative with inexpensive crafts, using papier-mâché made from old newspapers and an array of games and toys from their own imaginations.

Each family tried to make good of the bad and saw the benefits of the slower paced lifestyle the lack of funds had led them to. After making it through the withdrawal from malls, fast food strips, other stimulants and entertainment they had thought they could not live without, most individuals settled in for what the future held for them. Through January and February, Cathren kept her shop running as usual, open on weekends and prices as low as possible. On many an occasion, Cathren could tell when a regular customer was having a hard time of it and would sell items to them at the price she had paid, without letting on she had done so. The economy was not coming around as many had hoped. In the meantime, each family reduced spending, never making ends meet. Many homes fell into foreclosure, but families stayed in them anyway. Banks went bankrupt and gave up throwing people out of their homes. Cathren's neighbors had their phones turned off, and others sold their cars because they were not able to continue their monthly loan installments and payments on insurance rates that had continued to skyrocket, along with the consideration of increased thefts and carjackings.

Although everyone's pride was hurt one way or the other, most of Cathren's neighbors were in the same boat, and everyone paddled their way through, trying to lend a helping hand to those sinking faster than the rest. It was now usual for two or three families to purchase food together in bulk. Weekends they could be found cooking large pots of bean soups, casseroles, and breads such as biscuits baked and frozen for weekly meals. Many went together to farmers in the country to purchase locally grown food. The men and women who were gun sportsmen accustomed to hunting, dressing game and knowledgeable in the areas of preserving meats helped their surrounding neighbors. They readily shared their knowledge, showing others how to make it through the winter months during blackouts. One of Cathren's neighbors had a small grinder used for grinding grains that sat on the kitchen counter. Many families would buy a bushel of hulled corn, grinding it into cornmeal for cornbread.

Many in the neighborhood enjoyed gardening and working with families to start tomatoes and other seedlings indoors for spring planting. They had already built hotbeds for early lettuce crops that could be shared by the neighbors since fresh California lettuce was now a rarity. Tillers turned backyards into raised bed gardens as families prepared for spring planting for the first time during the ownership of their homes. Food shortages throughout the winter had stung families hard and a few dollars for a few packets of seeds would help them carry through the times when gangs cut food supplies off from other parts of the country and the rest of the world.

When St. Patrick's Day rolled around, green beer didn't. The neighborhood instead opted for a potato eye planting party. During the morning hours, neighbors met in Cathren's garage for a large breakfast and to cut potatoes for planting. Only one elderly neighbor knew what to do and instructed everyone. The planting of the potatoes took the entire afternoon that led to the St. Patrick's Day party that evening at another home in the neighborhood. Trips to the mall were out; gardening videos and comparing yard gardens were in.

CHAPTER FIVE

"Hello. Hello, is that you, Herb Downing?" Cathren asked over the static on the phone.

"Sure is! How's our girl?" Herb answered, and as usual he got straight to the point.

His tone of voice let her know he still thought of her as the young girl that always begged to hunt the eggs his chickens would lay in the loft of his barn. She knew she would never be an adult in his eyes, and Cathren liked that in a way.

"I've been waiting for you to put a call through. We've been hearing an awful lot about things up your way. We've been more than a might worried about you and the kids," he continued.

"I knew you would be. How is Martha?" Cathren returned.

"She is doing just fine, dear girl, but let's not be changing the subject here. Let's get back to you," Herb persisted.

"Yes?" Cathren sighed and thought that she really didn't need a lecture today, but she knew by the tone of Herb's voice that was exactly what she was in for.

"Now this farm next to me is sitting empty and seeing what's going on up there in Ohio, I believe a move down here by you and your family is in order. You did the right thing by keeping this farm in the family after your grandparents passed on. Your children have always been able to come back here once each year or so and feel their roots, but now you need the farm for more than that, you need that farm for your survival. Now, I'm going to put it to you straight. If you can get down here for spring planting, we will do all we can to help you

46

get a fair start on the growing season and give you all the pointers on growing marketable crops and enough food to make it through the winter. If you plant a large garden, there will be food to store for the winter months, and from what I've been reading and figuring on my own, things are going get worse before there's a turn for the better. Any time there is unrest or revolution in a country, you will find that people do starve and some to the point of dying, especially children. You want to avoid that."

Herb continued, "Child, you have never lived through a depression, and I can tell you the one I lived through was bad. I surely believe the last depression will look like a party compared to what is to come. People just aren't as independent as they were then. It would be right smart to act immediately. Now, I know you called to see about the land I lease from your grandpa's old place. It has a good-sized tobacco base that produces some income that could keep food on the table for you all," he told her with a frankness she had never before heard from his lips.

The audacity of Herb Downing's words caught her off guard for a moment until she realized he was being genuine. She also knew Herb would never have spoken to her of this unless he had confided in his wife of sixty years about what he planned to say. Herb and his wife were both in their eighties, but still worked on their farm with some help. Their lifestyle had been favorable to them, for their minds were still as sharp as they had always been, and they were "a well-read couple". They would agree on nearly any subject. Though Nate had spoken of sending Cathren away for her protection, she never gave a second thought of moving deep into the remote hills of Kentucky.

"Herb, I can't move down there. There is really nothing there for us. The children aren't used to that way of life. We live in a different world than you. We are suburbanites and city roamers. What in the world would Andrew and Marisa do on a farm in the middle of nowhere? My home is here, my work is here, and the children go to school here. I just don't see how things can get much worse than they are now. It just has to get better."

"Well, it's food for thought, anyway. You are luckier than most. You've got a place to stay if worst comes to worst, understand? Your children will come to know and love this part of the country. It may take some time, but mark my word, child, where you are, is no place to be," he told her. "Like I said before, you have never lived through a depression. I lived through the Great Depression and was overseas during war in the service. I know what I am talking about. I have seen much, and some of it was terrible. You need to protect yourself and your family. I am old and have seen a lot in my lifetime, and I have a bad feeling about what is to come shortly. Don't be foolish, child."

"I guess I do understand, and you may be right, but I don't see how we can possibly move right now. Marisa just could not leave now. She needs all the support she can get around our home and with friends we have here since Nate died. She is so fragile. I just do not know if we could make it in such a secluded setting. And there is my shop I would be leaving behind," she responded.

"Your grandpa's garden tools are still out back in the shed. The house will keep you dry and warm, though it won't be what you are accustomed to. The woodstove will heat the whole place on the coldest of winter nights. Don't be foolish about the matter. It is time to let go of things and get out of there while you still can," he sternly told her. "Promise me you will at least consider a move, if just for the summer. At least it will be safe here."

"I promise to give it some thought. I just can't see leaving my home. The children would be upset if we moved, it would be hard on them," she told him. "I am not going to take lightly all we have discussed today. You may be right. I just don't know if I could make that transition. I'll get back to you in a couple of weeks and we can discuss this again, okay? I need to think. Right now I am taken aback by your bringing the entire subject forward."

"You know we will be thinking about you. Now, you're a smart girl Cathren and you do know societies fall apart from time to time and then it takes time for them to heal before they are better again. You don't need me to tell you that our country has headed down the wrong path the last part of this past century. We made advances in technology like no other country has ever, but we managed somehow to leave our scruples behind and went backwards in many respects. When many of our streets are bloody from gang fighting in major cities across our land and they are able to block use of major highways from time to time, then we are steering into a strange direction. I know your gut feeling will tell you what to do when the time comes, whether you should stay in the suburbs or come home to the farm. Just think on it good, will you?" Herb asked her, trying to provoke a move on her part.

"Maybe we will be down for a visit in July or August. Give Martha my love, will you?" Cathren said, desperate for a change of subject matter.

"Sure will. In the meantime, I will start the seedbed for all the plants you will need if you decide to make a move. If you change your mind about coming, your plants will be here," he told her. "Now you take care, and if there's anything we can do, let us know, you hear? Bye now."

"Okay, bye for now. Love you both," Cathren ended the call. She hadn't been so relieved to end a phone conversation in a long time.

"How ridiculous a move to the farm would be!" she told herself. "I would have to sell or rent my home here in order to afford the move, and considering the real estate market, selling would be out of the question. It would cost an arm and a leg to hire movers, and then there was the risk of going on a trip now. How many times each day do I read in the papers that another car is hijacked with people in it? Do I need to take that sort of chance with my children, driving so far? All cities would have to be avoided. Some days it is safe to drive on the main highways, and some days it is not. I would have to drive most of the way on back roads. There would be less trouble on the back roads, as there have been few snipers or anyone throwing rocks or homemade bombs from overpasses onto innocent motorists on most of those roads." Her mind raced a minute before she dismissed the thought of moving at all. This was home. Ohio was home, and no one would force her to leave no matter how bad it got. In retrospect, the entire thought of moving was beyond ridiculous, and she hoped Herb would not call to bring the subject up again.

"I had better get down to business, or nothing will get done today," she said to herself. Cathren picked up her keys, jacket, purse, and gun, then left to prepare for the weekend at the shop.

The clerk behind the bullet-resistant glass and her present customer were discussing the headlines while Cathren made her midmorning stop at the corner food mart for a cup of fresh coffee and a newspaper. She knew the tale must be a gruesome one to warrant being the subject of discussion. For the most part, the populous had recently become shockproof when it came to atrocities on the streets. Many youths and adults seemed unconscionable during their acts of terror on individuals. Homes were broken into across the country and entire families were terrorized with regularity, so often that it now rarely appeared in newspapers or on the nightly news. Cathren recalled that as a student, many years past, the nation was shocked at the brutality in Truman Capote's *In Cold Blood*. The nation, once upset at such brutality, now merely sloughed it off as an everyday occurrence.

Cathren filled a Styrofoam cup with fresh hot coffee, picked up a paper, and paid the clerk with the bulletproof vest for her purchase through the bullet-resistant window. After fastening her seatbelt, she flipped open the paper to find out the reason for the conversation between the clerk and the other customer.

"Oh dear God, please no," she said out loud to herself. The headlines now reminded her of books in which she had read of many revolutions in countries where angry mobs would behead someone and place the head on a long pole then parading it through the streets. But this was not a history lesson on another country's revolution; it was a newspaper article about a real incident occurring the past evening just a few miles from Cathren's home.

Sickened by the article in the paper, Cathren drove straight home instead of running her next errand.

Cathren picked up her phone and put a call in to the one person she could confide in.

"Hello, Sharon, this is Cathren. Is Stew at the office?"

"Yes, he is, I'll connect you. I am going to put you on hold, Cathren," Sharon replied.

"Hello, Cat?" Stew asked. Cathren would not interrupt his work unless it was important. "Are you okay?"

"Not sure. Would you mind coming here for dinner this evening? I would like to talk with you," Cathren asked.

"You're not having dating problems, are you?" Stew asked jokingly.

"Don't be silly," she chided, then laughed. "Stew! Did you read the morning paper?"

"I heard a little about it on the radio on the way in. I am assuming we are talking about the same incident?" he asked.

"The paper reported that an angry mob attacked a group of people leaving a building downtown last evening. There were no authorities around to stop the attack. One gentleman at the scene was beaten mercilessly by a mob when he tried to deter the situation. By this time, people came flooding from out of nowhere as the disturbance worsened until a couple hundred individuals were involved in the fighting."

She continued, "A leader of the pack pulled out a long knife from his boot and continued to antagonize the gentleman that tried to stop the growing mob from their dirty work. He then turned and grabbed an innocent woman who had exited a movie theater and slit her throat, then proceeded to disconnect her head from her torso to cheering of the mob that started the incident. Innocent bystanders stood by helplessly. The mob then mounted the decapitated head onto an iron bar. The deviant group ran two blocks, threw the head in an alley, they then dispersed. By the time police arrived, all was over except the reporting and retrieval of the head with its final cold, stiff expression of terror. Authorities thought the incident occurred entirely too fast to have been spontaneous. Many believed a small, local terrorist group instigated the barbaric act, but as usual it could not be proven. And to top all this, in Pennsylvania an entire town was terrorized when gangs invaded a neighborhood. The gang closed down an entire street and removed people from their homes and killed people at random in front of their family members. Some women were raped in front of their husbands and children. My God in Heaven, what have we come to?"

"I was hoping you would not read the paper until this evening," Stew told her. "I'll be over after the office closes, say around six."

"Good, I'll see you then. Bye." Cathren hung up the phone with a sigh, then headed to the door leading to her garage. "Well, I am leaving right now. I am not going to let this incident keep me from my work. If those rats think they can intimidate me into staying indoors, they have another thing coming."

Cathren now took an attack on any innocent victim personally. "Tonight Stew and I can talk," she said to herself.

That night, Andrew looked through the window to see who was at the door. "It's Stew, its

Stew," he yelled, opening the door. "That new flight simulator we found at the computer store last week is real fun!"

"Well, is that so? Let's see what you've figured out since I was here last. Hi, Cat!" Stew greeted Cathren as Andrew pulled him to the room the computer was in.

"You guys go ahead. Dinner isn't quite ready," Cathren told them.

"Sounds great! I can't remember the last time I had a home-cooked meal," Stew replied.

"Well, that computer game you bought sure has made Andrew happy. It is such a joy to see him laughing again," Cathren informed Stew. "It makes me so happy to hear Andrew sound like a normal child again instead of the distraught little boy the past events have thrown him into. I can't say enough, Stew."

"It's my pleasure, Cat," Stew replied.

"Dinner is nearly ready. Marisa, time to get off the phone. Can you help set the table for dinner? Andrew, wash your hands," Cathren commanded.

"Cat, this meal is great," Stew kept repeating.

"It's okay," said Andrew. "Hamburgers and pizzas are my favorite."

"That's all you would eat if Mom would let you get away with it," Marisa retorted to Andrew. Andrew silently answered by looking at his sister and sticking his tongue out with food on it.

"That is enough, you two. When dinner is over, Andrew, you need to get into the shower," Cathren told him.

"But Mom! I'm not finished showing Stew all the tricks I have figured out on the new game he bought me," Andrew whined.

"You will still have enough time for the computer after you shower. Stew and I have some things we need to discuss this evening. Now off to the shower, young man, as soon as you are finished eating," Cathren told him. Andrew dutifully scampered off to the shower when finished. Cathren began her conversation with Stew.

"We can talk. You were always Nate's friend, and so I was always at arm's length," Cathren told him.

"I guess it was that way. Now we are the closest of friends," Stew told her.

Stew had told Nate that screwing around on his wife wasn't right, but at the time that came from the logistical point of view that Nate had too much money invested in his life to lose it all. Thinking back, Stew could not believe he had looked at Nate and his problems from that perspective. Now Cathren had become his closest friend, and Stew felt he was a part of her family. Stew thought that maybe these crazy times had created a weakness in him that invoked a desire to be part of a real family, her family. He felt warm and safe in this home. He treasured their friendship and the time he spent with them, and at times he found himself crossing an imaginary line of thought linking to her romantically. When his mind drifted this way, he automatically scolded himself, telling himself that she was still Nate's wife, and he would cancel his thoughts.

"Stew, do you remember the farm Nate and I bought from my grandfather's estate?" Cathren asked him as she poured a cup of coffee for him.

"Sure, Nate would never have gone for it but it was a great tax write-off and it was near the lake where he enjoyed boating," Stew told her, smiling.

"And besides, he did have some attachment to the place. He said it was peaceful there. Hmmm. I'd just about forgotten about the place."

"Stew, I lease the tobacco base each year to friends of the family who own the farm adjacent to the old home place. Each year I call Herb to set up the arrangement for the year's crop, but the conversation this year went to a direction that has provoked much thought about why I am even staying in Ohio," Cathren told him. "When I spoke with Herb, he let me know in no uncertain terms that I should move to the farm before things get much worse around here. He told me if I came down now that I could put a crop out myself and plant a large garden for the summer," Cathren informed him.

"Well, he does have a point about the safety of continuing to live here. There are dangers everywhere right now, but it is extremely dangerous here. I've got to be truthful with you: if it were not for my career, I probably would have already left and gone to a less populated area of the country."

Cathren was gripped by what Stew confided to her. "So, you agree with Herb?" Cathren asked.

"I do and I don't," he replied. "Listen, if the government continues to deteriorate at the rate it is going, it could get real nasty in the few months ahead. If the same thing happens to you that happened to Nate, what will become of your children? I don't mean to be cruel and I sure hate to see you leave the area, but maybe the man is right. It would be a breather for you and the kids to get away for a while, a vacation. And you do have to think what would become of them if you were gone."

"What about Marisa and Andrew? A move would be hard on them. They have made so many adjustments in their lives since Nate's death," Cathren told him.

"A move for the summer may be what the doctor ordered. Marisa is still devastated over Nate's death. She asked me not to tell you this, but I am going to, anyway. Marisa has called the office many times in tears since Nate died. She didn't want to burden you with it because of what you have gone through with Andrew's nightmares. I know she puts on a good front, but the child is terrified beneath that tough exterior. She is a mental wreck. I hate to say it, but all of you have PTSD at this point."

"Oh my Lord help us! We live in a combat zone now. We have what soldiers have when they live through the unmentionable overseas and come home. Oh dear God, now I realize what they go through. I have PTSD. Father in Heaven. I had not thought of it that way. After all I have read on Post-Traumatic Stress Disorder, I never related it to me or the children. We do have PTSD." Cathren cried uncontrollably as she confided in Stew. "I'm glad you've been there for Marisa. She was always her daddy's pet. I know this has been hard on her and I feel helpless when it comes to the loss of their father. I've heard her crying some nights in her room. I just don't know where to start repairing our lives," Cathren sobbed.

"You probably should consider a move, at least for the summer. This entire country has plunged into an internal war of some sort. You would think, with so much turmoil and fighting across the nation – all the riots, burning, and the like – that there was a civil war or revolution taking

57

place. The nineteen sixties were nothing compared to this. If there was a war, at least everyone would know there was a reason for all the fighting and the breakdown of society. Have no doubt about it, it's crazy out there," Stew said, shaking his head.

"I know. People are being robbed and terrorized left and right. I wouldn't dare send a child to crime-ridden schools and parks anymore, places where it was once safe," Cathren cried.

"I really hate to see you leave for the summer, but it would be in your best interest. And about the schools, I have to hand it to my ex-wife as far as my daughter's education goes. She homeschooled since the beginning and will enroll our daughter in a private Christian school this year since they have moved near one. My little girl has excelled on national tests time and again. What is it that a mother without a college degree can do with little money that public schools can't? They throw millions and millions into it each year and students are coming out not in the best of shape. I feel so sorry for teachers in public schools and what they have to deal with now." The discussion continued for hours until they both realized it was three a.m.

"Stay in Seth's room tonight. It's entirely too late to go out on these streets across town to your condo," Cathren told him.

"You're right. I can run home in the morning and get ready for work. Well, actually, it is morning already, but I need a few hours' sleep," he said as Cathren walked him down the hall to show him the room.

Cathren turned to her bedroom door. "Stew, I am so scared."

Stew put his arms around her. "I know, I am scared right along with you. It will be fine if we're extra careful, Cat. I do worry so about you and the children. There are a lot of decisions you need to make over the next several days."

Stew wanted to embrace her, bring her to his bedside, lie beside her, and hold her securely forever. He wanted to protect her. She had been through enough alone. Stew turned to close the bedroom door, hiding the tears in his eyes, when he felt the tender touch of Cathren pull him back to her. She pressed herself against his aching soul. He could feel his lips place a sentimental kiss against hers, one that turned quickly into the kiss of two needing each other.

Both let the surprise of finding each other pass quickly. Cathren lifted her arms above her and pressed her back against the wall outside her door. Stew was pulled tenderly to her, moving silently where she led him. Through the darkness they were against each other, ready for one another.

Stew's memory fled backward to the days before she and Nate were married, the days when he did wonder what a moment as this with her would be like, a moment he had thought would never exist. Stew pressed his chest against her bare breasts, pulling her toward him so they could be together as one. Cathren kissed his shoulders, moving under him, grasping Stew to bring him to her. Each looked into the eyes of the other simply to melt together. The embracing glance shook them into reality. Both burst into laughter: they were friends, not lovers.

"We just nearly ruined the best friendship two people could have. I love you, Stew! I truly do." Cathren held onto him. "But this is not right, is it?"

"No, it isn't. This would not ruin anything you and I have, but it would have made it difficult, or should I say embarrassing, for us." He laughed, relieved but all the same, wanting her in a way he knew could not be possible. "A short time ago I would have wanted to go on with this relationship we just nearly had, but now I know this is not the time or the place for us. Maybe someday it will be different. I just don't know. Both of us desperately reached out to each other in a way we need, but not now. We are literally emotionally strung out. I love you, Cat. You are the best friend any man could have."

"We need to be stronger to start a relationship, which requires commitment. Neither of us are capable at this time." Cathren told him. "I am so glad we have each other, Stew. We have a bond no one can break, ever!"

"We do! But you know, I feel just a bit awkward right now, buck naked and all," he answered, grabbing a sheet to cover him. "Do you mind if I use this? Love ya', Cat, but I'd better go before I do something stupid, like change my mind."

"No, be my guest," she told him. Stew smiled and slid out the door to across the hall to the other bedroom after closing her door behind him.

Cathren fell face first onto her mattress. "Well, there went my chance for sex since who only knows how long it has been," she whispered to herself before dozing into sleep. "Sometimes it seems like going without food. Absolutely unbelievable!"

CHAPTER SIX

Entering the kitchen in semi-darkness, Cathren found herself turning on the television for the six a.m. news and starting her morning coffee in a semi-conscious state. "Stew! Stew!" Cathren yelled, running down the hall to Stew's bedroom door, Cathren felt she ran a mile. Stew ran to the television as Cathren ordered.

"A live newscast from the street of your condo showed your building in flames. Authorities announced they suspected arson by a group of gang members who were harassing residents of the complex just last night. It might be a good idea for you to call the manager's office at the complex or the police department to tell them you were not in the condo last night. The way it appears on the news, they are searching for bodies," Cathren told him.

Stew immediately made several calls that put many of his neighbors and friends at ease. Gangs walked the streets, according to the reporter, shooting windows of vehicles parked curbside throughout the city. Cathren opted not to send Marisa and Andrew to school, ordering them to stay indoors and toward the rear of the house in case trouble found their neighborhood.

"The school sent the automatic message to my email. Classes will be on the internet today," Marisa announced from her room.

"Okay, thanks for letting me know. Go ahead and start your classes."

"I'm going to the office to see if there are any problems there before I go to the condo," Stew told them after he showered and dressed.

"Stew, you are so pale right now. If you really need to leave for the office, please be extra careful. If it gets bad just abandon your car then run back here. You know our home is yours until you get straightened around. You are welcome to store your belongings in my basement and garage until your condo has undergone repairs."

Marisa screamed, "I'm sick of all this. We never know when it is safe to leave the house anymore. This is just absolutely ridiculous. None of my friends are allowed to drive anymore. No one is allowed to go to a mall anymore. I am tired of metal detectors and being searched everywhere I go. I am just sick, sick, sick of all this crap!" Marisa slammed her bedroom door behind her.

Cathren could hear Marisa sobbing as she tried to clean the breakfast dishes. She called several places to cancel her appointments for the day. Many places of business did not answer their phones until later during the morning. Marisa came out of her room.

"Kids, do your best with your schoolwork today," Cathren told them. "I do need to run a few errands this morning and drop merchandise at the shop. That should not take more than two hours. I trust you to do your school work while I'm gone, Andrew. And, I am going to pick up your favorite pizzas for lunch. I need to buy some milk and a few other items in case there is more trouble this evening and the lights are out for a few days again. I'll see you later. Be careful. Love you! Bye."

CHAPTER SEVEN

"Don't lose it, lady, or I will blow your fuckin' ass to hell. Just act like you're my wife or whatever and steer that cart closer to my car here right next to your van," the voice whispered in her ear. Cathren's heartbeat thickened and numbness spread through her, enhancing her awareness of the danger in which she found herself.

"Now listen close. After I open the trunk to my car, we'll both load the groceries. If you fuck up, lady, you're dead meat. This gun stuck in your side is just itching to do away with its first body for the day."

Cathren did not hesitate to do as he instructed, for the gun he held plunged deeply into her flesh, sending flashes of pain from its metal tip. The gun in her purse could not help her. It would be suicide to try and defend herself. Her shaking hands grabbed the first paper sack full of groceries from the cart. The voice told her not to look his way as he repeated threats while she continued loading sacks into the trunk of his car.

The rear door of the car opened and a disheveled character dressed in gray slid onto the pavement, making the situation hectic for the gun holder. Something fell on the pavement. The three – Cathren, gun holder, and gray character – followed the sound with their eyes. While grabbing another bag, the holder had dropped his weapon. Angry, the gray-dressed character lashed his fists upon the one responsible for dropping the gun on the pavement as they grabbed for it. The gun went off, sending a bullet into one of the parked cars.

"You sorry bastard! This is the second job you've screwed up this week, you dumb ass," the gray character screamed from his six-foot-plus, heavy frame. Cathren stood, astonished, watching the two exchange slugs for a moment before she finally realized she could walk away.

She shook when one of them yelled to her, "Get into your van real calm like, you bitch. Dig around in your purse like you're trying to find your keys until I'm gone. Remember, there's a bullet waiting to be used on someone today, so play it cool until I am well away from here. I have your license plate number. I can find you. You so much as dare to report this to the police, I will find you and you will pay a big price!"

Cathren managed to shake her head forward in a yes motion to please them with the answer they wanted then proceeded to the driver's door of the van and opened it. She climbed into the van's captain chair and followed the instructions as ordered until she saw the assailants' car spin from the parking lot.

Cathren opened her door and stepped onto the pavement, but could only feel the ground shake beneath her. The sensation was accompanied by a deafening noise. She turned to the street, where hundreds of fearful faces ran in every direction as debris, smoke, and screams filled the atmosphere around them. She immediately lost her sense of time, and twenty minutes passed before she was able to put her keys in the ignition. Had someone told her it had been hours, not minutes that had passed, she would have believed the messenger. The mall across the street was in flames.

"Gosh, Mom! Are you sick?" Andrew asked while watching his mother throw up on the garage floor as she climbed from the van. "What did you get at the grocery? Where is the pizza? What luck! Can I call Joey and see if he can come over and play for a while?"

"Oh God! Mom!" Marisa screamed, grabbing a phone. "Stew, Mom is a mess. Please come now."

"Not now, Andrew. I don't have any groceries. Sorry. Would you shut the garage door, Honey? I still need to get the pizza. I will order it in instead of picking it up. Cathren clung to walls of the garage, feeling her way into the house until she fell into her bed. Her head and stomach swirling again, she ran into the bathroom, sending more contents of her stomach up again and again. She fell to the bathroom floor. She was suffering from a severe nervous breakdown. She had nearly died this afternoon and left her children parentless.

"Cathren, what's wrong?" Stew yelled, running down the hall to the bathroom. "Cathren, wake up! Marisa! Run and get some towels for your Mom while I try to get her into her bed. Thanks for calling me, kids. You did the right thing."

Andrew asked in a bewildered voice, "What's Mom doing lying on the bathroom floor?"

"She's all right, Andrew, she must have eaten something that upset her stomach. Did she say anything when she came home?" Stew asked them.

"No, but she was real short with Andrew and went straight to her room when she came into the house," Marisa told him.

"She's coming around, she should be okay now. You guys go ahead and watch some television or whatever. She will be okay. I can watch your Mom. Andrew, could you shut the door? It is okay, go ahead," he told them both while they stood not knowing whether to leave or stay but obeying Stew never the less.

"The kids are in the other room. Now, what is going on?" Stew asked.

"I was robbed outside the grocers a while ago. As soon as the robbers left me, a bomb went off across the street. I can't remember anything after that. I can't even remember driving home. I just got so sick after I pulled into the garage. Nerves, I guess. I'm so weak, I can barely hold my head up," she told him.

"I heard about the blast, I guess there were fatalities. You were lucky you weren't hurt. The center of the entire mall collapsed after the bomb ignited. It will be days before they find out how many people were in the mall. The scenes of the rubble on the news are devastating," Stew told her. "Marisa called a few minutes ago scared out of her wits. She thought you needed to go to the hospital. Maybe she's right, but I imagine all the hospitals in the area are packed about now."

"I'll be fine in a few minutes. Guess the shock of it all overwhelmed me. Would you believe the two robbers got into a fight because they nearly botched the whole thing?" Cathren laughed, attempting to stand. "Oh my head. Let's go into the kitchen I need coffee and aspirin."

"I'll fix the coffee, you sit at the table," Stew commanded.

"Stew, I can't take it anymore. I am going to leave tomorrow as soon as I can get out of here. Oh, I didn't get the kids lunch. I planned to buy pizza on the way home, but all this happened."

"I would like to disagree with you, but your decision to get away from here, though hasty, is a good one. I'll order pizza for the kids now. You just

66

take care of yourself," Stew told her, placing a cup of coffee on the table in front of her.

"Why don't you go back to work? I will be all right."

"Actually, I was on my way out of the office to try and get into my condo. There is caution tape around the building, but no one is around to enforce a no crossing rule because there are so many fires across town and then there was the bombing. I'm going to climb into a window and get what I can. I borrowed a truck from a friend, who said he'd help me. Sure you'll be all right?"

"Yes. I'll see you later. Be careful, Stew. Please be careful," she begged.

Stew hesitated, "I hate to leave now, but much of my property inside the condo just has smoke damage now and I know if I wait until tomorrow nearly everything will be lost to looters. Tell the kids pizza is on the way."

"Okay, Stew. We'll be fine here. I just don't think I can take this anymore," she told him. Stew smiled and softly kissed her cheek before exiting.

When she was able to stand without getting light-headed, Cathren began gathering all the boxes and bags she could find and started stuffing belongings into them. After an hour of packing, she decided to call movers to get estimates for the nearly two-hundred mile trip ahead of her. Cathren was not a superstitious person, but the timely conversation with Herb and all that had happened since was sufficient as an omen to induce a move from the city. The price to move her furniture was more than she could afford, so she dismissed that thought immediately. All she could think of was running. Staying away from here until fall would give her enough time to gain strength to cope again, she thought to herself. "I am not giving in," she told herself, " just going on a much-needed vacation."

"Mom! What are you doing? Have you gone bonkers or what? What are you doing with all our stuff?" Marisa squalled frantically.

Cathren explained the robbery and bombing as she silently tried to figure out how she could possibly break the news of the coming trip to Marisa. "Andrew, we need to talk, come and sit by your sister, please."

Marisa crossed her arms. "Mom, I don't need another lecture. I am nearly grown. These lectures need to be saved for Andrew."

"I have been thinking about going to Grandpa's farm to stay for the summer, but now I have decided that making the trip immediately instead of waiting until school is out for the summer would be a better idea. We are taking the boat from the garage and loading it with everything we need. Take as much as you want from your rooms. We will have Stew pack the computers so you can do your schooling from there," Cathren informed the two. "Andrew, take your bikes and all the toys you want. We can haul it all back in the boat when we come back this fall. You may pack all the fishing equipment too."

"Mom! We can't do this. What about prom night and the rest of the school year? I can't leave my friends until school *is* out for the summer," Marisa yelled.

"You mean we get to go to the farm when I get my clothes packed? Wow!" Andrew yelled. "I am going to pack my fishing equipment first."

"I've already made the decision to go as soon as we can get packed, and that is final! We'll probably leave tomorrow or the next day if I can make all the arrangements in time."

"Mom, I don't believe it. You would actually drag me to the absolute middle of nowhere on earth. Can't I stay with one of my friends till summer?" Marisa cried. "You have completely flipped out. How could you do this to me? You just can't do this. I'm not afraid to stay here and you shouldn't be, either. This just makes me sick. sick, sick, sick."

"Can I get my fishing tackle out of the garage and put it in the van?" Andrew jumped from the couch in anticipation of a "yes" answer.

"Go ahead, Andrew," Cathren told him. She was relieved that she did not have two children battling her about the move. Andrew sped to the garage.

"Marisa, I am so sorry, but we really should leave for a while, at least until it is safer here. I really do not think there will be a prom now. The school is already discussing canceling it. It will probably be worse around here when summer arrives. Honey, we don't have a choice. We are lucky there is a place to stay for the summer months. It will be fine, just wait and see," Cathren explained.

"This is crazy, Mother! Absolutely crazy! Please don't make me do this!" Were Marisa's last words before she ran down the hall and slammed her bedroom door again.

"Great! I will not miss that bedroom door slamming for a few months," Cathren cried. "This is going to be a long trip. I hope I don't hear this all the way to the farm. One thing is for sure: I will not be getting much help from Marisa as far as packing is concerned!"

Cathren continued to pack all evening. It was nine o'clock when Stew arrived with a truckload of what could be saved from his condo.

"I managed to salvage most of my belongings. We were able to get some furniture out and store it in the extra room at the office. The section of the building where my condo is located sustained the least amount of damage. I expect more when it begins to rain over the next few days because the roof to my place has burned through in several places. I need to begin washing my clothing. It all smells like smoke. I see you meant what you said. You have packed a lot since I left. How are you going to move all this?" he asked.

Cathren told him, "The price of hiring movers was too high, so I need your help backing the van into the backyard to the garage at the back of the property where the boat is stored. Nate and I never got around to selling it after the divorce. I can haul a good amount of our belongings in it. There will be plenty of room if we put the camper top on the boat instead of using the canvas cover. I will need to check the tires to see if they need air before leaving."

"Cathren, the more I think about this, the better it sounds. I am so glad you are leaving this place for a while," Stew told her and embraced her for the comfort and strength to help through the long night ahead. His heart saddened, for knowing his dearest friend, the woman he had learned to care for so much the past months was leaving him.

"I will waste no time. I'll hitch the boat and pull it around now so it will be easier to load," Stew told her, hoping to get started right away so she would not have time to change her mind. He knew she had made a good decision for safety, but, on the other hand, Cathren could be drawn to stay home, too.

Stew and one of the neighbors hitched the twenty-three-foot boat to the van then connected the brake and light wires. Nate had driven when the boat was being towed. Cathren rarely towed the boat, but she wasn't about to let Stew know that bit of information. She was afraid he would try talking her into staying until he could drive the van and boat to the farm for her. With the boat hitched to its rear, the van was finally parked in front of the house. Cathren felt a sigh of relief, then called Seth at the university.

"Mom, there is no way I can leave school now. It's still calm here. I've been careful, and most of us stay on campus, keeping to ourselves now, anyway. If you like, I can come to the farm as soon as finals are over. I would really like to spend the summer near the lake, anyway. Maybe I can get a summer job on one of the docks. Is that all right with you?" Seth asked.

"Not really. You know how I worry, but you are probably making the right decision. You really don't need to lose all the time and money spent at school this semester. I'll need your help this summer. Since I will be leaving what source of income I do have, we will have to plant a large garden. Most of Grandpa's garden equipment is still in the shed at Herb's. He and Martha want us to come down as soon as possible, and they are willing to help us get started."

"I'll be fine on campus. Besides, it is just a few weeks before finals, anyway. I don't think it will get as bad as the cities. Mom, I feel I can tell you this now. I am glad you are leaving. Several of my instructors say this coming summer may be very

71

bad for the entire country, considering the financial status of the government. I know Marisa is upset because she called me about forty-five minutes ago. I calmed her as much as I could. I explained to her that a lot of people may be hurt this summer in the cities and she needed to help you with Andrew as much as possible. Just don't let on that I told you she called. I told her I may be behind you getting to the farm. I have a feeling she may have her clothes packed shortly," Seth assured her.

"Thanks for talking with her. I know she is upset, and there doesn't seem to be any way for me to comfort her. I will worry day and night over leaving you. I don't know if I can stand it. Just try to get to the farm as soon as school is out. Bye, son." Cathren dissolved into tears again. Stew approached her and held her in another embrace.

"Listen, Cat. I don't have a place to stay. Would you mind renting your house to me for the summer until I get settled somewhere new while my condo is repaired? There is no better place I would like to stay. I will pay rent and the utilities until you get back home. How does that sound?"

"Stew, you are an angel in disguise. Nothing would please me more right now. It would be a pleasure letting someone I trust as much as you stay in my home and watch over it while I am gone. No rent, just pay utilities please. That would be so wonderful. God has blessed us through our tragedies. You are a true friend I will love and cherish forever."

Stew and Cathren spent half the night packing, loading, unloading, re-packing, and re-loading until neither could stay awake any longer.

Cathren gave Marisa permission to take anything she wanted from her room and to load it in the van to help ease the pain of the move. All of Marisa's "junk", as Andrew put it, took most of the room in the van.

Cathren filled the boat and put the top on. Stew drove the van to the gas station several blocks away and filled the van, along with the boat, with gasoline in case stations were closed on the way south and they would need to siphon gas for the rest of the drive. She counted on siphoning gas from the boat for use in the van if need be; though she had never siphoned gas before, she had seen it done.

"Cathren, I believe it would be in your best interest to leave around four in the morning. That seems to be the quiet part of the day. Most rebel rousers have gotten all their troublemaking in by this time and there are no crowds for them to blend with at that time of night. If you leave then, it will be near daylight when you get to roads you do not know. You will be well away from any places where there is likely to be trouble. I have two maps marked with the safest route for you to take since a GPS will try and divert you to highways. Use the maps."

"Thank you, Stew. This means so much to me. I have something to ask of you. I need someone to keep my shop open during the weekend hours. I know by the time I pay someone an hourly wage, I won't make money, but the important thing is to keep the business running until I get back."

"I think we can work out something that would be favorable for both of us. My sister lost her job and, as you know, she has children to support. I have been helping her make ends meet. My investments are not doing as well as they should due to the economy, so my help is limited right now. She has been unsuccessful finding new

73

employment. She asked me to be on the lookout for a job. This will be perfect for her. She can put in hours through the week and I can help stock through the weeknights. I'll fill in for her if her children need her at home when the shop is open." Stew was eager to take over the shop for Cathren. "Many of my clients have had to make serious cuts business-wise, so I expect many of them to negotiate with me over the next several months to cut the cost of my services to their companies. I will have to oblige them if I want to retain their business for when times get better again. My running your shop for the next several months will be a learning experience for me and income for my sister."

Juggling jobs would be hard, but since Stew was no longer a weekend party animal, Cathren knew he could handle it. Stew was still maturing in ways Cathren never thought possible and he had become an admirable human being.

It was getting late into the night, and Cathren was still stuffing boxes where no more could be stuffed. Then she began cramming clothing and other articles between boxes and bags. Stew yelled across the yard, "I need to go next door and help Jim with his new computer program. I'll be back in a few minutes." Cathren knew he would fit well in their neighborhood because Stew was amicable and already making friends. He was truly a people person.

Fifteen minutes had not passed when Stew yelled for Cathren to come outside to the driveway. Stew stood smiling in the middle of the yard with the ugliest creature she had ever seen at the end of a leash. Her neighbor Jim stood behind him, smiling.

"What is that?" Andrew asked. "It looks like one of those potbellied pigs."

"It is," Jim told him.

"Can I pet it?" Andrew asked.

"You sure can," Stew told him.

"Whose pig is it?" Cathren inquired.

"Yours," Jim chuckled. "A friend of mine raises them on his farm outside the city and gave Stew a good deal. It is young, healthy, and friendly. They make good pets."

"That's not my pet, no way!" Cathren rebutted.

"Mom, please. Can we keep it?" Andrew pleaded.

"No, Andrew! What would I do with a potbellied pig?" his mother snapped. Andrew moaned.

"Come here." Stew pulled Cathren inside the front door. "It will do Andrew and Marisa a world of good. It is going to be hard on them this summer, and the pig will keep them company. I've a friend that keeps his in their apartment that is two stories up. It gets on the elevator with them when they take it out on a leash. It's even house trained!"

"Get real, Stew. I can't haul a pig all those miles tomorrow. You've got to be kidding. What would I haul it in? Or should I just let it crawl around in the van the entire trip?" Cathren was growing irate with Stew.

"Jim has a cage for it to travel in. Please, for the kids?" Stew pleaded.

"I just can't believe you are trying to talk me into this. I don't have anything to feed it. I can't take it."

"I bought a twenty-five pound bag of special feed from the man that raised it. It will last a while. What do you say?" Stew asked.

Marisa walked out the front door and caught sight of the pig. "Oh, look at the cute little pig," she exclaimed. "Cara Terrell has one and it stays in the house. Mom, can we have one?"

"If we take that as a pet, the responsibility is yours and Andrew's. Understand?" Cathren angrily turned to Stew. "You discuss their responsibilities concerning this pig with them! This was your idea."

Stew smiled and told Cathren, "Of course I will. Well, I guess you are now the proud owner of a potbellied pig."

"Kids," Stew addressed Andrew and Marisa, "take the cage into the garage for the night. The pig will rest well there, just make sure it has snacks and water. Here, let me help."

"When you are finished, make sure you are off to bed for the night. You will be busy tomorrow taking care of that pig all the way to the farm," their mother informed them, rolling her eyes is disgust.

"Listen to your Mom, guys, and head for bed in a few minutes. I'll finish putting the rest of your boxes in the boat for you, deal?"

"Sure, we will go right to bed if we can get out of doing the rest of that stuff, won't we, Andrew?" Marisa asked her brother with a smile.

"Sure, sis," he answered.

"Thanks Stew." Cathren was glad he would finish loading the boxes instead of the children, who would fight going through the motions of it as they were emotionally and physically drained.

CHAPTER EIGHT

Cathren stretched her arm to press the snooze button on the alarm, then promptly fell back into a deep sleep. It had been after midnight before she could halt her racing mind over all that needed to be done before they could leave.

There were coolers to pack, and the cat had to be loaded, along with the latest addition to the family. Everything from the last pot, the dishes to the broom ran through her mind. She felt foolish at dwelling on such trivial items because she knew they could be stopped along a country road and stripped of everything in their possession, including their lives. It happened to others on occasion. The nightly news exploded with such stories, only to be forgotten by the next day in time for another explosive story. To make matters worse, many small insurance companies had recently gone bankrupt from paying out backbreaking funds needed to make good on commitments to their customers. Some insurance companies were now only insuring structures and not contents. Theft was so rampant that it was impossible to keep up with all claims anymore. Piece by piece, the system was falling apart. Societal and government dikes were full of leaks, and as soon as one drip or gush was repaired, ten others trickled through, a burst then a flood of problems.

Stew knocked on Cathren's door. "I need to make sure you are up and out of town by dawn while the area is quiet." He continued, "The Saturday weather report was calling for rain in the morning, clearing by afternoon with warm temperatures. It could mean trouble in the making on the streets if the weather is nice. Rain may make it safer as far as crime, but it would make it harder to pull the boat. If you could cross the Ohio River shortly after daylight, hopefully it will be clear, and you should have smooth driving conditions to the farm."

Stew started a pot of coffee. By the time Cathren showered, he had the thermos filled, in the van and a full cup on the table waiting for her.

"Is this crazy or what? When I wake in the morning things don't seem so bad. Maybe I should stay here after all," Cathren told him. "I'm uneasy and unsure about making this decision so fast."

She sipped her coffee and waited for Stew to respond.

"No, it is not crazy. This is no time to be unsure about the decision you have made. There isn't a soul in the area who wouldn't like to be in your shoes right now. This is the perfect opportunity, and you need to take it." He continued, "It is shaky all over and I just don't know what is about to come down, but I sure feel something. Besides, you need a good vacation. The opportunity exists. It would be foolish not to take a break. This government debt isn't a late-night talk show joke anymore. Instead of dealing with issues to help save the economy, the government just let the debt get bigger and bigger. Now it is beyond controlling. It all may fall apart at any time, and when it does it is going to be bad, real bad. It is clearly best for you to get the kids away while you can. If things are better by fall, then no sweat, you will have had a nice vacation in the country." His words were confident, but Stew's voice shook, and the look in his eyes let Cathren know that he was not optimistic about the future.

"You know, I really get tired of living in fear day and night. My stomach is in a knot each time Andrew and Marisa are out of the house. I am so afraid for them. We're still so keyed up over Nate's death and every other violent act around us. Maybe this is the best thing to do."

"Yes it is. And this is why I think now is the time to get away. Please, have no doubts," he told her. "I will be there to visit soon. I need a vacation and would enjoy boating."

"We'll be outside looking in. Surely, the economy will pick up a little by fall and everything will calm down. If the area isn't peaceful by August, I may stay for the winter. Keep that to yourself. Marisa would die if she knew I said such a thing."

"Enough of this, you need to leave in the next half hour. There won't be much traffic early in the morning. There was trouble along the interstate last night and it appeared to be organized by gangs. It's beginning to look more like terrorist groups or guerilla warfare instead of isolated incidents related to gangs. The confiscated arms were made in an underground factory. State troopers will be thick, and that will be to your advantage. I plan to follow you to the Ohio River," Stew informed her.

"Good, I hate to ask you to do anything else for me. You've done so much already. I am so thankful for you," she told him.

"And I'm thankful for what you've done for me. It will be lonely when you're gone. I've become so close to Marisa and Andrew. They have helped me understand my own daughter. They have been good for me," he told her.

"Time to leave! Marisa! Andrew! Load up! Let's hit the road," Cathren told them, standing outside their bedroom doors. "You can go back to sleep in the van."

Cathren did not look back to the house as she turned onto the next street. The van was so full there was little room for animals or humans. Cathren already realized that Stew was right about the pig. Andrew and Marisa were fascinated by it and were attached already. It would help the transition from suburbia and city life to life on a farm. Cathren yawned. The boat was so full it felt as if it would pull the van backward. It was clearly overloaded. She hoped it wasn't obvious to Stew that she could not tow a boat well. She planned to avoid backing up anywhere because she would really be in trouble then. Getting to the country posed no problem because there was virtually no traffic.

The van and boat were slow, so it was well into daylight before they approached crossing the Ohio River into Maysville, Kentucky. Cathren pulled into the parking lot of a church along the roadway, got out of the van, and walked to Stew's car. Marisa and Andrew were sleeping, and she tried to be careful so as to not disturb them. The farther away from home Marisa was when she woke, the less traumatic it would be for her.

"I think it will be okay now. Please go back home. I don't want you to get caught out later in the day," she told him. The air was damp and cool. Dark clouds hung low over the countryside, announcing that a cold rain was on the way.

"I agree. Just be careful and try not to make any stops until you are well into Kentucky. Do you have enough money?" he asked.

"Yes, I do. Nate's insurance has helped a lot. It keeps us from drowning, anyway, since there is no more child support."

Cathren embraced Stew. Tears ran down their cheeks. Neither could speak. Cathren climbed into her van and pulled out of the church lot. Stew stood alone, watching helplessly until they were out of sight.

The river current had begun to lessen its grip on the morning fog, allowing it to rise toward the hilltops surrounding the river, when Cathren caught the reverent sight from the van. She praised God for their safety to this point of their journey south. She could now see the Simon Kenton Bridge that connected Aberdeen and Maysville. They drifted on in the foggy mist until they came close to the turn onto the bridge. She remembered having been told that guards would be standing near and on the bridge. She was assured this would be a safe crossing. All bridges crossing main waterways were guarded now. There had been too many incidents of gang members trying to destroy the highway system. This sort of thing always happened in other countries, or so Cathren thought, anyway. She never dreamed this could happen here. Could this turn into a World War Three nightmare? "Yes," she whispered to herself, "it could."

"What was that noise? Marisa! Andrew! Wake up. Oh my. I'm losing the boat. I can't control the van. We're all over the road." Cathren felt sure she had been caught in crossfire as she tried to gain control of her swerving van. The men guarding the bridge ran to safety, running far from where they thought the swerving vehicle may be heading.

Marisa woke.

"Mom, what are you doing? We are going to wreck." Instantly realizing the danger of the situation, she sat screaming.

Cathren braked slowly, beginning to feel the van stabilize. The rear of the van and boat weaved across one side of the road and then the other less and less as Cathren continued lightly touching her brakes. Repeating, repeating. The van and boat seemed tamed and stopped of their own volition in the middle of the intersection at the entrance of the bridge. With arms draped over the steering wheel and head leaning forward, Cathren shook uncontrollably.

One of the guards managed to accumulate enough nerve to approach the van, for he too was not sure gunfire had not been the cause of the commotion. "Are you all right, lady?" he yelled through the closed window. It took all she had to muster to nod.

"Unlock the door," he told her. She unlocked the door and he helped her from the van onto the pavement. "You sure gave us a scare! Is everyone all right?"

It was visible to him that this was another family headed south. The sight was common now since a good part of southern Ohioans had Appalachian roots.

"We need to get that tire changed in a jiffy, before traffic builds up. Just calm down. It's going to be fine now. We can get you back on the road here in just a few minutes."

Cathren's legs would barely hold her. She still shook uncontrollably. Several guards came to her aid and within fifteen minutes the tire was changed. She was thankful Stew had fixed the spare the night before.

"I thought it was gunfire at first." Her voice shook.

"We wondered about that, too," one of them told her.

"There, you will be ready to be on your way again in ten minutes. Just drive slowly, like you were when approaching the turnoff at the bridge. It's a good thing you were driving slowly or you might not be here to tell about it," he informed her.

Cathren dug into her pocket and pulled out money to pay the men for their help. She told them she would appreciate it if they would let her pay them, but they refused.

"Looks like you're headed south to family. A lot of people have the same idea now," one of the men told her.

"I'm headed to the family farm. No one wanted it when my grandfather passed away, so my late husband and I bought it," she told him.

"With the way it is getting in Ohio, that is probably the best investment you ever made," he told her. "My wife and I moved from the city to a farm south of Maysville a few years back. It's a big adjustment from the conveniences of the city. It will be hard for you at first, but hang in there and don't give up. Good luck."

"Thanks, I'll remember that." Cathren got back into the van. She tried hard to keep from exposing to Marisa how scared she was of crossing the bridge. Now the crossing seemed as frightening as the blowout. Her hands still shook, making it difficult to hold onto the steering wheel. Cathren was relieved when she was finally driving through the picturesque, winding Maysville and back onto the country roads that would lead her to the farm. The long drive to the farm was still ahead of them.

She was putting the miles behind her at a pace she felt comfortable with.

"Mom! That pig just peed again. Oh, yuck! Now it's pooping in its cage. Mom, it smells awful. Can't we stop for just a minute and let it out so it can poop outside?" Andrew spoke sleepily.

"I need a break. There's a place I can turn off just ahead. I can see it from here. It's right next to a creek. Andrew, put the leash on the pig when I stop the van. I'll take the cage and rinse it in the creek and let it dry before we're on our way again. How is the cat doing in its cage?"

"Still sleeping."

"Good. This is a nice spot for stretching our legs. We still have a good way to go," their mother told them.

"Mom, do we really have to do this? I mean, this is crazy. I don't want to live in that old house on the farm. It only has one bathroom and the inside is not decorated except for that hundred-year-old wallpaper in the kitchen," Marisa complained.

"We just have to remedy the decorating part when we get there. It is something I have wanted to do for years anyway. It needs a good coat of paint inside and out. It could be a cute, homey little place with a little TLC," Cathren told her while rinsing poop out of the pig's cage in the creek by the side of the road.

"Can we get back in the van and get to the farm?" Andrew asked. "I want to show it to the pig."

"Sure, honey. Let me wash my hands with the soap we brought with us and we will be on our way. I remember a small restaurant a few miles down this road that serves a great country breakfast. How about it? We can stretch a bit and have plenty of energy for the rest of the trip. Your pig is going to love the farm and the cat, too. We'll be there soon."

CHAPTER NINE

"Finally! Look, Andrew, do you remember this road? The lane is just beyond the curve. Oh dear, now the tricky part. I made it through the gas station, now let's see how I do on the lane. This is going to be a real pill. Here goes whatever is to be!" Cathren told them as she negotiated the turnoff onto the lane.

The van and boat jiggled over ruts where strong southern storms had washed the gravel to one side of the drive. Cathren tried her best to pull to the left, avoiding the ditch that was necessary to keep heavy rains from completely washing away the gravel. The pig had done its business in the cage again and the smell had become unbearable. Andrew and Marisa bickered for the last one hundred miles, adding to the already tense drive. The cat still snoozed, oblivious of the commotion during most of the trip.

The air grew heavy and damp. The sky threatened rain. Cathren had done well avoiding bad weather thus far. Under a heavy sky, the threesome climbed out of the van and walked to the front door. Cathren slid the key into the lock and pushed open the door. Cool, musty air greeted the new residents. Marisa gagged at the smell.

"Yuck, Mom! I'm not about to go in there unless it smells better. This smells as bad as the pig poop in the van. I can't believe this. I could be home still in bed like normal people should be!" Marisa complained.

"Okay kids. Gather a few small branches lying under the trees over there. Watch for copperheads and rattlers. It is not like home. I'll start a fire in the woodstove. Marisa, I'll put some cinnamon in a pan of water on top of the stove. That will clear the musty smell. The warmth of the stove will get rid of the dampness fast."

Cathren grabbed yesterday's paper from under the seat in the van, though she had not yet read it. After shredding it and placing it in the woodstove, she laid the gathered kindling on top of the paper and lit the fire.

In a matter of seconds, smoke billowed from the inside of the stove into the living room, rushing into the kitchen and throughout the house.

"Everybody out, Mom's caught the house on fire," yelled Marisa. They ran through the back door into the yard, choking from smoke inhalation.

"Marisa! Take Andrew down by the barn. I have to pull the van and boat away from the house. Hurry!" Cathren cried. Cathren haphazardly backed the boat down the drive before it jackknifed and she could move it no further. She jumped from the van and was running back to the little white frame house when she caught sight of a red Ford pickup turning into the lane toward the house. From the truck jumped a middle aged man with a couple days' beard growth, unkempt hair, and greased jeans.

"What's going on?" he yelled.

"The house is on fire. I tried to light a fire in the woodstove and smoke billowed out," Cathren cried, barely getting her words out.

"Did you check to see if the damper was open before you lit the fire?" he calmly asked, trying to determine the problem.

"Yes, I checked that first." *How stupid does he think I am?* She wondered to herself.

"When was the last time someone used that woodstove?" he questioned her again, trying to narrow the cause of the fire.

"It has been at least three years that I know of," Cathren said, shaking.

"Man alive, lady. This place could burn completely down." The man ran to his pickup and drove it through the yard to the lowest side of the front porch. He climbed onto the porch roof from atop the truck cab then onto the house roof.

"Birds' nests," the man shouted from the roof.

He climbed back onto the truck bed then tied a rope around the handle of a black metal toolbox only large enough to hold a few screwdrivers and a hammer. He emptied the box contents on the ground and replaced the tools with rocks from the driveway and closed the box. He climbed back onto the roof and lowered the box into the chimney, pulling the box up then down again and again. Within seconds smoke started to rise from the chimney instead of the back door. The man continued to run the small toolbox up and down the chimney until it was clear of debris.

"The chimney is clear now and shouldn't give you any more problems. The old man who used to live here replaced the whole thing before he died a few years back," he told her.

The tall, dark man with salt-and-pepper hair climbed back into his pickup before Cathren had time to introduce herself as the new resident for the summer. She felt incredibly stupid over the incident and walked back into the house to open all the windows and doors.

"Well, I just doubled my cleaning chores now that I have managed to smoke up the place. The place doesn't smell musty anymore, that's for sure. The water pump isn't on yet, so we need to drive to Herb and Martha's to see if he can stop by to prime and start the pump. I am not sure the cell phone will work here," Cathren told her children. "Let's get into the van after I get the boat disconnected and we will see what else I do to embarrass myself into hibernation."

Cathren turned onto the road and headed to her nearest neighbor's home. She knocked on the front door, and Martha answered with the same hug as always. Herb went to the barn to get the necessary tools for priming the pump.

"Cathren, make sure you don't start a fire in the woodstove until I clean the chimney. It will only take a few minutes," Herb instructed her. "It is probably full of birds' nests or raccoons."

"I already made that mistake," she sheepishly told them. "A man in a red pickup stopped and rescued the day." She went on to tell them what happened.

"That's Kent Freeman. He owns the place that backs up to the other side of our farm," Martha told her. "Real nice fella'. He and his wife split up last year. He served in the military overseas and finished college after they bought their farm. At first, they visited the farm on weekends several years back, but then after he finished school they moved here. His wife found someone else on a visit home last summer and they were divorced right away. He keeps pretty much to himself. He doesn't socialize much even though some of the single women his age have tried to snag him."

"After he cleaned the chimney, he didn't stick around long enough for an introduction. I didn't know if I offended him or what," Cathren told Martha.

"I doubt it. He's easygoing about things, but he stays busy working. He was probably in a hurry.

He always gives a hand when you need it, and he'll stop by once in a while to borrow a tool or two. He's plain-spoken, even though he reads a lot. Mr. Milford, our postman, says he doesn't know how one person could read so much stuff. Says Kent gets more reading material than the library up town. Of course that's an exaggeration, but it makes the point," Martha said to her.

"If he stops by, will you tell him I intend to pay him in a few days?" Cathren asked her.

"You can forget that. Now *that* would offend him. If you are here any amount of time, you'll get the chance to return the favor soon enough," said Herb.

Cathren followed Herb back to her place. It took two hours to get the pump primed and running again. They let the water run through the faucets for several minutes until it ran clear. They unloaded the van and set the contents on the floor of the kitchen. Marisa put their sleeping bags on the floor in the living room while Cathren went outside and gathered several pieces of the wood Herb had left on the porch for the evening. Andrew made sure the pig was safe in the cage outside the kitchen door. By this time, Cathren was beyond tired. All three promptly fell asleep by nightfall, but not before Cathren could fall onto her knees and give thanks to the Lord and asking for his help.

CHAPTER TEN

Sunday was spent cleaning, unloading, and unpacking. The old refrigerator she and Nate had purchased at an auction when they first bought the farm was small, but it worked.

Marisa and Andrew ate doughnuts for breakfast from snacks packed in the van. They headed outside to play with the pig. The cat snoozed in the corner behind the woodstove, content with her new warm spot on the hearth. Marisa and Andrew claimed the two small bedrooms on the first floor as theirs. Upstairs was an unfinished room used mostly for storage. A door off the kitchen concealed the steep, narrow steps leading to the second floor. It led to a room that fell to an angle toward the eaves of the roof and left only a couple of feet of vertical wall space, giving the feeling of attic space. The front side over the kitchen near the steps was built several feet toward the center of the house, leaving a good-sized closet for storage. Andrew and Marisa set up the portable television in the kitchen, quickly discovering that television reception in the area was poor, a problem that went over like a thousand lead balloons.

Cathren finally had the coolers unpacked and discovered her cookware in the cuddy cabin of the boat. It took the entire day to begin cleaning the house and to unpack half the boxes. For dinner that evening, Cathren fixed biscuits, country ham, grits, fried eggs, fried potatoes, and sausage gravy. A southern meal settled their frayed nerves. They felt ravenous after their first full day on the farm. The second night soon surrounded the farmhouse. It promptly put the three refugees into a deep slumber in their sleeping bags again. Silent stars kept watch over the household while the potbellied pig huddled on the back porch surrounded by bails of straw from the barn.

The cold antique hardwood floor beneath Cathren's feet made sure it would not take an alarm clock to completely wake her at the crack of dawn. It was chilly, a sure indication that the fire was nearly out and needed a good stoking. Cathren had learned the skill of banking a fire from her grandfather so that it would hold warmth through the cool morning hours of a spring morning. There were a few hot coals left.

She had been too tired for a change of clothes the night before, so she had slept in the clothes she had on. She heated water for morning instant coffee then stepped outside to check on the pig.

Wet dew sprinkled across the bluegrass waiting for morning sunshine with the background of a perfect Kentucky sky. Redbud trees announced spring through their brilliant reds from the front yard up to the surrounding Appalachian foothills. Cathren climbed up the rear unit of the boat, unsnapped the dew-covered camper top. She crawled over the engine cover and into the boat to dig through a few remaining boxes left unpacked. She tried to remember where she put the coffeemaker because drinking instant coffee was already getting old with the first cup. After rummaging through the third box, she found the coffeemaker and a can of coffee. Twenty minutes later, Cathren came to life while sipping a strong cup of java.

She walked through the yard and found several pieces of wood Herb had left outside the day before. No sounds of civilization could be heard. All was quiet. She shook at the sight of a pristine, crisp Kentucky daybreak. Dew, still clinging to each blade of bluegrass, began to sparkle as rays of light were sent tumbling over the hillsides before the sun would fully show itself. Budded maples, wild cherry, sassafras, mimosas, and oaks waited their spring coming out, letting some spring wildflowers celebrate their time in the sun before they were shaded by the deciduous forest for summer.

Cathren imagined her soul flowing to where logging roads could be seen spiraling through the surrounding hills, where spring foliage had not yet turned into the blanket of green that would soon hide those very roads. In weeks to come, the woods canopy would turn into a protective green shield, keeping undergrowth from the harm of the southern sun during summer months ahead. For now, these very foothills hid Cathren away from the world she had left in their morning mist.

Chattering birds chorused in the air with a promise of safe days ahead. Morning shadows shortened with each moment the sun climbed over the eastern hillsides. Cathren had forgotten how a Kentucky morning could mend a soul, fill a sad heart with happiness, and massage the mind into perfect harmony with nature.

She could not think of a better way to begin her day and would like to have wakened Marisa and Andrew to share it with her, but she knew they would not have the same appreciation of this special moment she did. In fact, she thought comically, they would more than likely ruin its calmness with the complaint that it was not quite time to wake for their lessons. Instead, Cathren's dew-soaked feet carried her back over the threshold of the house with an armload of kindling for the woodstove.

The morning was consumed with making a list of errands and chores for the family. A trip into town was needed to order the phone installation, buy groceries, and a visit to the local library for cards so Andrew and Marisa could begin visiting. It would help supplement their homeschooling curriculum since she did not think it wise to enroll Marisa and Andrew into a local school so late in the school year. Cathren let her children sleep a while longer than usual. When she did leave her refuge for town, she saw that the children had started their lessons for the day.

By the end of her shopping trip, most of the town knew Carl McCarty's granddaughter was visiting and, by appearances, planned to stick around for the spring and summer months. Much of the errand-hopping was done around the town square housing the old county courthouse. Cathren could still remember from her childhood the creaking courthouse floors and large ten-foot-high pine doors that led to each county office throughout the old three-story red southern brick building. The wooden, backless benches still stationed themselves along the sidewalk of the courthouse square where much of the community news changed hands.

A good two hours passed before Cathren was on her way back to the farm. As she made the curve a few hundred yards beyond the town limits, she saw the sign advertising "free puppies". Cathren knew what the farm was missing and it would comfort Marisa's heartache for home. The eight-mile drive back to the farm could not pass fast enough for Cathren's excitement.

"Hey guys. Load yourselves in the van. I need your help picking out something," Cathren ordered.

"Mom, we're not finished with our work," Andrew told her.

"There is a sign at a farm near town that says "free puppies" on it. Would you like to pick one from the litter?" Their mom asked. "I remember Grandpa McCarty saying a farm wasn't a farm without a good dog, and that a mixed breed was the healthiest and most loyal of all dogs. I would say they are mixed if they are free."

"I'll choose a pup. Andrew can stay and finish his work. I'll finish when I get back," Marisa told her mother.

"I want to help choose," Andrew squealed. "Don't leave without me. I need to put my shoes on."

Cathren turned into the drive with the sign. The lady of the house came out the front door. She conversed with Cathren for several minutes while Andrew and Marisa tried to choose a puppy.

"Mom, I want the black one and Marisa found a spotted one she likes. Can we have two instead of one?" asked Andrew.

Cathren didn't have the heart to say no to Andrew's pleading eyes or the puppy in his arms, so she nodded. Besides, Cathren had just purchased a dozen hens and one rooster from her new acquaintance, Mrs. Jarboe. Another trip into town was required for the purchase of puppy food and chicken feed before the trip back to the farm. Herb was busy unloading firewood and two buckets of coal when Cathren returned.

"Chickens! Old Mrs. Jarboe's been tryin' to sell those hens to someone for three months. It costs more for the mash to feed those critters than it does to buy eggs off the shelf at the grocers." Herb, hoping he hadn't hurt Cathren's feelings, quickly commented. "On the other hand, eggs from a free-range chicken taste a heck of a lot better than those from one of those chicken factories. They will be organically grown, so they are healthier, too. When you get your first dozen, we will make a point of having a breakfast of fresh eggs and country ham. There is nothing that tastes as good as farm fresh eggs for breakfast in the morning."

"I'll be the hostess for breakfast. It'll be the first get-together here. How does that sound?" Cathren asked.

"Sounds like a good offer to me. Now, to other business at hand. It will soon be time set out the crops. Since you are on the farm this early, I don't see any reason why you can't raise crops this year. Martha and I will do what we can to show you the ropes, and it will give you a little income for the winter. If you go back to Ohio in the fall, you can take what you raised with you. Raising tobacco is hard work, and you can't sell it 'till right before winter sets in, but it'll help pay the winter bills if you stay. This place still has a tobacco base. I also need to tell you there is a church school uptown the kids can attend when they want. They can ride the regular school bus, as it makes a stop at the church where the school is. They work with homeschooled students who want to attend certain classes, such as geometry. You might give it a try," informed Herb.

"Marisa and Andrew have no friends here. I think that is a wonderful idea. I will look into that immediately. Thank you so much!" Cathren was beginning to plan ahead.

"You might consider planting bell pepper plants, too. There is an organic farmers' market about thirty miles from here where produce can be sold if you go that route. They can provide a source of income. We'll talk about that later in the week," Herb said.

"I'll do my best not to disappoint you," Cathren told him. "I really do appreciate this. I want to repay you in some way."

"You already have just by being here. Martha and I aren't getting any younger, and it's a comfort to know we've got good neighbors close by. When I need to pick up equipment and supplies for the farm, I worry about leaving Martha out here by herself. Her arthritis makes it hard for her some days, especially during fall and winter months when it is damp out. Having you nearby while I'm gone will be a comfort."

"On the condition we stay here," Cathren said to him.

Herb smiled. "Huh! By the time you get settled in, youngun', you won't give a second thought about going back up north again. Guess I better head back to the house. I'll be over sometime this evenin' to plow the garden for ya'll. When it dries a good bit, I'll disk it, then you can plant what you want for the summer. See ya' later." Herb climbed into his pickup and drove out the lane.

Tobacco, peppers, *garden,* Cathren thought to herself. She couldn't believe she would be so busy already. Spring and summer promised to be full.

The serviceman from the phone company pulled into the drive to connect the phone line and internet to the house. Cathren was eager to get her phone installed so she could put a call through to Seth, for it was the voice of the person she had regretted leaving in Ohio that she needed so dearly to hear. Cathren feared he may change his mind about a move south. She hoped he was still looking forward to coming to the farm for the summer.

Marisa and Andrew began studying at eight a.m. Tuesday morning and finished their work by twelve o'clock so they could ride with Cathren into town again for more supplies. Cathren needed drywall patch for the upstairs wall, her future bedroom.

The trip to the hardware store for the drywall patching materials and wallpaper for the upstairs bedroom and kitchen took longer than she expected because Marisa went through nearly each book before choosing a paper for her room that was in stock. Cathren didn't regret letting her help choose the décor because Marisa had gone the entire morning without complaining about the trip south. Marisa's desire to decorate her room at the farm was a welcome relief to her mother. They made a stop at the material store across the street to purchase cloth for curtains matching their wallpaper selections.

While exiting the material store, Cathren noticed several men sitting on benches located on the square outside the courthouse. This was not an unusual sight since the county seat was the hub of most agricultural communities in this part of the country. People were taking advantage of the nice weather to exchange general information on or around the courthouse steps. Cathren wouldn't have paid much attention to the men across the street, but one gentleman caught her eye. It was Kent

Freeman. Clean-shaven and dressed in khakis and a plaid shirt, his appearance was much different than it had been the day she met him on the farm.

Cathren was secure that she went unnoticed, but she was mistaken. Kent always kept an eye out on his surroundings, a keen sense acquired when he found himself surviving the jungles and deserts during his service to his country. He was glad Cathren was on the farm for a visit; it would put a little excitement in life to have a green city person transplanted to the country. This should be good entertainment, he thought to himself. He could not help but chuckle under his breath over the incident with the woodstove, a story he kept to himself.

Cathren gave Marisa and Andrew money for lunch at the café across the street from the courthouse then she drove to Simm's Farm and Garden Supply on the edge of town, where she checked out seed and bedding plants, pretending to genuinely know what she was doing. She knew she was in the heart of gardening country, unlike the nurseries that catered to suburbanites back home who had to be baby-stepped into gardening a few flowers on the front lawn. She purchased seed for squash, corn, beans, Swiss chard, lettuce, and a host of other garden varieties to set out after the garden was disked.

To the side of the seeds and bedding plants was a row of rotor tillers for sale. The rear tined one in the back row was like one of her neighbors back home used in his garden. Her former neighbor was so excited how easy it was to use that he had every adult on the street come into his garden to give it a try. Cathren remembered how smoothly it ran and how the garden soil felt like silt after the tiller went over the clods of dirt.

The salesman approached her to see if she was interested in buying one. Ten minutes later Cathren signed the receipt for the tiller, though she'd only tried the one at her neighbor's property, hoping the money she would save by gardening would reduce living expenses the coming months. The salesman reassured her it would be delivered the following morning and that it would pay for itself if she planned her gardening well. Cathren bought flower seeds and plants in addition to the garden seeds already purchased, then went to the café where the children were having lunch.

"Mom, that man who helped us when the chimney smoked us out ate his lunch at the booth right behind us. Some woman sat with him," Andrew told her.

"We greeted him and thanked him for helping us out the other day," Marisa told her. "The woman he was with is pretty with very expensive clothes on."

"He wanted to know why we were not in school. We told him we went to a part-time school at home. We said when the crime was too bad our school closed and the teachers taught over the computers through conference software. He said we had a good idea there, that several families around here homeschool and there was a group that met in town that we could join. He said they announce their meetings in the local newspaper," Andrew told her.

"Good. It was nice of him to tell you about the group. He must have been having lunch with his girlfriend. Are you nearly finished with lunch? I need to stop at the library on the way home to check out some books on gardening, so I can figure out what to do with all these seeds I just bought.

Between the internet and books, I may have some success," Cathren laughed. "Tell me about your shopping. Did you find anything interesting?"

"I bought perfume at the drug store and Andrew bought comic books. I think we're done with our meal, let's go back to the farm and check on the animals," Marisa suggested. Her mother could barely believe the comment came from her daughter.

When Cathren arrived back at the farm, she placed a call to Seth and left a message for him to call when he returned from his classes. As soon as she placed the phone down, it rang. She answered.

"Hi, Mom," Seth said to her.

"That was fast. I didn't expect you to call back right away," she told him.

Seth answered, "They said I walked in immediately after you called. Is everything all right?"

"Yes, it is going quite well so far. Marisa and Andrew are adjusting better than I thought possible. Marisa is still upset, but they are so busy unpacking and taking care of their animals that there's little time for them to think about leaving. How are you?" she asked.

"It is pretty calm here, as opposed to what is going on in the cities. It got pretty wild last Saturday night. Stew called and told me not to come home for the weekend. Trouble had already started when he arrived in town after he followed you to the river," informed Seth. "I plan to get out of dodge as soon as finals are over. I plan to check on the availability of jobs at docks on the lake, maybe pumping gas this summer."

"That answered my next question. We will put the boat in when you arrive. You can do some fishing and exploring if you like. You could use some time on the lake to relax," Cathren said.

"Yes. Would it be okay with you if Susan came along for the trip? Her father retired this winter and her parents have already left to spend the summer in Canada. Susan doesn't really want to stay in Canada the entire summer."

"Fine with me." replied Cathren. "Give me a call when the arrangements for your trip are finalized."

"Sure. And you don't need to send any money for the trip. Susan and I have enough to make it. I have to hang up. Someone is waiting in line for the phone here. My cell phone is out today. May have been cell towers sabotaged. So many parents are calling the school to see if it is still calm, it is hard to talk on a phone long without someone else needing it. Even though most of us have cell phones, parents still call dorms and apartments."

"I am so glad you are doing well. Love you. Bye," Cathren told him. Cathren was relieved Seth planned to spend the summer on the farm and that Susan would be coming too. Now she needed to put a call through to Stew.

"Hello? Stew?"

"Hey Cat! How are you?" he asked.

"I'm okay. I just spoke with Seth. He told me you asked him to stay away from the house because there was trouble last weekend. Are you alright?"

"Sure, but it got a little rough last weekend. Apparently some of the gangs were fighting over turf throughout the weekend and it got pretty nasty on the streets. It was all-out warfare for a while. Some of the gangs are still struggling to gain control over certain areas around here. During the fighting some of the grocery stores were ransacked again and left devoid of food. The newspapers reported that several grocers decided to call it quits and not reopen because of this."

"Thanks for calling Seth," she told him.

"I'm glad you're not here. Some of these gangs are creating their own little draft system in the areas they control. If you don't cooperate, the gangs can make it pretty miserable for you and your family. Some gangs are posting a twenty-four-hour guard around the areas they claim to control while other aggressive groups try to expand their territory, resulting in bloodshed. Cathren, I just don't see how this is happening in the United States." Stew sounded depressed over the situation.

"I'm glad we are not there, too. I was so afraid for the children, and with good reason. Stew, I don't have to lock my doors when I leave the farm. Seth is still planning to stay on the farm this summer. I will be glad when this semester is over and he arrives safely, which leads me to one of the reasons I called. I have made the decision to have all our belongings and furniture sent here. It has been such a relief to not be afraid while walking on a town street. I didn't know how bad it was at home until I left. Could you hire a mover and have the rest of our things sent? I know it will cost an arm and a leg, but I am going to go through with this. I do not want to drag Andrew and Marisa back to that hell until all this is over. That may happen in just a few months from now for all I know, but I would feel better if I called this home for a while," she said.

"Cathren, I really hate sending your things south, but you're right about this. I may be able to save you money on moving your furniture and the rest of your belongings. One of my clients owns a small trucking business, and he hauled my furniture from the apartment to the house when he had a spare truck around. His trucks make several trips south each week to pick up loads of produce to bring back north. Sometimes a truck is empty on the way south. He may haul your things to you. I can leave a message at his office right away. If he has a truck going out, he usually goes where it is safe to send drivers. I'll see what I can do. And speaking of money, do you have enough to live on? Cathren, I know you have a lot of pride and would not ask for money if you were starving."

"Yes, Stew. I can survive. As you know, I was still the beneficiary of Nate's life insurance policy when he died. If I am very careful, I can make it last a while longer. If your client could work something out for me I would appreciate it. Every time I turn around I need something that is sitting nearly two hundred miles away, whether it is the food processor or my good sweeper," Cathren told him.

"If he makes a run, it could be anytime, even tonight. I'll hire someone to help pack the rest of your things this evening. This will be a good job for my sister, she is still looking for some extra work," Stew said.

"That will be great. I'll call Seth and tell him to drive down when finals are over and not worry about picking up all his clothes at the house. Listen, I know you are busy. Good luck with the shop this weekend. Bye now, take care," she concluded.

"Cathren, I miss you and the children." Stew paused. "Bye, Cat."

"Mom, can I call Chad now that you are finished making your calls?" Marisa asked.

"Sure, but don't stay on the phone more than fifteen minutes," Cathren quite firmly told her.

Andrew teased, "Marisa's calling her boyfriend, ha! He probably has a new girlfriend by now."

"Mom! Would you make him shut up and get out? Now, Andrew, before I wring your neck. Mom, do something with him," Marisa yelled.

"Andrew, mind your manners. Get your fishing pole out of the barn. Didn't Martha and Herb say they would take you fishing at the dock this evening? They should be here any time, so get ready now before you get into trouble and lose the privilege to go," warned Cathren as she turned to the sound of a vehicle in the drive. It was the delivery truck from Simm's Farm and Garden Supply.

"I live down the road from you all. Since the tiller was ready for delivery by the end of the day, I volunteered to drop it off early," the deliveryman told her.

"Yes, I am glad you could deliver it earlier than scheduled. The garden is in this direction. They told me you could give me a few pointers on how to run this," she told him.

"I will be more than happy to show you." He could tell she was in dire need of instruction and told her she would be glad she purchased the one with the electric starter. He left Cathren tilling on her own when he felt sure that she knew how to run the tiller. She finished tilling a small section to the side of the big garden that Herb would work up. Soon she found an old rusty hoe in the shed behind the house and figured it was better than nothing. Cathren got the seeds and fertilizer out of the van then began planting peas, onions, lettuce, and a few

105

potato sets. She would wait until Herb could work up the rest of the garden before planting more. She had forgotten to put on the brown jersey gloves she bought at Simm's and her fingers began to blister after she used the hoe for a short while. When she walked into the house to get her gloves off the table, she found Marisa still on the phone with her boyfriend in Ohio.

"Marisa, I have been outside for an hour. The phone bill will be sky high. We have limited long distance hours with our plan!" Cathren told her, and Marisa reacted with a quick good-bye to her boyfriend.

The afternoon was quite windy. Herb thought the wind had dried the soil enough to work up the garden, so he finished that job before they took Andrew fishing at the dock. Cathren planted three rows of cabbage and other cole crops and still had plants left. Martha had raised them from seed and had at least a hundred extra, so she told Cathren to take as many as she wanted because Martha planned to turn the extras under during the next couple days. Cathren could not bear to see them all destroyed, so, in her naïveté, she took them all. Martha had commented about how beginner gardeners could never let extra plants be turned under, and how Cathren would learn soon enough. Cathren continued planting through the evening until she was too tired to carry on and hoped to make it to bed early. She decided the garden needed to be larger.

"Mom!" Marisa yelled from the kitchen door, "Stew is on the phone." Cathren ran to the phone.

CHAPTER ELEVEN

"Cat, I spoke with my client a few minutes ago. He has a load to pick up in Alabama at noon tomorrow. He is loading your furniture this very minute. They plan to run straight through the night, so you need to stay up till around two in the morning. You'll need someone there to help unload because they're in a hurry. Can you come up with someone?" he asked.

"I'll call Herb. He'll know someone I can hire," Cathren told him. "Oh thanks so much."

"No thanks needed, you know that. I need to hang up since I'm helping them load the truck along with my sister and her teenagers. It's going fast. Bye."

Cathren looked around at the small home of her grandfather's, trying to decide where to put everything. She called Martha to see if they knew of anyone who could be hired to unload her furniture when it arrived around two in the morning. Herb told her not to worry. He would be there around one o'clock with someone. Cathren set her alarm clock for twelve so she could get some rest before the truck arrived. It would be a long night.

Cathren startled when the alarm went off at the stroke of twelve. She got up and stirred together a coffee cake to bake so it would be warm when the truck and help arrived. She made sure the barnyard and outside lights were on so the driver could easily find the house.

Herb arrived at one o'clock sharp with a helper. Cathren turned crimson when she saw Kent Freeman standing at the door, as she was still quite embarrassed over their first meeting. The two men sat on the rickety chairs at the card table in the kitchen eating cake and drinking coffee. Cathren could not tell if this man minded being in her home in the middle of the night to unload furniture and her family's belongings.

Cathren participated in chit-chat with the two gentlemen. Herb repeated the stories Cathren had heard many times of her grandfather and his childhood days with his friend Herb, the Depression, and the time the Tennessee Valley Authority built the dams that resulted in reservoirs to provide electricity, improving lives in the region from the electricity it provided. He recalled that many of his generation were still extremely upset because the government built the dams that drove many of them from their homes.

Herb told of the small towns that were moved from the path of the future lake and that foundations of buildings could still be seen in some reservoirs when water was low in late fall, that a few local residents still refused to fish or boat on the reservoirs to this day. Herb maintained that the dams were for the good in the long run, and a person would have to be a fool not to accept that after all these years.

Cathren was refilling cups with coffee when the phone rang, it was Martha. The truck had passed Cathren's lane and stopped in front of Martha's after realizing the mistake. Martha had gone outside and had showed them where to turn around. By the time Cathren put the down the phone, she could see the lights from the truck turning off the road toward her house.

"I'm so relieved my furniture made it. There have been so many robberies on the roadway, I was afraid it would happen to this shipment." She sighed with relief.

"I think you have had your fair share of trouble this past winter. I didn't doubt that your things would get here safely," Herb assured her.

"Looks like we've plenty of work ahead of us," said Kent Freeman when the truckers opened the rear door of the trailer. She offered the truckers fresh coffee and cake. They declined, but did ask if she could put a couple pieces of the cake in a bag to take with them when they left. They were on a tight schedule and needed to unload her furniture and belongings quickly.

Within two hours, the semi was unloaded. The kitchen, living room, and porch were so full that one could barely get around the furniture and boxes. Some of the boxes had to be placed in the van and others in the yard for the time being. The large chest freezer had been difficult to unload and had required them to remove the kitchen door from its hinges. Boxes of books were strewn across the couch in the living room. Cathren recalled Martha telling her that Kent Freeman enjoyed reading. Cathren noticed him looking at titles of books on top of boxes when he carried them in from the yard.

"Well, I believe it is time for this old man to hit the hay. If you don't mind, I'll be on my way. See you all," Herb announced as he exited the back door toward his pickup, leaving Kent Freeman to bring the last five or six boxes in from the yard.

Cathren got out her purse to pay Kent for his help.

"I didn't expect pay and I don't want it. I told Herb that when he asked me to help. Didn't he tell you?" Kent asked.

"But I mean to pay you since this is the second time you have helped me in a tight spot," she told him.

"I tell you what, I saw a couple books I would like to read sitting in that box over there. Would you mind if I borrowed one or two for payment?" he asked her.

"Take as many as you like. It will take me until fall to get into reading again. I'll never miss them," she told him. "I buy too many books, anyway. I have a weakness for books.

"Now that is a deal I can't refuse. It is forty miles to a good bookstore. If you don't mind, I would like a piece of that coffee cake for later today," he told her.

"I'll carry the coffee cake to your truck while you carry the box with books," Cathren said while cutting the cake. "Books and cake are really lousy pay for all the work you've done since I arrived here. If there is anything I can do in return, please let me know. I really put you to the test on the roof the other day. That entire roof could have been on fire. Boy! Did I ever feel stupid! I am indebted to you. Thank you."

"You are welcome. Guess I better be going now," he said, getting into his truck. Kent seemed embarrassed by the thanks Cathren gave him.

Cathren watched as Kent Freeman left the farm. Thankful for good neighbors, she walked back into the house, stepping over boxes to the crowded living room, and moved boxes from the couch to the floor. She pulled a blanket from the top of a box, made her bed on the couch, and promptly fell asleep with the security of being surrounded by her possessions, until a few short hours later.

"Andrew, this box is some of your stuff. Don't throw that, it's mine and it will break, and besides it may land on Mom if you throw it," Marisa yelled to Andrew, waking her mother.

"Chill, why don't you! I'm not going to throw anything. I found another box of your stuff over here," said Andrew.

"There's more stuff on the porch," Cathren told them with eyes still closed. "Much of it is yours, so get it in your room as soon as possible. It may rain this afternoon. What time is it anyway?"

"It is eleven-thirty. We already fed the animals. The pig loves it here. She sniffs all over the ground with her nose looking for something to eat. She loves those mints we have on the table in the kitchen," Andrew laughed.

"Mom, I didn't get much sleep last night with everyone banging around out here," Marisa complained. "Can we forget our lessons today?"

"Yes, I think that would be a good idea considering the mess we have. We can resume lessons tomorrow," Cathren told them. "You can help organize this stuff and we will chalk that up as home economics!" She laughed.

Cathren walked into the kitchen and plugged in her newly delivered thirteen-inch television she kept in her kitchen at home. The reception was good this morning. She turned it on. A big story had just broken. A reporter from Washington D.C. introduced pressing events of the hour. Cathren listened while scrambling eggs for breakfast.

"The federal government has just presented the news media with an early morning press release. It states that no Social Security checks will be mailed for a thirty-day period. And at the present time the government will not be able to fund at least half of its welfare programs or a host of other social programs for at least a sixty-day period, beginning immediately. It has also announced that amounts owed to recipients will not be made up to recipients once funding is resumed. Those waiting for their checks at this time will not receive them and will not receive any funds for that period at all. All checks scheduled for next week will be canceled. Along with these facts, as talk is rampant, including one which postulates that the federal government may not be able to meet its payroll beginning the month of July. Of course, this is just a rumor circulating in Congress and is being discussed in several committees at this very moment. This does indicate that the situation for the government at this time is critical. Stay tuned for additional information throughout the day. As it stands, this is the only information the news media has been presented with at this hour. Hopefully, additional information will be forthcoming shortly. This is Marie Walt reporting to you from Washington D.C. Now back to your regular morning news broadcast," the journalist announced.

"Looks like we got out in the nick of time! Things will get wild in the cities now," Cathren informed Marisa when they sat at their kitchen table that had been shipped from Ohio just hours before, but Marisa seemed more interested in the color of her newly-painted nails than the newscast.

"Oh, to be young again," Cathren commented. Turning to Andrew, she said, "Make sure you brush your teeth after breakfast."

"I found my toothbrush when I unpacked my stuff," Andrew informed.

Cathren fumed at the thought and asked, "Do you mean to tell me you haven't brushed your teeth since you have been here?"

"Well, I sneak and use Marisa's toothbrush when she's outside." He laughed, looking straight at his sister.

Marisa jumped from her chair and ran toward Andrew. "That's absolutely gross, you little brat! I'm going to get you!" She chased Andrew out the back door and through the garden. Cathren watched as Andrew climbed a tree too far and fast for Marisa to reach him. Marisa marched back to the house and in through the door.

"I will get after him and give him extra chores, just calm down. I have an extra toothbrush still in its wrapping packed in the bathroom toiletries I will find for you this morning," Cathren told her, but it was hard for her to keep from thinking about the news report from Washington.

The morning news did not surprise her. It was to be expected sooner or later. Calls from an over-taxed public to Congress, the President, and state legislatures and governors to control spending fell on deaf ears. Taxes grew at an alarming rate with each a squeeze of life out of the Nation's economy. "And now this," Cathren whispered to herself.

Cathren looked at the washer and dryer sitting in front of their respective hook-ups. She squirmed behind them, plugged in the dryer, and slipped the white vent hose over the galvanized steel vent leading outside. She then screwed the hot and cold hoses leading from the washer to the spigots sticking out of the wall. She plugged the washer into the electrical outlet and shoved both appliances into place. In order to save on the electric bill, she decided to use the dryer for emergencies only.

Before long, several loads hung on the line, drying in the warm spring sun. A red pickup sped by, and the driver blew the horn and waved, it was Kent Freeman.

Late afternoon saw billowy clouds pushed from the heavens to be replaced by a dark, rumbling, moisture-filled cumulonimbus from the west. Cathren had forgotten how fast a storm could brew here. It reminded her of the many times she and Nate would be in their boat on one of the reservoirs during vacations. The same rumbling would send an experienced boater back to the docks or into a cove to drop anchor. A storm pushing in behind warm air on a spring or summer day was nothing to take lightly here when warm tropical winds met northerly cool air.

Storms still came, but Nate is gone forever, Cathren thought. A knot grew in her throat and tears formed in her eyes at her thoughts of the loss. Her shoulders fell low as she walked toward the baskets to gather clothes off the line before the rain fell. After carrying the basket of clothes into the house, she sat on the couch and slept, oblivious to the downpour of rain outside.

Cathren woke half an hour later to the noise of Andrew unloading his possessions in his new room. The rain pattered on the tin roof and dampness began to cling to the household air, so she lit a fire in the woodstove.

"Thank you God for the rain," Cathren said aloud. "This will help the seeds I planted in the garden to sprout the next several days."

After the storm, Cathren and Andrew fed the chickens and checked for eggs. They found six hidden in the barn loft. The pig was nestled in her blanket on the back porch. She rose to see if there were treats for her, too. The puppies were already used to livestock, so they had few problems adapting to their new home and the pig. They were sleeping in a cardboard box close to the back door. When evening fell, the ladies of the house went about moving furniture from one position to the other. The old couch was transported to Marisa's room, making way for the couch from home. Outdoor furniture was on the porch. The porch walls needed painting, but would have to wait because money was tight and there was much work to be done inside.

Cathren vowed to start on the upstairs first thing in the morning. Her bedroom set still sat on the porch, mattress and all. It was covered with plastic, but it needed to be indoors as soon as possible. Exhausted, Marisa and Andrew settled into sleep. Cathren had forgone the late news. She really didn't care to listen about outside turmoil anymore. She was gladly falling into a sweet repose here on the farm, and it was welcome.

Rain began falling again. It was impossible to fight sleep with the lullaby of rain falling on the tin roof that lured eyes to close. "Oh Kentucky," was Cathren's closing thought on that evening.

CHAPTER TWELVE

Stew was safely indoors when the upheaval began on streets across the nation. Swarms of belligerents filled the streets in protest of the government announcement early in the day. It was more an excuse to cause disorder than concern for loss of income for others. It was an excuse for looting, robberies, and the intimidation of innocent people.

Hearing the news when he woke in the morning, Stew called the employees from the office and told them to stay home. They would resort to teleconferencing. The company was learning to survive in that manner. Stew made a quick dash to the grocery to stock up on canned goods. He purchased fuel for his camp stove and lanterns. He decided not to be left unprepared in case the power went out again. He was proven right.

Gangs threw homemade bombs into the local electric company's substation again. The coming weekend promised to be a long and tedious one. He worked in the backyard garden with a pistol strapped inside his jacket. A siege was on for the city and he hoped it would be a short one.

"Hello, Seth?" Stew asked over the phone line, "Was it calm at your end of the world last night?"

"It stayed quiet here. I saw on the news that it got pretty tough in the cities again last night. You safe?" Seth asked.

"Sure, no problem, I'm tough!" He lied. "I will be glad when your classes are finished for the school year. I really do want to get you out of here before the summer heat sets in. We need to make plans in a couple of weeks. I hope the roads will still be passable to the south by that time."

"I know. I have heard rumors around town. It seems the wilder it gets elsewhere the more sober it gets here. Nearly all students stayed on or near campus during spring break. When we hear the news reports of uprisings across the country, you can see it in the faces of students here on campus. They're scared, you can feel it," Seth told him.

"I have heard that most urban areas look like ghost towns today, that urban and suburban dwellers were getting good at smelling trouble in their areas, so there is not the usual drain of workforce from the suburbs to jobs in the cities today," informed Stew.

"The news reported this morning that Wall Street opened heavily guarded, trying to ensure the safety of those willing to hold the nation's markets together. Police forces and the National Guard were trying to cope with overtime needed to pay officers for the twenty-four-hour a day effort to keep streets calm. Some officers have to catch a little shut-eye now and then on cots at their respective stations," Seth told him.

"Lines at grocery markets here run front to rear with guards in parking lots to ensure the safety of customers to their vehicles. Food is a valuable commodity since one never knows if food will be able get through from other parts of the country. I hear ships full of fruits and vegetables from Central and South America lay rotting at anchor in many shipyards on all coasts because of rioting. People

117

are buying tanks of propane for their gas grills. Gas station attendants are helping customers who stand in line for hours on end to fill containers with kerosene and gas. I'm glad you are safe, so I will let you go and I will be in touch tomorrow. Good-bye for now," Stew ended.

Stew knew most of his new neighbors were home preparing. Some families boarded windows that faced the street. No one felt they were overreacting. Media blitzes on the television leapt from one city to another, ensuring conformity on all fronts and revealing the norm of the times.

On this morning, Cathren's stomach grew uneasy worrying about Seth. She couldn't eat breakfast. She knew early that staying busy would be her only comfort. She patched the bad places on the walls upstairs and set out rollers and brushes to paint the yellowed ceiling above her.

After spending the morning painting the ceiling and windowpanes in the bedroom she was creating, a trip to town was necessary to pick up the wallpaper that was on order. It was business as usual in a small town of less than two thousand souls. No media could be found in this sleepy agricultural-based community. Occupants of the cities never gave thought to their brothers here. They were and would always be two different worlds and each glad of it. Cathren was glad she was in this world now. No one was boarding up windows and doors. There was no line when she walked into the grocery. The restaurant on the square was full of people discussing the local news, which primarily consisted of who was sick and which family had the latest addition.

A new baby, the location of the next revival or brush arbor meeting, and the weather were news here. The local radio station always announced the name of persons well enough to have left the hospital. An announced revival in town gave Christians a chance to discuss scriptures in a place where they were rarely taken out of context. Such is the rural south.

And the weather? Weather ruled the lives of the county's residents. It was only last year when the more humid than usual summer wreaked havoc on fields of crops. Wheat could not be harvested in July because the fields were too wet for a combine to enter the fields without getting stuck. When the weather was bad, tourists and boaters who usually evacuated from cities and surrounding states stayed home, not spending money on the docks, local stores, and restaurants. Weather is king in communities like this across the nation with a reverence and love for the earth and its moods.

On this day, the fragrance of lilacs swirled in the air as Cathren drove past homes back toward the farm after getting the wallpaper. She left the windows open in the van to feel the warm spring wind on her face while driving through the countryside. The drive to the farm showed a museum of peach, pear, cherry, and apple trees that would bear fruit for their curators during the coming months. Cathren remembered her grandfather would barely let an apple go to waste; the ones not canned for pies or made into applesauce would be frozen or dried for apple stack cake. Something useful would be made with the last fruit to hit the ground, the one that always reminded Cathren of Robert Frost's poem about apples put by for the winter months to come.

The painted ceiling seemed to have dried since the morning hours, and lunch was finished.

Andrew typed his lessons on the computer and Marisa sewed a sundress for a school project. Hours passed quickly into the evening then to midnight, when Cathren finally finished papering her room. Marisa and Andrew were still awake at the television, so Cathren drafted them into helping her pull her mattress, box springs, and bed frame up the steps. Cathren also dragged her nightstand up the steps and plugged her alarm clock in next to the bed. The dresser and chest of drawers would be tackled in the morning because she was much too tired for more work. The cool night breeze mingled with spring scents flowing through the upstairs windows. Cathren drifted to sleep while trying to absorb a little information from a book on the fundamentals of growing a variety of garden seeds so she wouldn't be a complete idiot when Herb and Martha were trying to give her pointers on her new farm adventure.

CHAPTER THIRTEEN

"Stew and I are making arrangements to come down as soon as finals are over. Susan plans to drive her car, so she and I will follow Stew. I think he would like to get some boating in while he is there." Seth told his mother.

"Are you planning to take the back roads down?" Cathren asked.

"So far, yes. Our finals will be over shortly, so expect us then," Seth told her in a breath. "We will probably cross the Simon Kenton Bridge in Maysville, as you did. The scenery is beautiful that way."

"I guess you will be leaving at a good hour when there isn't much going on outside, won't you?" she asked.

"Yes, no need to ask that, Mom. Susan's mother and father aren't real happy about the trip, but they don't want her to stay here, either. They know she will be much safer on the farm during the summer. We even thought about finishing our senior year by commuting to a school down there if it doesn't cool off here between now and then. Would that be all right with you?" Seth asked.

"That is a good idea, and it is fine with me. I hadn't thought of that." Cathren was delighted at the thought. The way their finances stood, a school costing less might be better in the long run, but she didn't have the heart to tell him that. She had planned to help him finish college if it took everything they had to pull it off, but she would worry about that this summer. Now she just worried about their trip south.

Saturday proved to be good for planting more garden seed. Cathren noticed the greens she planted earlier were growing fast and could be eaten soon. She planted about six varieties and couldn't wait to taste the first harvest.

Herb plowed a large patch on the edge of the field for sweet corn. She bought extra seed because raccoon, deer, and other animals would raid the corn patch when the corn ripened, though he planned to place an electric fence around the corn plot. She remembered her grandfather complaining about the animals eating more than their fair share of the crop when she was a girl. She thought how good the corn tasted when they picked a dozen or two at the peak of the afternoon when the sugar content was reputed to be at its highest. Cathren never knew if there was any truth to that tale, but she always downed at least three large ears at dinner. Uneaten corn would be cut off the cob and warmed with a little butter in an iron skillet for lunch the next day. She wanted to do the same thing for her children, not just for the taste but for their survival.

Cathren looked down at her hands that were barely recognizable. They were rough from work done inside and out. She could not remember the last time she had had a manicure. That was the last of her worries now, she thought, as food needed to be stored for winter because there would not be much, if any, money to spend at the grocery store.

Tomorrow was Sunday. It was time for her family to begin attending church services in town. Cathren decided to attend the church her grandfather had attended.

"Yes," Cathren informed Andrew, "you do have to take a bath for church tomorrow. Now! It is getting late, now hop to it, kiddo!" Cathren demanded. She couldn't believe how much Andrew hated bathing. Getting him into the tub was winning a major battle. He loved the outdoors, here especially since he had two dogs and a potbellied pig that thought she was one of the dogs following him around the farm. Cathren worried about copperheads and rattlesnakes and was relieved the dogs and pig were with him whenever he roamed on the surrounding acreage. It was always hard to get him into the house at dusk.

Cathren was nervous the next morning as she prepared for church. She didn't want to overdress or underdress for the morning services. She also hoped Marisa and Andrew would meet new friends. Cathren was cut off from her friends she left behind in Ohio and she had been so busy with the farm that a social life was out of the question, so Sunday morning worship at church would be a must for the family.

She knew all eyes would be on them when they walked in. She hoped Andrew would put on his best behavior and that he wouldn't have to visit the bathroom every five minutes, as was his custom during church at home in Ohio if he could get away with it. Marisa was not pleased about having to meet a new set of strangers, but when they walked into the church, Cathren chose a pew near the middle of the sanctuary that happened to seat Marisa next to a teenaged guy. "Things are looking up," Marisa whispered to Andrew.

After communion the minister spoke the closing prayer. One of the ladies of the congregation made a point to talk with Cathren. Cathren told her she recently moved to her late grandfather's farm. That encouraged the lady to introduce to her many others who connected Cathren with her grandfather. Some of the members remembered when she accompanied him as a young girl. These conversations gave Marisa plenty of time to strike a friendship with her new mystery man. All the other young ladies her age had already left the church, giving her a monopoly on the hunk she sat next to. Andrew passed a ball in the churchyard with one of the member's sons. Cathren was relieved the morning ended on a note of success.

The following days flew by because there was so much work to be finished before hot weather set in. Seth was due in anytime. News reports revealed a constant struggle for the economy to stabilize. With each rise in unemployment, there was a reduction in the tax base the government relied on to survive. Government services continued to dwindle, and many thousands of the unemployed were bureaucrats. Many were of the opinion that these cuts should have been made years ago in order to save the government from its sad demise. The number of people on the government payroll, from farm subsidies to the public educational system funds that never made it to children in class rooms, amazed those who cared to know. In education, no one stopped to think that the money earmarked for education should go to the classroom and teachers, nothing else if at all possible. No wonder the system was falling apart. There were too few productive people left paying taxes. The productive part of society was so heavily taxed that there was very little motivation to be more productive, or the production jobs were sent overseas because government regulations and taxes drove them there. The more productive a person the past years, the more they were penalized for being productive. It was a madness that confiscated taxpayers' earnings, keeping them from investing.

Every now and then, a tax protest group would rise but would be squashed by the bureaucratic nonsense the taxpayers supported more than ever with higher taxes. Government was too greedy and selfish.

Many thought a government so bankrupt that it could no longer support itself and its addictions would be the answer after all. It would have to cut off its own evil arms that raped the pockets of every productive man and woman in the nation. This would no doubt cost many lives, as it was doing in the streets now.

Occasionally Kent stopped at the farm to ask Cathren questions about news she heard from friends in the north and he borrowed more books to read. Kent and Cathren were patriotic and hurt for their country in its present condition. They both knew it was inevitable, but they feared the outcome. They wondered if the United States would remain as one or break into smaller regions with a weakened central government that founders of the country intended in the first place. They agreed all states and their regions should have more control over the way they were governed. There were a million and one ways the tide could turn over the next year and as many factors involved in determining the future of the country. As already seen in the cities, the process would be painful, whatever the outcome.

Kent was sitting on the porch one evening when Cathren answered the phone. It was Seth. They would be leaving shortly before dawn and Stew was still coming. "Oh, Mom! Susan and I have good news to tell you. We were married this morning in the chapel on campus," Seth told her.

"You did what?" Cathren cried, upset that she had not been present at the wedding, but she was careful to hold her tongue. "I am truly happy for you both. Congratulations! We will celebrate. But why get married right now? We could have thrown a wedding for you."

"We weighed the pros and cons of getting our families together and decided on this. We had a lot of friends from the campus with us. Susan's dad isn't in the best of health since his heart attack last year and we thought it would be too much. We had a small ceremony with friends," he said.

"I am sure you made the right decision." Cathren paused to hold back tears. "Is Susan there?"

"Yes, would you like to speak with her?" he asked.

"Yes, put her on."

"Hello?" Susan said, unsure of what the response would be on the other end of the line.

"Congratulations! Welcome to the family." Tears were rolling down Cathren's cheeks by now. "I wish you all the happiness in the world, and I am glad for both of you and me, too, because I now have a new daughter."

"Thank you, Cathren. We called you first. My parents don't know yet."

"They will no doubt be shocked, but they will be happy for you, I am sure. They may sound upset with you at first, but they will come around and realize you did the right thing. Parents like to give their daughters away, but to tell the truth, I don't know if we could have pulled off a nice wedding right now with the way our families are spread across the country and the prevailing conditions," Cathren reassured her.

"That's the conclusion we came to. I guess I better call my parents and tell them the news. We will see you some time tomorrow. Bye," said Susan. Cathren sat on the chair in the kitchen crying aloud when Kent walked in.

She cried. "If things weren't like this, we could have a real wedding for them. I feel cheated, and they are cheated. I just feel terrible and happy at the same time."

"They sounded happy on the phone, didn't they?" Kent asked her.

"Yes, they were elated," she cried.

"Well, that is what counts, isn't it?" Kent asked, and Cathren nodded. "They are old enough to make their own decisions, and they apparently have made a good one. You like the girl?"

"Yes. She has been so good for us, especially when Nate was murdered last year," She sighed.

"Come on, let's go for a walk," he told her. "You can get yourself pulled together, and when we get back, we can tell the good news to Marisa and Andrew."

"I just feel so bad because I was not there for them!" She cried along the path behind the barn. Kent and Cathren silently walked onto the old logging road behind the house. Kent held Cathren's hand and took the lead.

"This walk sure was medicine for the soul," Cathren said, entering the back door to the kitchen a half hour later. "Hey guys. Guess what! Seth and Susan were married this morning on the campus. We are lucky to have Susan in our family now."

"Oh boy! But that makes another girl for the family," Andrew laughed.

"My wedding is going to be a huge one with a cake of seven layers," Marisa told them.

"Where are they going to sleep?" Andrew asked. Cathren hadn't thought of that yet, so she didn't respond.

"See, everything is fine. I am going home now to leave you folks alone. If Seth has any trouble on the way down, give me a call," Kent told them. "You take care."

"I doubt that I get much sleep tonight. I won't have a gift ready for them either," she said. "But their safe arrival is the most important item for the moment. I will see you tomorrow, Kent."

CHAPTER FOURTEEN

Just after noon a U-Haul Truck with Stew's car in tow pulled into the lane. Susan's car followed. Cathren ran to them as they stopped at the house and hugged all three as soon as they climbed from their vehicles. Cathren unleashed the strain of the past several hours with her tears.

"How was the trip?" Marisa asked.

"It was fine. We were afraid we wouldn't make it at one point because a fire that was started by gang fighting blocked the roads on the way out of town. It turned to our advantage because troublemakers didn't stick around. After we got into Kentucky we made pretty good time," Stew told her.

"Dinner is ready to put on the table. Come in and rest a bit before you unload your things. Stew, are you staying with us for a few days?" Cathren asked.

"Sure, I would like to get some fishing in if that is fine?" he asked.

"To tell the truth, I have been so busy, I haven't gone to the lake since we arrived. Andrew has fished with Herb several times, and they did well. Let's clean up the boat this evening and put it in tomorrow morning. I have boat fever, and a day on the lake is well deserved for all of us."

After they had lunch, Cathren presented Susan and Seth an envelope with the receipt for a motel room paid in full for the rest of the week. She told them she planned to leave the boat tied at the dock for a couple weeks for them to use at their leisure. Cathren tried to see that they would have some sort of a honeymoon. After dinner, they unloaded their contents into the barn where it was dry, then drove fifteen miles one way to return the U-Haul. Upon returning, the newlyweds packed for the night at a motel on the lake.

Stew checked out the boat and readied it for the summer. Cathren loaded the fishing equipment and life preservers.

"Did you put the drain plug in the boat?" Cathren teased Stew.

A few years ago Stew had backed his boat and trailer onto a launching ramp and into the water. He nearly lost his boat because he forgot to screw in the drain plug before he launched his new sport boat. Luckily, there were plenty of people on hand at the launching ramp and they managed to get the boat to shore before it went under water. Lucky for Stew, the bilge pump had not flooded and it pumped out the water, with help from a few buckets. Stew's friends never let him live this down. It was always a conversation piece during boating season. It did not matter how many times the tale was told – it was still funny each time it came into the conversation.

Recognizing the dig, he smiled back. "Now, would I forget a thing like that?"

Cathren went into the house to call Kent to see if he would like to go boating in the morning. His answering machine clicked on and she left a message. As soon as she put the phone down, Kent drove down her lane. He stepped from his truck with a package wrapped in silver and white wedding paper with a large bow on top. Along with the package stood a young girl. Cathren assumed it was Kent's child with his ex-wife, but she didn't know she would be visiting.

"Thought I would bring this by on my way back from Lexington," Kent told her. "This is my daughter, Julianna. I met her at the airport just hours ago. Julianna, this is our new neighbor, Cathren. In the yard playing is Andrew, and he has an older sister whose name is Marisa."

"I am pleased to meet you, Julianna," Cathren told her, but Julianna's attention turned immediately to the potbellied pig running toward Cathren to beg for a treat. Frightened by the pig, Kent's daughter ran to him.

"Daddy, Daddy! It's coming after me. Help, help!" screamed his daughter.

"It's a pet, Julianna. Watch Daddy feed the pig a piece of candy," he told her as he pulled a pack of hard candy from his shirt pocket. The pig immediately recognized that Kent had a treat for her and turned its tiny hoofs in his direction. He fed her the candy and rubbed the pig's belly. The pig relished the attention.

"Daddy, can I pet the pig?" Julianna asked.

"You sure can, pumpkin. Come here and I'll show you her favorite spots to be rubbed."

Julianna cautiously approached the pig and let her father steer her hand behind the pig's ears. Then he gave Julianna a piece of candy to feed the pig. "Looks like this pig has found a new friend," Kent said, smiling at Julianna.

"Feed her once and you will have a friend forever. I think she likes you, Julianna," Cathren told her.

"Kent, come here and meet our friend, Stew, whom I have told you so much about. Stew, this is Kent, my neighbor. I've told Kent all about you and how much help you've been for us."

The men shook hands and carried on a light conversation while Cathren went into the house to make a fresh pot of coffee and to retrieve cookies from the freezer. One of Cathren's ways to cut costs was baking in bulk and freezing extras, as the family could no longer afford store pastries. As long as the chickens laid eggs and she had sugar, flour, and a few other ingredients on hand, something could always be stirred together and baked. Cathren called the men into the house for coffee. The pig followed Julianna to the porch, so she stayed outside to keep it company and got acquainted with the dogs and cat, too. Kent walked into the kitchen first

"How long will Julianna be visiting with you?" Cathren inquired of him.

"It may be a permanent move for her. I'm hoping so, anyway. Her mother is working long hours and is now required to do a good deal of traveling for her job. Her new husband wasn't thrilled about being a stepfather, much less having to babysit while his new wife was out of town on business. We're discussing letting her stay with me on a permanent basis and visiting with her mother when she has the extra time to 'deal with her,' as she put it," Kent told her.

"It would be a pleasure for Julianna to visit us often. Let me know if I there is any way I can help. By the way, I tried to call you about the time you pulled into the lane. We are going boating in the morning. Would you and Julianna like to come along for some fishing?" Cathren asked him.

"Thanks for the invite, but I've got work waiting at home this very minute. Martha is going to watch Julianna tomorrow so I can tend to business. Can I take a rain check?" he asked.

"Sure, there will be the entire summer for boating," she answered.

Stew spoke, "I am still tired from the trip. I am ready to relax and forget about problems in my city."

Kent asked, "I am familiar with the problems that plagued cities in other countries during war. Would it be possible for us to talk a little on the subject before you leave?"

"Sure. You may be able to help me. It's really hard to describe what it feels like to live in fear all the time." Stew went on to tell about conditions at home. "There is so much disruption in our daily lives that it is a struggle to make it through each day. Each morning I have to turn the news on to see if it is safe to drive through town. Some days I have to re-route my usual drive to the office because gangs have blocked off certain areas of the city. They have either made a mess of certain streets by morning or there is still fighting and looting going on from the night before.

"There are so many underground gang organizations pushing small gangs over the edge to commit heinous crimes that it's hard to know whether it is worth walking out the door at times. I don't know how people with families cope with the worry. Last week an entire bus of children was held hostage again for an exchange of ammunition. Some neighborhoods have completely stopped sending their children to schools and are teaching their children in homes and churches. I just don't understand why anyone would use children like this," Stew told them with a sense of loss for the way things were.

"Who or what do these gangs consist of?" Kent asked him. "They don't sound like patriotic militia types."

"I wish we did have a militia strong enough to deal with these gangs. At least a patriotic militia would want the country to get back to the basic principles it was founded on and would have compassion for all men, whoever they may be.

"Most of the street fighters seem to be youths to adults ranging from ages fourteen to sixty. They fight over anything that trips their trigger, whether it be drugs, stolen items, control over turf, race-related incidents – the list goes on and on. It's a madhouse because there doesn't seem to be anyone in control. I fear someone will come forward and gain control of the nation's cities. That could lead to an extension of a Third Reich type insanity." Stew paused to drink his coffee. No one spoke.

Stew began again, "You know, at first, I thought this phase would pass like the demonstrations of the Vietnam Era did when society peacefully slid into the easygoing late seventies and eighties, but I see differently now. This recession or depression is like no other before it in the States. There is so much dissent and so many lines drawn on so many issues with no compromises in sight. These disputes are fed by the unemployed and uneducated who are easily lured and directed by no-goods standing on the sidelines, open-armed and making all sorts of promises to the discontented. Life as we knew it when we grew up is over. It is a whole different ball game out there, and the rules are changing with each inning. I'm glad Cathren and the kids had a chance to get out when they did."

"Under these conditions, I really don't feel comfortable with Seth going back to school this fall.

I'm hoping they commute from the farm and stick it out here for at least a year," Cathren told Stew.

"The way it looks, I don't think it will be safe enough to go back if he wanted. We've already discussed this," Stew told her. "They are seriously thinking of staying in Kentucky for a while, and I have encouraged them to do so."

"I will probably give them the upstairs to stay in. It will be crowded, but summer weather will keep us outside a good deal of the time," she said.

"I'll see all of you later," Kent told them. "Julianna needs to go home and rest from her trip. It looks like she and Andrew are buddies already."

"I'm glad. Come to think of it, I need a few minutes rest, too. Stew, you're staying in my room upstairs tonight. I'm going to sleep on the couch in the living room. Listen closely and you will hear the whippoorwills singing their nightly song before you go to sleep. Kent, let me walk you and Julianna to your truck. It will be such a nice evening to stay indoors with Stew who will be leaving for home soon."

CHAPTER FIFTEEN

Cathren climbed in the boat and Stew backed it down the cement ramp into clear blue water. Seth unhooked the bow from the trailer and gave it a shove. The lower unit had plenty of room, so Cathren lowered it then turned over the motor for a smooth start on her first try. Slowly, without a wake behind it, she steered the boat into the slip she rented as she waited for the rest of the crew to park near the commercial dock lined with every size of houseboat, pontoon, and pleasure boat imaginable on a reservoir.

Stew, Susan, and Seth bought fishing bait on the dock with Andrew in tow. Marisa, determined to get a deep tan to display at church on Sunday, dowsed herself in a combination of tanning oils. Andrew easily talked them into steering toward the cliffs a couple miles upstream from the dock where crystal waters afforded visibility downward many feet. Andrew wanted to watch fish grab onto the hook he would cast, but fishing near the cliffs turned out to be quite poor, so they trolled into a nearby cove and fished for bluegill, that seemed eager to latch onto Andrew's hook. Stew caught a smallmouth bass. The rest settled for bluegill on their hooks. A crane soared over the boaters and landed on the shoreline nearest the boat. Spring sun bore down, delivering warm, summer-like temperatures that were accompanied by the gentle lapping of miniature waves and a light breeze against the fiberglass hull.

"Sitting on this boat is making me very sleepy. I'm going to rest in the cabin for a few minutes, if nobody minds." Stew pulled his fishing line in, then went below where the gentle rocking of the boat ensured a restful nap.

Waking hungry, Stew persuaded the rest of the crew that they needed a piece of homemade pie at a waterfront restaurant on the lake that had a longstanding reputation for great southern desserts. Cathren hoped the southern specialty, apple stack cake, would be on the menu as it had been when she and Nate took the children in for ice cream during summer afternoons of boating.

"Andrew, can you remember which cove to turn into for the dock that has the nicest restaurant on the lake?" Stew asked.

"I think it is that way." Andrew pointed. Stew nodded and steered the boat in that direction.

Once they had arrived at the restaurant, Cathren said, "This coffee is delicious, and they do have apple stack cake on the menu today. Looking over the water from this lakeside diner brings home so many wonderful memories, and here we are creating more good memories. I wish it could last forever."

"This is the most beautiful lake I've been to. The water is so clean and clear. The surrounding hills are so beautiful they hardly seem real," Susan told them.

"It looks as though we may have the lake to ourselves this summer. Did you see all the boats for sale on the bulletin board when we came in?" Seth asked.

"I noticed. I dread the thought of having to sell our boat. We sacrificed so much through the years to save and buy it." Cathren shuddered when she spoke the words. "So many good times with you children on our boat. I couldn't bear to part with it."

The crew spent the rest of the day cruising the lake and visiting two more docks before calling it quits.

"Mom, look! Garfish. Man, look at the noses on those fish. YUCK!" yelled Andrew as they pulled close to the dock. "Will they bite me if I get in the water here? Marisa said they can take a man's leg off. Is that so?"

"No, they will not bite. Marisa, why do you tell him things like that?" Cathren asked her as they pulled into the rented slip.

"He deserves it because he can be such a brat. The next time he listens to one of my phone calls from Ohio on the extension, I am going to skin him alive," Marisa threatened.

Cathren ignored the bickering between the two for the time being. She was glad that life was getting back to normal for her children. The strain of living in constant fear that had been depriving them of their childhood was weakening. Cathren had heard what those conditions did to children during times of war, and now she knew firsthand. The dose they had received before leaving their home was enough for her to bear witness, and she secretly prayed for those of the world who lived their entire lives in a war zone.

Marisa claimed it was getting late for good tan rays, and Andrew's nose already sunburned. Back at the house half an hour later, Marisa and Cathren began cooking dinner. Stew and Andrew filleted the fish they would have for lunch tomorrow.

After nearly five days of relaxing activities, Stew decided he could face going back into Ohio.

Cathren regretted having Stew depart, for his contentment the past days surmounted his alertness to the possibility that a tragedy could occur at any given moment. Sad for his departure, she packed his lunch for his way home and gave him baked goods that would last several days. He and Cathren had already shopped at a grocery in town to stock up on hard-to-find items. The small town didn't seem to show a scarcity of essentials. Stew planned to barter with some items he bought in Kentucky, including plenty of flour, cans of evaporated milk, and other food. Stew drove home with those things that could not be found when roads were blocked by gangs into the city.

Stew rented the same truck Seth had brought to the farm. Stew's towed car and rental truck were full for the trip to Ohio. He listened to the radio, made calls from his cell phone, and kept a CB on to catch the latest news as he approached the Ohio River, for if there was trouble he planned to stop at a campground and sit it out until it was safe to drive home. Cathren made him promise to call when he stopped for the night or arrived home so she wouldn't worry.

Marisa and Andrew spent that evening on the farm helping Seth and his new bride start filling the upstairs room with their belongings. A predicted and welcome rain fell on the garden. The accompanying cool air soothed sunburns and aching muscles as they painfully found out why local farmers wore straw hats to shield themselves while working their fields in the southern sun.

Stew called late that evening to tell of his safe trip home. He unloaded his stash and put it all in the basement in the crawl space under the kitchen. It would not be discovered if someone broke into the house after he placed cement blocks to cover the hole to the crawl space. As far as he was concerned, they could take anything in the house but the food. Food was more valuable than gold during intense violent outbreaks in the city. Four weeks passed on the farm after Stew's departure. Marisa and Andrew finished their lessons for the summer, except for reading books. Cathren finished freezing rhubarb and rhubarb pies for the months ahead. Early peas were picked and hulled, leaving Cathren, Susan, and Marisa's hands sore before Cathren decided to buy a pea sheller. Lodi apples filled several bushel baskets, waiting on the kitchen floor to be made into applesauce. For winter pies, the women of the house already canned quarts of apples.

Clearly having more than enough, Cathren still found herself picking up the last apple from the ground, just as her grandmother and grandfather used to do. At one time she poked fun at this habit, but now she realized it was the survival instinct that never left him after the Great Depression of the 1930's. Though times were good for him during his later years, he passed that survival instinct onto her, and it breathed through her every action. She realized now the farm had been their grocery store. During most of their life together, a grocery was just a place to buy essentials needed for canning such as salt, sugar, spices, canning jars, and the like.

Cathren grieved sorely at the passing of her grandparents. Her grandmother died years before her grandfather passed on. She had felt they were gone forever. She found that was just not true. With every turn and every thought that carried her through the days, she recalled the thoughtful training they gave her of farm life when she visited during many summers. It was as though they knew she would need their guidance in her lifetime. She now knew her grandparents really were not gone, but with her to carry on to the future as they knew it would be. It was their grandparents before them who knew to teach them the necessary skills to pass down from generation to generation. All of it came back to her, little by little. She had learned something of farm life; not enough, but some.

The attic space behind the bedroom upstairs still held dozens of canning jars sitting next to the old pressure canner and kraut shredder her grandmother used, just as if her grandmother had stored them for Cathren's use. Cathren felt a strange shiver go down her spine.

Cathren had already decided that the kraut shredder would stay put because the food processor sitting in the kitchen downstairs would do the job in a fraction of the time it took her grandmother to shred cabbage for kraut. She also decided not to use a crock to make kraut as her grandmother did but to use the canning jar method Martha told her about.

Summer days filled themselves with canning green beans, cutting corn off the cob, and storing everything the family could during harvest. Tomatoes came in by the bushels for the simple reason that they had planted far too many in the first place. Paste tomatoes were strained into thick sauces for pasta while standard varieties provided quart after quart of juice and canned whole tomatoes for soups, stews, and even tomato jelly.

Depressing news continued to filter to the farm through the media, detailing the deteriorating economy and social unrest. With each news report, the inexperienced farm family understood more than most in the surrounding county the necessity of "laying by in store" for the coming winter, the expression Cathren had heard from her grandfather's lips many times when it came to the farm and church.

Marisa kept in contact with friends in Ohio by mail and e-mail, though at times it would take several weeks for a letter to get through to a friend or vice versa. Outbreaks of violence deterring mail delivery in the cities was a sad situation. Often mail delivery was hampered because postal delivery persons were robbed or the postal service payroll could not be met.

When the family ran to a screaming Marisa, who they had thought had fallen on the rocky lane, they found the harshest of letters managed to find its way into their country mailbox.

When Susan saw a letter in Marisa's hand, it was obvious the content was responsible for the hysterical outburst.

Correspondence from home brought Marisa many a shock. One former school friend of Marisa's had been killed in crossfire while walking into one of the local teen hangouts, and other friends were injured during the same incident. Shootings from stray bullets were still an everyday occurrence in the city of their old home. Only time helped Marisa learn to cope with her losses.

Marisa fell into the deepest of depression at the death of her friend. Her family could do nothing to console her. To see her in mourning over such a senseless killing again, leaving them with a harsh reminder of Nate's demise, was too much. Marisa's eyes showed emptiness through agonizing days and nightmarish nights that didn't seem to want to end.

Cathren still no longer doubted her decision to move to the farm after that day, for she knew Marisa would have been with her friends in the crossfire of battle had she kept her little family in

142

Ohio. Cathren gave thanks to God for the protection he had given her daughter and for the wisdom to leave her old home when she did. The most recent of letters from her friends told of food shortages in the city. One of Marisa's friends complained of eating entirely too much salad, as it was the first crop from their postage stamp yard and there was little money to buy groceries even if there were any stocked on store shelves. A couple years ago, lots of parties with friends and brand name clothes from the mall had been where confidence came from for Marisa. Now her source of confidence came from her family and their struggle together.

Marisa's letters from her friends gave her an eerie perspective when it came to problems at home. Marisa had left her friends in a war zone and in many ways the guilt of leaving them still haunted her. Marisa understood that now she was a refugee.

Kent found farm work for Seth in the area and eventually Seth found a dock on the lake that needed help pumping gas and selling bait to fishermen. Seth got the job, and before long, the owners became aware of his knowledge of computers and the experience he had received at jobs during the summer in previous years. He was eventually drafted into the office to network the computer system and to teach the employees how to use the software he installed to enhance the business.

Kent also showed Seth how to use a chain saw. Susan watched her new husband fell dead trees and stack them for firewood. According to Herb, Cathren needed about five to six cords of wood to keep this particular house toasty during the coming winter months. Seth already had two cords stacked and seasoning behind the barn.

Martha told her that coal put out the best heat but it was dirty and would make the walls and curtains filthy if she burned too much of it, and that a man generally came around with a dump truck full of the black rock in the early days of fall. Herb usually took the entire load if enough neighbors kicked in to split the cost. If he could buy the entire truck full, he would get a better price, so Cathren opted to buy part of a load. Cathren figured it would come in handy during long winter nights with no man around to cut firewood, and it would last for years stored in the coal bin her grandparents had in the barn out back.

There was rarely a day that wasn't spent preparing for winter. When they took the boat out for swimming, they also fished. Fish were filleted then frozen for meals later in the season. Cathren and Susan even tried canning some fish, which turned out to be a success on their first try. The canning and preserving books Cathren purchased in town earlier remained open and in use for most of the summer.

"Mom," Seth yelled to her from the house at dusk, "there is something going on at home. There's a special report on the television now."

"What have you heard?" she asked, while running toward the house.

"Phone service has been cut throughout major cities across the nation, both landlines and cell service. Apparently, some of this was planned by terrorists wanting to gain control of the government. I think our university is in one of the areas affected. There were power outages reported also. Some areas are completely void of information going in or out," Susan informed her.

"I will try to get through to Stew and a few others this very minute," Cathren told them, grabbing onto the phone in the kitchen.

"Nothing! Darn it! No answer from his cell phone either. Stew should have stayed here with the rest of us. Andrew, I want you to get your shower now," Cathren told him, but she really wanted him out of the room so she could talk more freely with Seth and Susan. This extent of trouble greatly disturbed her. Kent's truck pulled into the drive to tell them of the news he had heard minutes earlier.

Julianna accompanied him. She jumped from the truck and ran to the pig, then went on a hunt for the rest of the animals. Coming to Cathren's was one of her favorite pastimes.

"Have you heard the news?" Kent asked them. "The evening news reported mass blackouts in cities across the country, and phone service is reported to be out in parts of the country. Some major airports were stormed early this afternoon, and travel in and out of larger cities like New York and Chicago have nearly come to a halt."

"How could this happen?" Cathren sat down in a chair close to the television, watching it intensely. "Look at the flames in that city. Is this going on everywhere?"

"From what I have been able to find out, it is. Fighting in the streets between gangs has escalated to the engulfing of entire towns and cities. Gunfire is everywhere, even in parts of cities and towns where you would least expect it. Gangs are fighting with residents of homes in suburbs. Some families that do not have guns to protect themselves have been completely thrown out of their homes onto the streets while gangs moved into their houses and took what they wanted. There is no one willing to fight for homeowners to get property out of gang members' possession. All hell has just broken loose," Kent told them.

"Kent, why don't you stay for dinner this evening? I would appreciate it, as I am afraid of the news we may hear from home," Cathren asked of him. He agreed.

The phone began ringing. People from church and others with whom Cathren had become acquainted called to see how they were coping with the news and to express their concern. One caller owning a ham radio offered his assistance to locate friends of hers if the situation lasted much longer. Cathren could not help but cry with each call offering help, and the gut feeling that this was the end of the country she loved so much.

Kent remained until Julianna was too sleepy to stay awake any longer. Little more information was available, with the exception of a few individual accounts. Nothing could be done but wait for word from Stew, for it could be suicidal to travel through heavily populated areas to find loved ones during this dangerous time.

"Well, this confirms it. Susan and I have decided to enroll in classes at the college town fifty miles north of here. We sent our applications in as commuting students this spring and have been accepted. We will try to schedule classes for one or two days each week to cut down on driving time." Seth told his mother. "We would really like to find a place of our own to live."

"There was an older mobile home in the paper this week. Herb mentioned it to me. He said Ted Jarboe's mother lived in it on their place, but she could no longer stay by herself. It is small and twenty years old but clean and well kept." Cathren had noticed the strain on the newlyweds having to live in close quarters with another family, but there was really nothing else that could be done at the present time. As usual, Herb and Martha understood the family's need and made appropriate suggestions.

"Would you be interested in driving to their place in the morning to check it out? You could have it moved to the farm. The best place would be where the county road runs on the northwest side of the property. You wouldn't have to spend much on a driveway there."

"That would be great. We looked at some rentals near the campus and they're a bit pricey. We have managed to save a little money, but I don't know if we can swing it. It would be worth looking into," Seth mentioned with Susan agreeing.

"I start a part-time job tomorrow waiting tables at the dock restaurant. It's only seasonal, but it will help," Susan informed them.

"I know it has been a strain for you to stay here with us in a small house like this. Older, used mobile homes don't sell for much if the buyer has cash to close the deal and a little land to put it on. Herb said he would help us put a septic system in with his backhoe, and the electric lines run on the roadside. The only problem would be water. You may have to haul it for a while until a well can be dug, but you are welcome to use the washer, dryer, and shower here. You will be roughing it for sure, but it will be your own home," Cathren told them. "It measures only fourteen by sixty-five."

"My parents said they would help us financially when the time came since they did not spend money to throw a wedding. When we find out the cost of the mobile home, I'll call them to see what they think about helping us," said Susan.

"I am running low on cash, so I spoke with Herb about selling a few trees out back. Grandfather had the sellable ones marked years ago. Herb suggested a buyer at one of the local sawmills that would give me a fair cut of the deal and would help me manage the wood lot for future sales years from now. I need to pay off a few bills, anyway, and some of the money can be used as a wedding gift from me," Cathren said. "I'll call the Jarboe family in the morning to set an appointment for tomorrow evening. It is going to be a busy day tomorrow, and I am a bit tired. You guys try to rest well. We have a lot to do the next several days. Plus, I'm hoping to hear from Stew. We'll talk more about it in the morning."

The fourteen by sixty-five was clean and in excellent shape. Cathren had intended to bargain on the price until she found out the refrigerator, stove, and stacked washer and dryer were included with the sale. She offered a deposit to hold the home for five days and the Jarboe family agreed. Everyone parted pleased with the deal.

One more stop had to be made on the way home, Cathren needed to make the final agreement on the trees. The owner of the saw mill agreed to cut the trees that were previously marked when her grandfather had considered selling them to the same sawmill before his death. With the deal made, Cathren told him of the situation with the mobile home. Having called Herb to see if Cathren did indeed own the farm, he had no qualms about giving her a check for the amount for the trees, since it was customary to pay for the trees before their removal by a reputable forestry consultant.

They shook on the deal, and Cathren was relieved to know she had money to buy the mobile home because she sure didn't want to lose her deposit.

"Oh, that smells terrific, Marisa," exclaimed Susan as they walked into the kitchen after negotiating a deal on the home and trees. "I want the recipe for the pasta sauce you're making. Would you like to go with me and Seth to choose a spot for our new home while the sauce is simmering?"

"Sure, let's go now. The sauce won't be done for another hour or so anyway. It can simmer. I see Seth is already outside waiting for us," Marisa said, observing her brother standing near the back door with his arms crossed, contemplating the purchase they had made.

The lane past the barn forked off toward the field on the right where Herb bailed hay each summer. They followed the natural drive used for farm machinery that led to the other side of the farm where there was road frontage. It needed little gravel because the earth was sound enough to be used even during the wettest of weather. Large sassafras and maples shaded the lot near the county road with wild broom sage dotting the field edge along with wild blackberries.

"This is the perfect place! Could a better view be had in all of Kentucky? Oh, Seth, look to the west where the sun is falling to the horizon. The hues of pink, yellow, and orange that cloud the sky over the mountains can be seen miles away. Would this be a good place to pull the mobile home into?" Susan asked.

"I believe this would be perfect. We could build a deck and eventually have a roof installed over it to make a place to sit and watch sunsets," Seth agreed.

"If we put it here, a garden can go over there, and flowers can be planted around the yard next to the home. I don't think I can wait. How soon do you think we can get started?" she asked.

"I talked with Herb on the phone and we will try to get started the next day or so. It isn't supposed to rain, so Herb may be able to bring the backhoe tomorrow morning and begin digging a septic system. I'll drive to the courthouse and get the permit for the septic tank, and then call an electrician. I can get all that done before work in the morning," he told her.

"That is settled, so let's get back to the house for dinner and celebrate," Marisa said, turning back toward the house. After choosing the site, Susan called her parents and asked to borrow money for a septic system and electricity. Her father asked to speak with Cathren, who explained the purchase of the trailer and what was needed. She also told him that the farm would be passed down to the children and she would deed Susan and Seth an acre of land immediately since he and Susan would be making improvements on the land. Susan's father said he would call back in an hour or so if the lines were still working. He was surprised Susan had gotten through at all.

Fifteen minutes later, the phone rang. It was Susan's father.

"Your mother and I have decided that since we did not throw a large costly wedding as we did for your sister, we will wire you the money. The money will not be a loan but a wedding gift, and the money we would have used for your schooling this year. Hopefully this will cover what is needed for your new home and schooling. If you fall short, don't hesitate to call us," her father told her. "Now I need to speak with Cathren again."

"Oh," Susan cried, nearly unable to speak, "I love you and Mom. Thanks for the support you have given me through the years. Here's Cathren."

"Yes?" Cathren asked.

"Hello? Cathren. I want to thank you for going all-out for Susan. We really do appreciate it. We have been so worried about her safety the past year."

"You have a nice daughter, and she is a joy to have here. I really hate for them to leave the house, for they have been great company, but I know they want a place of their own and this is the only way for the time being," Cathren told him.

"We told Susan enough money would be wired to them, that this was a wedding gift and school money combined. It should take care of their needs. Now to you: how are you doing?" Susan's father asked.

"We will stay here for the winter instead of taking any chances home in Ohio. We are fine now that we have settled in," she told him.

"We have decided to stay here at our cabin on the lake instead of going back to the city. We thought the move you made was wise. I just hope the winter is not harsh this year."

"I hope not for all our sakes. We have been working hard to get ready for the winter. Our lives have certainly changed. We'll be praying for your well-being, and please pray for us during these times. Susan is still here. I will hand her the phone. Take care and God bless," Cathren said before handing the telephone to Susan. Just then, Kent Freeman pulled in the lane.

"Hi there," Kent greeted with a smile.

"Hello Kent. Where is Julianna?" Cathren asked.

"Martha asked her to help bake cookies."

"I'm glad you stopped by. Come on in and I will fill you in on what we have been up to," she told him.

"I stopped by to ask something first," he said.

"Sure, my story can wait," she responded.

"There is a restaurant about twenty miles from here that overlooks some beautiful scenery over the lake. Would you like to ride there with me tomorrow and have dinner?" Kent's voice wavered as he asked.

"Yes, I would really like that," she said. "I have heard it is a wonderful place for dinner at sunset. What time should I be ready?"

"Around three-thirty. That will give us plenty of time to stop and enjoy the scenery," he told her.

"I would like that. It would be nice to go out for an evening. Tomorrow at three-thirty is fine." Cathren was not sure whether she had been asked for a date or if two friends were going to spend some time together, but either way it felt great to have plans with someone for the evening.

Kent was turning to tell Cathren good-bye when their hands accidentally touched. The palm of his hand slid over her shoulder as she lifted her other hand to his cheek. It had been so long since she had felt the touch of a man against her that Cathren forgot to take her next breath when he pulled her to him. Unconsciously, Cathren reached her arms around his wide shoulders, her lips to his. Neither spoke for seconds. Kent turned to leave.

"Would you mind if I ask a personal question before I leave?" he asked.

"I wouldn't mind in the least," she answered.

"I know Stew is so close to you and you have feelings for one another, but I just for the life of me cannot tell the sort relationship you nurture for each other. I know there is a great deal of love and admiration you have for him, and I know he feels exactly the same toward you. Did I just overstep my bounds a minute ago? Would Stew take offense to what just happened between the two of us?"

"Wow, I was not expecting that sort of question. Let's go for a short walk so I can tell you about Stew and I," she told him.

"Sure," he answered, not certain he really wanted the answer.

"Stew and I have known each other since our college days. And you're intuitive enough to know Stew and I are extremely close, so close that at times since Nate's death we feel like one when we have had to reach deep into our survival mode, so to speak, with everything we have had to face together. We did at one point attempt a romantic relationship. We realized how wonderful our friendship was and that we were just friends. We even discussed that our attempt at a relationship as a couple was very bad timing at that point in our lives and that we should hold off. We were afraid if we made a romantic leap at that time we could ruin our friendship, and we were right," she continued. "I will always love Stew and will always be there for him, as a constant friend with whom I have bonded in a very positive way. Out of desperation and loneliness, we nearly destroyed our friendship. We are friends forever, but not in the sense I believe you are asking about."

"I want us to always be friends no matter the type of relationship we're in, is that clear?" he asked.

"I understand completely. We are adults and seem to be content with our friendship with one another. You are a wonderful person, a good father, and a great neighbor, and I am so glad we met when we did," she told him.

"Same here, and I think I should leave now with this conversation standing on the up note it is. Have a good evening, Cathren."

An understanding had been met between the two. Kent had fallen for Cathren at first glance the very day she started the fire in the woodstove. This was a woman who had left everything for her family. He admired her bravery.

Cathren thought about how wonderful it was they had become such close friends in recent months and how she so looked forward to his company and their conversations. Cathren did not know if she could stand the wait until after three-thirty tomorrow.

 Since her arrival on the farm, all she could think of was the survival of her family. Even leisure time on the lake was spent by fishing for food. Her concern dominated her being. Newly found feelings for Kent came as a surprise to her. She had not thought this could exist for her. It stirred her but did not frighten her as she thought it would if such a time arrived before she left this Earth. A binding friendship and trusting relationship had been molded with Kent Freeman, the kind of relationship she had felt was never meant to be a part of her life again.

154

"I am so glad everyone is gone for the afternoon," Cathren whispered to herself. "I just am not going to get any work done today. Where is that dress I packed away?"

Grateful that Seth and Susan were preparing for the move of their mobile home while the other two volunteered at the church, Cathren rummaged through several boxes that remained unpacked from the move south. Most of her jewelry was still hidden in a box somewhere. She changed six times before deciding what to wear that evening. She nervously pranced around the house, trying to make sense of her feelings of contentment with this man, acting like a schoolgirl. She tried to remind herself to calm down, to be mature about this dinner date. But her mind fled to the feelings of a deepened friendship mature enough to ripen into a healthy bond between two responsible, caring people who had been set adrift and were now sailing into one another. They were two drifting vessels bumping together in a storm while searching for safety, finding a safe place to anchor in the most beautiful and serene of harbors, Kentucky.

Cathren often thought about the way she had cut away natural feelings and had hidden how a woman should feel, feelings she thought the divorce had destroyed. Similar circumstances held Kent. Failed marriages caused both to be unable to commit fully to another relationship. Neither felt they could weather such a storm again; both were cautious, bent on avoiding the repetition of past mistakes.

Kent Freeman arrived on time, not in his pickup, that Cathren had thought was his only on road vehicle, but in an early seventies red Corvette convertible.

"I haven't ridden in a car this old for years. Is this yours?" Cathren asked.

"Sure is. When I got back from war I swore I would get one of these and keep it for the rest of my life, and so far I have been able to hang on to it." Kent walked to the passenger side and opened the door for Cathren.

"I've tried to keep it off the road as much as possible through the years. You don't mind riding in something this old, do you?" He smiled.

"Are you kidding? This is a treat. I may not want to stop once we get on the road. Makes me feel young again." She slid into the passenger's seat, glad to get off the high-heeled shoes she had grown unused to wearing.

Kent saw Cathren acting gaily as he never saw her. From the beginning he knew that, after meeting her on a more casual basis, it would be best if he remained a neighbor and friend until she was able to find herself. She abandoned her home in Ohio out of fear, and the damage from personal problems was evident. Her wounds had been in need of mending before she could go on with her life. That would take time. He chose to wait. He realized her children were hurt, too, and if he did come into the picture at a bad time, it would surely have a negative impact on their well-being. Kent continued to bide his time for the children as well as Cathren.

Kent's marriage was always in need of being saved and left Kent emotionally drained from the beginning until after the divorce. His relationship with Cathren seemed comfortable with no pretenses, and he now understood his daughter's mother never really had time for her or Kent. She didn't really want a child in the first place, but thought it might help the marriage float. It didn't. After Julianna was born, she really didn't want to stay married to Kent. Her desire was to go back to the lights of the city to work at her former profession, clearly without Kent.

Taking Julianna with her when she left proved to be a big mistake. She did love her, but she didn't have room in her life for Julianna. When Kent and Julianna's mother split, he contemplated a custody dispute but knew Julianna would be permanently damaged by a court battle. Given his ex's tendencies, he betted on her getting Julianna out of her life, anyway. His prediction had come to pass.

"I'm taking the scenic route when I turn off the main road here," he told her as he veered to the right. "There's a waterfall about a mile ahead."

"These cliffs and overhanging trees remind me of the Smoky Mountains. This is breathtaking. Oh, Kent, this is perfect. I didn't know this was here. What a ride you've taken me on. Are those the waterfalls?"

"Yes. We can't get the best view here. We need to walk a few yards to the path leading to the overlook. There is parking to the left," he told her as he turned off the road onto the gravel lot. "You can feel the cool mist as soon as you walk toward the falls. This way to the path." He pointed. "There's a story that a Native American maiden came upon a white man who was laying ill upon this very ground near the top of the falls. She was afraid at first, but then saw he was in need of medicine. She spent the afternoon gathering herbs on the side of this very hill and administered her knowledge of the plants in the forest to heal this white man she had found. She nursed him several days, hiding him all the while, fearful that warriors might come and kill him. He was finally well enough to travel on his way and her heart was broken, but not for long. He rode back into the Native American village one day to ask for her hand in marriage. He asked to live with the tribe so she could be near her family.

"The tribal leaders and her father listened as she confessed that she had helped this white man and that she had felt the creator would look ill upon her if she let him die. The chief agreed and felt her deeds brought good fortune to the tribe. They also agreed to the union of the two, for the white man had been a great warrior among his people. The chief said the white man would be an asset to the tribe, and he was right.

"It is said that when a couple pure of heart, as she and the white man were, come to this very spot, they will be much praised with happiness all their days together. They say many of the Indian maiden and the white man's descendants still live in this area and are all good neighbors."

"That beautiful legend makes the mist surrounding us feel as though that Indian maiden is visiting this very moment, telling me she will protect me and she has lifted the problems of my world from my shoulders for these few seconds so as to strengthen my weakened heart. Her enfolding mist makes me feel she is inducing me into a utopian world, making me drowsy with the sensation of protection Eden once held. These mountain falls are the caress of her arms around us and whoever else may need her. Kent, I must be losing myself from reality. Do you feel her, too?"

"Sure," he said, putting his arm around her shoulder and pulling her close to his side. No one else was visiting the falls. It was all theirs. Kent turned to press his lips to her. With a sigh, he pulled his lips from hers and used his hand to lay her head against his chest to feel her close to him. The maiden's mist continued to engulf them.

"You seem to belong in this natural setting," he told her.

Cathren's soul was stirred. "Yes. Standing here on the very ground of that event fills my being as nothing has ever done before. I can stop searching for something I have always needed. I realize now I am the whole person I have so desired to be my entire life. I found it here in Kentucky and the mist of the waterfall of my ancestors. I know now I will come here often."

Framed with locally quarried stone of light sand tones dashed with sweet honey blends and blushing gold hues, the lodge nestled itself into the mountainside so as to permit its lodgers to cast their sights above the incandescence resulting from the evening sun's last dash of exotic rose radiance upon the waters.

Quarried steps created the walkway leading to the lake. The descent ended where clans of fishermen met nightly, dockside with their worn lawn chairs, coolers, and bait. An earlier shower allowed cool and warm air to mingle on the surface of the blue lake where miniature clouds still lingered. Hummingbirds busily caught the last sunlight of the day on flowering trumpet vines hanging from a trellis on the landing. The sun leisurely lowered itself beyond the horizon, disappearing behind the mountains surrounding the lake.

Cathren strolled alone toward the end of the dock while Kent conversed with local fishermen. A grandmother and her grandchildren sat silently holding onto their poles. She pulled an entire stringer of fish from the water in response to his question and smiled at her catch.

Kent caught up with Cathren. "I have an idea. Let's walk to the restaurant and order dinner to go. Then we can walk to the end of the dock and buy a couple cane poles and bait. Let's rent a houseboat for a few hours. Those tied there have obviously not been rented."

"That *is* a wonderful idea. It would be a shame to miss the opportunity to view this beautiful evening from a houseboat."

Kent paid the boat rental fee while Cathren purchased snacks and beverages before calling home to check in.

"Hello, Susan. Kent and I will not be in until late. We decided to stay, enjoy the weather and do some fishing."

"Fishing? Oh, how romantic!" Susan laughed.

"I guess that came out a little funny, didn't it? It has been so long since I have been on a real date I can barely speak of it as it is. Strange. Ha! We are renting a houseboat and having dinner on the lake. Is Marisa home yet?"

"Yes, she got in about an hour ago from her picnic date with the guy she met from church. She seems very happy and looking like a teenager should. Poor girl, she worries so about friends back home, I am glad she is making friends here. Andrew is outside on his bike. Don't worry. Everything is fine here, really. Have fun!" Susan told her.

Relieved, Cathren walked to the boat rented by Kent to find a white tablecloth with dinner served upon it along with wine. Free of stress for a few hours, the two launched the houseboat and headed for a cove beyond sight of the lodge.

The aluminum hull of the boat permitted them to pull to shore and tie off to waterside trees and anchor the rear in clear water that hosted underwater terrain dropping dramatically a few feet from the pebbled shoreline.

Kent anchored while Cathren placed the snacks on the kitchen counter and started coffee on the propane stove. She walked to the rear of the houseboat then out the double glass doors onto the rear deck, leaning over the iron railing to splash a handful of the acres of water floating around her. Kent arrived onto the rear deck to be with her. A pontoon boat lingered by them, continuing westward toward the last light of day.

"It is so peaceful here. I could stay here forever just listening to the whippoorwills with their evening song," she told him.

"Me, too!" he whispered, moving silently behind her, wrapping his arms to envelope her, placing his hands on her waist, then kissing her hair. He did not want to push her into a relationship too hurriedly, but could not help himself from wanting to hold her close to him.

"Is this all right with you?" he asked, though he was afraid of the answer she might give.

"Yes, of course. You have been the greatest friend a person can have since I arrived here, and I have grown closer to you than I could think possible." She turned, then closed her eyes and tilted her long neck back, breathing in the remainder of the day, a breath that lifted her shoulders and breasts upward until a soft exhalation flowed, slowly and thoughtlessly as the current in the waters swirling around the boat.

"It was so lonely here until you arrived. I know how much you want to run back to Ohio, I can feel it and see it in your eyes, your homesickness. I do understand it's your home. I have been so afraid you may pack and leave at times that I dreaded driving past your farm, fearing the house may be empty."

Kent's facial coloring turned rose then crimson in his determination to let her know how he felt, to lay his feelings before her so she could examine them and his intent. "I know you have a strong and independent head of your own or you wouldn't have been able to move and make the new start here with children in the first place, but now I am asking you if you would consider staying here with me."

"Well, Kent, right now I have no intentions of leaving here. It has been wonderful for me and the children."

"I am sorry, I wasn't clear about what I meant. Oh, Cat," Kent managed to sputter out apologetically, "What I really meant to say was—"

"Look at me, Kent. After the friendship we have developed and the feelings we have for one another, I would find it hard to pull myself away from you. I hadn't expected anything like this to happen. I came here for my children's safety, fully expecting to spend my life alone. I just wasn't looking for anything like this," she told him.

"Anything like what?" he asked her.

"Finding a friend like you," she told him.

162

"You know I am in love with you, don't you?" he asked.

"Kent, I love hearing those words. I never want to be without you. I just cannot commit myself to anyone right now. After the excruciating pain my divorce caused, I never thought I would be able to trust a man again as I feel I can trust you. Your sense of strength and kindness fulfills and calms. Our relationship fills me. The type of love you speak of takes commitment that I am not sure I can measure up to at this time. I am so sorry. I don't want to hurt you, especially you of all people," Cathren whispered to him, knowing she probably just destroyed the most important relationship she had developed with a gentleman during her entire life.

"I can wait. I have waited a lifetime for a woman of your spirit. I trust your instinct about this, and I will not bring this up again. If you ever feel you are ready for us to make that commitment, please tell me. I will let you be the judge for this, and I'll stand waiting for your acceptance till the day I leave this earth. Now let's sit on the deck and enjoy the evening together. I just want to hold you and talk. As much as I love you, I want you to be comfortable, and let me know if I am rushing the development of our relationship. I know moving has been rough for you. I will always be here for you, Cathren. I know we haven't known each other long, but I want to let you know that, in the future, if you decide we should spend our life together, you have a standing proposal for marriage from me to you. Anytime, babe."

"Moving here was a godsend, and the angels had you waiting for me. Kent, in many ways we are already one." Those were her last words for hours

163

as the couple silently clung to one another, surrounded by the sound of waves lapping the shoreline and the sight of distant campfires on the water's edge.

Kent held tightly onto Cathren, showing his love for her in the physical realm as well as in the marriage of their spirits, desiring to feel her breasts against his chest. He wanted to love her through the night and wake before daylight finding her next to him, content in having found this new life together. He could only wait until she was ready.

Dawn had yet to arrive when they returned the boat to the dock. They climbed into the waiting Corvette. Kent left her at the front door when they arrived at the farm. He kissed her, not wanting to leave. But he knew he must, for Cathren was still fragile from her divorce and Nate's death.

Cathren walked into the silent house. Exhausted, she sat for a few moments on the edge of her couch. She wanted Kent with her.

"Mom, you slept in. It is ten-thirty!" Andrew yelled up the steps. "I fixed my own breakfast and fed the animals by myself."

"Good, thanks, Andrew. I'll be up in a few minutes." Cathren felt only minutes had passed, but in actuality it had been hours since Kent left her. Cathren put on her robe and walked to the kitchen when she heard the familiar sound of Kent's truck pull into the lane. She ran to the door.

"Kent, I am so glad you stopped by this morning," she said to him without a greeting.

"I have this bait for Andrew," Kent told her, looking a bit disappointed after Cathren's refusal of last evening.

"I couldn't rest well when I got home this morning," Cathren told him. "I left something unsaid last night. I'll just get straight to the point and you can tell me what you know what it is about you and me that feels so right. We haven't known each other long. This is crazy and rash, but here goes. If that proposal still stands, could we drive into Tennessee and get married in a chapel in the mountains?" she asked.

"I can't believe what I just heard. Are you sure of this?" he asked.

"How soon can we leave?" she teased. "I nearly made the mistake of my life last evening. This is what I want. I am not afraid to love again. Like I said, I have not made a decision as rash as this about marriage but now I know life is too short. We do not know if we will be alive tomorrow with the turmoil around us. Our lives have been destroyed. We have seen warfare, you overseas, and me in my own home state. We cannot wait to move on. I need you in my life. I would be crazy to pass you by. Can we leave now?"

"I'll be back in an hour," he whispered to her. Cathren called the others into the kitchen to tell them the news. Susan was still home and Seth arrived for lunch.

"You should go ahead and marry him, he's here practically every chance he gets, anyway. You have a date with a guy once and are going to marry him. I am beginning to wonder who the adult is here, geez...." Marisa mumbled throwing her hands in the air, eager to get back on the computer to her boyfriend with whom she had been chatting with online nearly all night.

"But, Mom! You're running off and getting married without anyone there," Seth told her.

"I think it is a wonderful and romantic idea," Susan said, giving Cathren a consenting look. "Seth, look who's talking when it comes to getting married without family around."

"But that means I will get another sister. I don't need another sister if Julianna acts like Marisa! That is what happened to my friend Gary when his dad got married. Yuck!" Andrew commented.

"You are right. It is just hard to think of your mother getting married. You could not have found a nicer man than Kent Freeman. We'll watch over things around here. Don't worry about Marisa and Andrew, they will be fine," Seth assured her.

Cathren rummaged through her clothes and found an outfit she had worn to a dinner party the past summer. She packed the rest of her things. Kent pulled into the lane as she finished. Susan made finishing touches on Cathren's hair before Cathren greeted Kent as he waited nervously for his bride-to-be.

They were in Tennessee just hours later, ready to become man and wife. The stream beneath the wooden bridge leading to the log chapel babbled swiftly over its rocky pathway. The lowering evening sun sent shafts of brilliant colored beams sparkling over the woods and the cabin that the couple entered to exchange their vows.

"I now pronounce you husband and wife. You may kiss the bride," announced the preacher. "And might I add, as I rarely do after a ceremony, that given a good sense of the personality of those marrying in this chapel throughout the years I am quite pleased to know this couple will no doubt have a long and happy marriage. I know they will cherish their love until their days on this earth have ended and they are called home to heaven. Amen."

A moment later, the ceremony ended. Cathren looked at Kent. "Did we really do this?" she asked.

"If we did, do you have any regrets?"

"No!" She giggled.

"Well then, we did it," he said, smiling.

"Hmmm. That makes me Mrs. Freeman now, doesn't it?"

"Sure does, and it sounds nice to me, Mrs. Freeman. You know, that engagement period sure was a long one. What took us so long to go through with it? And to top that, we don't know where we plan to live yet. My place or yours?" he asked.

"Considering our lengthy courtship, I really haven't had time to work that into my schedule, my dear husband. Any suggestions?" she asked him.

"We should wait until we get home, and then I will let you make the decision for us. You can go through my place and yours, then compare the pros and cons of both. I'll follow you where you lead me, Mrs. Freeman, but wherever you decide, I think we will need to build on a room or two. Our family just expanded."

"Build on. Do I oversee the work?" she asked.

"Sure thing!"

"Oh, Mr. Freeman, I have chosen well. You are absolutely too easy."

Kent teased back, "Let's get to the chalet we rented and I will really show you how easy I am, Mrs. Freeman. "It has been years since you or I visited the Smoky Mountain region, yet it is as enchanting as ever. I know memories were happy ones of years past, and we should let those memories carry us into a world of happiness again."

Kent carried her over the threshold. She made him promise not to turn the news on while they were there. She didn't want the turmoil in the most populated parts of the country to ruin her honeymoon with Kent. This would be their time to relish together as two that had just become one. The mountains still did their job of blocking out the rest of the world, providing a temporary refuge. Reality still had to be met, but it would be with a renewed freshness and a reserve of strength. Days wandering through the mountains strengthened them.

A week passed quickly and the couple felt the need to see their loved ones. During the final drive through the Smoky Mountains in the direction of home, they knew it was time to turn on the radio and make calls to fill themselves in on the latest events of the world around them.

Their absence saw Kentucky citizens officially form a volunteer militia to guard the borders along the Ohio River where heavily armed gangs crossed bridges connecting the two states to raid homes and businesses in Kentucky. Most utilities within cities in Ohio were being cut off for much longer periods, usually caused by powerful gangs or the federal government trying to regain control of certain regions. Crime overflowed over the Ohio River, and it needed stemming.

Guerrilla tactics undermined any real effort to maintain peace among streets of heavily populated areas. Kentucky had no choice but to begin guarding its northern border along the Ohio. Most realists were not surprised by the current events.

Reality set in quickly on the journey home. The newly-wedded couple stopped along different locations to buy supplies for the coming winter.

Kent, concerned with the possibility of a seed shortage for the next spring planting season, purchased enough seed for several families to barter. Cathren bought an assortment of items to ease the job of storing food for winter. She had not realized how time-consuming it was to store as much food as possible for the winter months ahead. She now understood why few women had worked outside the home in the past, or men for that matter, when there was a rural farm to run. It was quite simply impossible when food gathering and storage was the central key for the survival of a family. She was also surprised at how close her children became since their survival now depended on each other.

Everyone worked in sync. If Andrew and Marisa didn't gather the eggs from the loft in the barn, baking would be delayed and the others would not be able to finish their chores, which would ultimately make Andrew and Marisa have to help the others to make up for lost time.

Kent commented to Cathren he was glad she had insisted on taking her van for the trip into Tennessee. By the time they finished their stops for supplies, the vehicle was full to the ceiling, for they knew well of the deteriorating economy and what it could bring over the coming winter months. There could be fallout throughout the foothill region.

The semi pulling Seth and Susan's mobile home sat along the road, waiting for final instructions from Seth, when Kent stopped in the drive. The newly married couple had already stopped at Martha's and Julianna was with them.

"Back to work!" Cathren smiled to Kent, viewing the mobile home sitting in the drive.

Kent stopped the van and climbed out, letting Cathren drive on to the house. He spent the remainder of the day helping set the mobile home in place. The electricity was not connected. The young couple used a generator. There was no running water, but Susan and Seth gathered as many of their belongings as could be hauled until it was dark. They were ready to spend their first night in their new home.

It was getting late, so Marisa told Julianna she could sleep with her. Julianna was elated because she idolized Marisa. Cathren led Kent to her room upstairs to spend their first night home together, for Cathren had already decided that this would be their home for now.

Cathren rested in his arms while Kent silently lay awake. His thoughts ran to how much preparation was needed for the coming winter. He was glad he could be with Cathren now, to help take care of the things a man could provide for his wife and to appreciate the things she did for him, a willing and loving team.

Seth and Susan soon found new friends, who volunteered to let them stay near the campus in the event of inclement weather or trouble in the area. Thus far, the area remained peaceful, but Cathren wondered if it would remain that way if the cities a few hundred miles to the north did not have food during the winter months. Would there be raids to the farm communities to the south, east, north, and west of heavily populated areas? At least Seth and Susan only needed to commute two days each week. Cathren's mind rolled night and day contemplating the what-ifs that could happen throughout the world around her, unable to get a full night of sleep.

The federal government remained financially strapped through the summer, resulting in more branches of the government shutting down. One could only wonder why the government had kept growing during the latter part of the past century into the new century, continuing to spend when impending doom was in sight.

Many wondered how any government would be able to survive, and, if it didn't, who or what would be doing the governing in future. It was the opinion of most that this was no way for the first decades of a new century to begin. Many were thinking less of those in trouble areas and more of protecting themselves if gangs spread to the countryside.

Counties to the north continued organizing small militias that interacted together to protect their borders if raids came. Kent attended several meetings at the local county courthouse to help develop a community plan if raids came to their area.

The county sheriff did an excellent job communicating with residents, though there was no budget left to work with. He knew the importance of delegating and branching out to all parts of the county to keep the community intact, to enlist help, and to keep tabs on events around them. No one thought this, and other planning, was paranoia. This was reality to be dealt with.

In the meantime, Cathren rarely heard from Stew. He had his own problems trying to survive from day to day. His father passed away, and dealing with the estate took much of his time. Stew sent a letter stating he would like to buy Cathren's house in Ohio if she was willing to sell. She could no longer see any reason to hang on to it. Going back to Ohio was now out of the question. And she figured it would be years before the cities calmed, anyway.

Cathren sent two letters to Stew telling him to get an appraisal on the home in hopes that at least one letter would get through. She realized real estate prices had deflated according to the market value, but this would be the only chance she would have to sell the home. Stew and his sister wanted to buy the home with their inheritance from an aunt and planned to share it. His sister could no longer support herself and her children. Further, Cathren's old neighborhood was safer than other areas.

Many, including Stew, were tied to the cities because of their jobs, though cuts in pay were the norm. A small paycheck was better than none, especially since welfare rolls and unemployment benefits no longer existed to fall back on in the event of a job loss. The fat domineering federal government had lived out the worst fears of Thomas Jefferson, and now the people would pay for letting a large central government eat their rights and income with still increasing taxes and no accountability.

There wasn't time for Kent and Cathren to relax now. Tobacco needed harvesting, along with crops he had on his farm. Cathren seemed to be canning from daylight to dusk, along with sewing outfits for the girls' fall wardrobes. Julianna had grown so much during the past weeks she could no longer wear any of last year's school clothes her mother sent with her. Julianna also became a new light in Cathren's life.

Kent provided a stable environment for Julianna, always being there when she needed him and never giving the impression she was in the way, as her stepfather let her know. Julianna's mother

172

fulfilled her maternal obligations by sending a few winter clothes and school supplies, and that was fine with Cathren.

Seth continued to hold his job at the dock on a part-time basis that helped pay the electric and gas bill. Susan no longer worked in the restaurant since most tourist business, what little there had been during the summer, ended for the season.

Along with most families in the county, Susan busily stored the harvest from the garden. She and Seth purchased an upright freezer for their mobile home. They were proud of their newfound independence and wrote letters to friends about their new life together. Life in the backwoods was new to them, so they ordered gardening books from seed catalogues and checked out numerous books from libraries on self-sufficiency. Susan purchased an entire stack of magazines on self-sufficient gardening and survival magazines at a garage sale for winter reading.

Labor Day kicked off the beginning of cooler evenings, notifying many garden plants it was time for them to give way to kale, peas, winter greens, and a host of other plantings able to tolerate fall and winter temperatures.

Pumpkin vines turned dry and brown, having fulfilled their obligation for the summer by growing a bumper crop for jack-o-lanterns. Cathren began gathering Hubbard, butternut, and other winter squash varieties that would keep for the better part of winter in a cool, dry place. Kent started adding a new bedroom on one end of the house for Andrew and decided only a gourmet kitchen would do for the addition at the other end of the home. He wanted to get both rooms under roof before cold weather began. The remainder could be finished during the winter months ahead.

Several cords of seasoned firewood promising a warm and cozy winter sat carefully stacked in the backyard. Chimney smoke could already be seen rising from the house on chilly, damp mornings. The cat remembered how nice it had been next to the woodstove before summer arrived months ago and curled itself into a soft sleeping ball for the cooler times ahead, walking away from its corner occasionally only for a feast or to visit with other members of the household.

Coziness nestled in the household where, upon entry, friendly smells of a meal cooking mixed with the scent of fresh-baked bread in the bread machine lured family members inside for hearty food and good conversation. Life held goodness for them on the small mountain farm.

CHAPTER SEVENTEEN

"Hello," Cathren answered the ringing phone. She knew it would be a local call because utilities in the north were out again, according to the news last evening.

"Hello, Cathren, this is Sheriff Chaney. Would Kent happen to be around? I've got to come out that way, so I thought I would stop by and have a chat if you don't think he would mind," he told her.

"Oh! Hello, John. He won't mind, I'm sure of that. I'll walk out back and tell him you're on the way from town. He's due for a break anyway. If I'm not back by the time you get here, come on in the back door and have a seat." Kent and John had become good friends through the years, and Cathren felt comfortable enough around him to let him make himself at home when he and his wife stopped on occasions for a visit.

"I'll do that. See you all in a bit," he said before hanging up.

Cathren found Kent running the bush hog on the edge of the field, waved him down, and ran toward the tractor.

"John Chaney just called and is on his way out to have a chat with you. I told him you wouldn't mind coming out of the field, that you were due for a break, anyway," she yelled to him over the noise of the running tractor.

Kent nodded his head and pointed, indicating he would be putting the tractor away, bush hogging along the side of the field in the direction of the barn.

Cathren followed him so they could walk together to the house. He jumped from the tractor then walked toward her to give her a kiss. His scent of sweat from working in the field was familiar to her now, but the look in his eyes was not. She didn't want to know the reason for John's visit. After living in fear for so long in the city, she had developed a keen sense of smelling trouble brewing. John pulled into the drive as Kent opened the back door to the kitchen.

"There's coffee on the stove, go on and wash up. I will put cups on the table for you and John. I need to get some things done outside, so I'll leave you two to talk," Cathren told him.

Overhearing her, John said, "Cathren, you need to hear this. What I have to say will all be out in a couple of days, anyway. Law enforcement in the northern part of the state has received some disturbing information the past couple of weeks. At first, it was written off as a rumor because the same information was intercepted some time earlier, but no action was ever taken."

John got up from his chair and stood by the kitchen table and continued. "Rumors of gangs spreading their wings deep into the neighboring states gave little cause for concern until recently. Now reports are coming in from several different sources, and they have astounding similarities to other sources of information received across the country."

"Are you trying to say the gangs are becoming more aggressive and plan to make tighter strongholds throughout the areas they control?" Kent asked.

John looked seriously into Kent's eyes.

"Well try this on for size, Kent: these people are saying a revolution is in the making." Cathren put her cup down and Kent stood up. The three sitting in the room had discussed this possibility in the abstract at earlier dates.

"A radical international left wing group has been trying its best for years to get a foothold in the formation of a revolutionary wing here in the states. These groups are by no means interested in a democracy, but would rule so that they would end many of our freedoms. And what's worse, they will probably receive a lot of help from socialistic-leaning members of Congress and radical judges throughout the judicial system.

"With the economy as it stands and with all the discontent, particularly of those having to do without their monthly allotments from the government, it hasn't been hard for this radical left wing group to infiltrate street gangs. The Left Wings, as we've been calling them, are well-trained in terrorist tactics and are making a good impression on gang leaders. They have been able to teach street gangs the art of making their own munitions in underground factories and are financing them. Large arsenals have been cached in dozens of locations across the nation."

"Where are the CIA and the FBI while all of this is going on?" Cathren asked.

Chaney replied, "There is so much discord in the government itself that it is easy to say neither organization is very effective anymore. It is also rumored a few radicals have infiltrated the CIA and the FBI and have proved to be quite helpful in steering investigations away from the Left Wings."

"I know there have been accusations flying in news reports about this for quite some time, but nothing was substantiated. Why are you bringing it up now?" Kent asked, though dreading the answer.

"We live so far south I really don't see why any of this would concern us. And besides, I washed my hands of all this when I moved here and decided to make Kentucky my home." Cathren became tense at the thought of becoming involved. She had kept her children distant from any large city on the farm, in a place so far into the country she felt no radical on earth would be interested. As far as she was concerned, the turmoil of this twisted society was concentrated in heavily populated areas, the areas she had sworn out of her life. If those people wanted street wars and the rest, she had no control. She was out of it.

"These gangs that used to be at each other's throats on the streets during the past few years have now become allies against the rest of the country, and that's where the Left Wings come in," John continued. "They have been quite clever in their endeavor to bring gangs across the nation into alliances with one another. The Left Wings believe they will be able to gain control of the government when they get the support of the people through whatever means it takes and plan to ultimately set up a government of their own liking."

"How does this affect us?" Cathren was getting scared at the tone of this conversation. She knew the discussions of the possibility of defending their region from the spread of gang control if deemed necessary. Her voice shook as she said, "I've been through it. Those people are absolutely ruthless. You could be killed if you get involved."

John interrupted, "I know, and I really regret having to tell you this, but by all accounts the Left Wings are planning to launch assaults across the country shortly and plan to gain control. State leaders are aware of this now. Kentucky has sworn to defend itself and the Constitution from this possible incursion. Kentucky will probably do what it can to protect its borders. Sheriffs from each county have met several times in recent months to discuss the rumors. News reports today have confirmed heavy fighting in Washington D.C., New York, Chicago, and all major cities in California."

"Do you mean our government is already in the process of a genuine physical end?" she asked.

"That is a possibility now or in the near future. The Commonwealth of Kentucky, Tennessee, and every other state in the union may be making the decision as to whether they wish to be a part of the new government if our present government falls into new hands. The Left Wing group has some real radical ideas on how this country should be run, like more on the line of what Vladimir Lenin and Joseph Stalin had in mind. They probably won't let up without a fight, which brings me to the purpose of my visit." John had dark circles under his eyes and his shoulders told of pressures pushing hard on him. "Kentucky is still forming its own militia of men willing to volunteer their services to this cause. This cause could be an independent nation if the Left Wings actually do gain control of the United States government over time and scrap the Constitution worse than some court rulings already have. If they are able to take over our government, all depends on how aggressive a campaign they can muster. As it looks now, they plan to push hard," he told them.

Cathren turned angrily to Kent. "And you? You've known more than you have let on, haven't you?"

"I have been aware of certain information. I am so sorry. I didn't want to put you through this if it could be avoided. I was hoping the tide would turn and you wouldn't have to be burdened with this sort of news," Kent told her. Cathren poured herself coffee and told them she needed to go outside to be alone.

Cathren walked through the woods and stopped to see Susan and a new kitten. She did not tell Susan about the conversation Kent and John were having at the house. John's car was gone when Cathren turned toward the house from behind the barn. She was still upset from the conversation she heard between Sheriff Chaney and Kent. She felt betrayed that he hadn't confided in her.

She walked in the front door instead of the back, as usual. He had watched her walk to the front of the house and heard her footsteps on the wooden porch. She swung the screen door open and walked into the room. Kent leaned against the doorframe leading to the kitchen.

"I am sorry, but I didn't want to tell you how serious it was getting until I had to. You just looked so pitiful and scared when you first came here last spring. You had the same shell-shocked look in the eyes of a mother I met after her home was destroyed and family members killed, when I was overseas during wartime. I just could never forget that look, and I recognized it in you the first time we met. I am so sorry. For your sake, I did not want this to come to our doorstep. I just never dreamed it could happen here, but it has. Again, I am so sorry. I wanted to protect you from what I knew to give you more time to heal." He tugged her close to him and kissed her forehead and rubbed her back and shoulders to ease her tension. She pulled away and confronted him.

"I'm furious with you for not telling me. Is that one of the reasons you have been leaving the television and the radio off lately and making excuses to do something other than listen to the news in the evenings? And you have been keeping me occupied through the days, too, and when you catch me trying to listen to radio stations from major cities late at night, you turn down the volume or turn the radio off. And to think of it, you haven't brought a newspaper home in two weeks. In fact, on Sunday mornings you have been volunteering to buy a paper between Bible class and worship service and each time you told me they were sold out," she scolded. Her mood changed from anger to apprehension. She could not help but reflect back to Ohio before she left her home. She had not carried a gun in her purse since shortly after her arrival on the farm. After a few weeks of carrying it here, she no longer felt the need for it in her new environment. Cathren had unloaded it and locked it away.

"And what did this visit from John have to do with you?"

"They'll be asking for volunteers shortly. There is a list of veterans being contacted to help form some sort of defense to prepare for the worst scenario. I'm on that list," Kent told her with regret in his voice. There could be all-out war across the country as had already been seen in the cities.

"No! A thousand times no!" she screamed at him in no uncertain terms. "You haven't made any promises to them yet, have you?" Her voice rose to a maddened shriek. He had no choice, but to hold her shoulders and look deep into her hurt eyes.

"Not yet," he said, looking directly into her eyes.

"What do you mean, not yet? You can't be serious. We need to stay out of this. I don't want any more of this. I moved the children out of that situation and married you and that is that! This has been so perfect. Why ruin it? Oh please. Just stay out of it!" Cathren said, screaming and begging.

"I may not be able to, Cathren. There may be a volunteer draft where one's services are formally requested, but not legally required. None of the veterans I have talked with want this, but they are willing to serve if worst comes to worst. All we can do now is learn how hard these left wing groups go for control and how far they plan to push their border south, that is if they do gain control of neighboring states or areas."

"I just cannot talk about this anymore. This is entirely too much to handle. How can you do this, Kent? You could be killed!" Cathren yelled at him before she turned and slammed the kitchen door, exiting the house.

Beginning that evening, Cathren listened more intently to the late news on the radio when she could get broadcasts from the East Coast and Chicago and she logged onto websites she had grown to ignore since her move to the country. She had been taking the out-of-sight-out-of-mind attitude while nestled in her farmhouse, but that approach would not work any longer.

Political debates started during early evening hours and lasted till near daybreak. Each program pondered what had gone wrong with the country, what was responsible for societal unrest, why crime was so out of control, and what could be done to go about fixing the situation. Stations continually reported where the latest fighting was taking place, where the next uprisings were expected, and speculations on what would happen. Many thought national monuments like the Lincoln Memorial or Capitol Hill would be targets, but the Left Wings were reputed to have asked militant gangs to leave national monuments alone because such destruction would deteriorate morale in the event the Left Wings took over the government. They felt the transition of power would be easier with the national monuments intact.

The Left Wings were trying their best avoid appearing like the bad guys, choosing rather to be conveyed to society as saviors of the country, though they were instigating killings. They could finance gang violence and were becoming quite powerful by doing so.

The media concentrated on the warring at hand. Countrymen and the world watched, listened and were numbed by it. As highways were closed off by the militants, the nation ran to grocery stores and banks, trying to prepare for what may come. Most were attempting to store food away for the winter months, but skyrocketing inflation ensured the lack of funds to do so. Families still devastated over the past winter's heating and food bills were already blocking off rooms in their homes to conserve heat or to cope without a supply of heat during the cold months ahead.

Many cut down trees in their backyards for firewood. Most families were now armed to try and defend what they had left after past lootings from rioters.

State and local governments tried to curtail the availability of arms to individuals by passing new laws and ordinances, but these had little effect.

A handgun or rifle was the only defense a man or woman had to protect their families from harm. Making matters worse were certain ever-greedy politicians, who would sell their mothers' soul for the almighty dollar. They sold munitions to certain foreign countries that in turn sold them to the Left Wings. Some politicians dealing with defense contracts resorted to these secret sales of munitions to these radical gangs, padding themselves in the event the radical Left Wings did indeed take over the government. This would no doubt ensure future sales to the new government since they had supported their cause. The companies and a few unscrupulous politicians played both ends against the middle.

European countries and Japan held worldwide conferences on what should be done about the situation in the United States. Debates weighed heavy as to whether European or Asian armies should send forces to bring sanity to American society. Many European leaders felt it was their responsibility to return the favor of sacrifice that Americans had granted them during World Wars I and II. Others did not see any point wasting European lives. They argued that times were different now. Many thought the United States would have to work out its own problems, despite the threat the Left Wings and gangs posed. The Left Wings were building large prisoner camps in case of all-out war in the areas they now controlled.

All agreed that the economic problems in the United States had an impact on the rest of the world financial markets. No one volunteered to intervene out of fear of what terror the radical, all-powerful Left Wings could wreak upon their soil.

Increased living costs made it harder to make ends meet for most, especially when the low-paying garment factories would lay off workers by the thousands, sending local jobs to third world countries. These very companies sent back their garment products to sell in the states. Down went rural economies, along with many local companies, when the economy went sour for the region impacted. Residents of these type rural areas were used to these sort of ups and downs in the nation's economy, though this most recent was worse than the depression of the 1930's, but they would cope as they had always done. In this type of region, the traditional family still held strong and continued to sanction its standards, pronouncing a firm foundation and stable way of life in communities where little changed from one generation to the next. As rumors of war and a revolution flourished, so did the rumors of a Kentucky militia forming to protect its way of life. Cathren doubted anyone could ever take Kentucky from Kentuckians. Kentucky land was as precious to a Kentuckian as his or her own blood.

Kent opened the door to the root cellar that was carved into the hillside behind the house, then walked into the six-by-eight cement room. The vent in the ceiling kept moisture down, leaving the small storage space dry and cool for potatoes, sweet potatoes, and other root crops brought to storage during the final days of harvest.

On Kent's left, shelves stood filled with bushel baskets of freshly dug Kennebec and sweet potatoes. Braided onions hung from the ceiling to cure for winter cooking. Rear and side shelves were lined with jars of canned tomatoes, green beans, shell out beans, relishes, a half dozen different varieties of pickles, and a host of other canned vegetables that would ensure many a winter feast.

Working quart jars of a mixture of shredded cabbage, vinegar, water, and salt sat on the floor atop a plastic sheet for easy cleaning if they spilled over as the ingredients transformed into a delicacy sauerkraut no canning company could ever imitate and market. Kent smiled and let out a small chuckle as he counted the quarts of working kraut. Cathren, to him it seemed, had gotten over-enthused when it came to making sauerkraut from the dozens of cabbage heads splitting from overgrowth in the garden. She found it too hard to let them go to waste; therefore, a hundred ten quarts of kraut sat on the cement floor and lined shelves, leaving little room for a person to maneuver.

"I don't know what in the world we are going to do with that much kraut," he whispered to himself. He lowered his head to get out through the five-foot high door and closed it behind him.

Cathren walked from the front of the house toward the back door.

"Looks like we have enough stored for the winter and then some. I will need to haul a few head of cattle for butchering in a few days. Three are already sold to families in town. I'll have one butchered for us the same time," Kent informed Cathren. "The Mann family asked me last spring if I would like to buy a hog. It nearly slipped my mind. I told them how I wanted it butchered, wrapped, and frozen at the time. They'll be calling when it is ready."

Kent worked from daylight to dark, working both farms to try to get ahead in case he had to leave when bad weather set in. Little trouble was anticipated until after the end of the year, when it

186

was possible main highways would be cut off and food would not be able to get to grocery stores in the cities.

"Kent, you need to get the freezer from your place because the one here is completely full. I could use the other one any time now," Cathren told him. Cathren, teaming with Marisa and Susan, had had success with preparing food for the winter, although it was haunting to know that the motivation for Marisa's hard work was the news sent from her friends back home as they described how hard it was getting hold of food. Her friends also wrote of other shortages that aggravated their everyday lives. Marisa made the remark many times that maybe some of her work could pay off if she could get food to a few of her friends' families when winter struck.

"My upright freezer will fit well beside the refrigerator in the kitchen. I'm going to bring my refrigerator and put it in the tack room of the barn. It will keep bushels of apples crisp for the better part of winter. Oh, I forgot to let you know that the generator will be delivered in a couple days. If we lose electricity the generator will automatically kick on once it is installed." Kent was not leaving a single thought of survival left unturned in case something happened to him and he left his new wife and their children behind. Even as he prepared for the worst scenario, he spoke little of it except during evening hours while listening to the news.

"Did Richard and Abby call back about renting the house at my farm?" Kent asked. Richard, a young, hardworking man, had worked for Kent during hay season for several summers and had recently married. Kent also knew Abby's parents and was glad to rent his former home to them at a low rate, since he knew Richard would take excellent care of the house.

"Abby called to tell us they will be over this evening to pay the first month's rent and to get the keys. She is so excited about it," Cathren told him. "I told her we would finish moving your things by tomorrow evening."

"I'm relieved someone will be there. I sure hated letting the place stand empty through the winter months. I will have to put most of the furniture in the unfinished part of the house for the time being. Andrew needs his room worse than we need our new space."

"Seth should be back in the morning. I'll see if he can help you get the rest of the furniture moved tomorrow."

"Good. We should be able to handle it. I can store some things in the tack room," Kent told her in a strained voice. Cathren could see the weight of so much worry bearing on his shoulders. Cathren had learned by now that when Kent's proud shoulders rounded themselves and when the middle age lines stood more prominent on his forehead, he needed rest, but for now he pushed on physically and mentally for the future.

"Mom. You got a letter in the mail today. It's from Ohio," Marisa yelled from inside the kitchen door. "It's on the table."

"Okay, Marisa, I'll open it when I get in."

"The return address is Stew's," were her last words before she shut the door and started her nightly phone marathon with her newfound friends in Kentucky.

Stew rarely sent letters, but when he did they were full of information he thought Cathren would be interested in hearing. Sometimes, he just sent large envelopes full of newspaper clippings to keep her in touch with happenings in Ohio.

Cathren opened the letter. This time it contained only one newspaper clipping. She read it before reading Stew's letter. The article was cut from a newspaper with a heading unfamiliar to her. The heading sported the name *The American Wing*. It informed readers that it would be the only paper published in the city and surrounding suburbs where Cathren was from. It also declared the printing of any other newspaper illegal for a period of at least six months or until civil order was in place. These orders came from the new elite, and they were making promises to restore sanity to the streets of America. It urged all America to stand behind them in the endeavor.

Cathren was unable to believe the article. "How could any good come from suppressing free speech?" she said to herself while shaking her head in disbelief. "So this is what things are coming to. If free speech is gone today, then what would be gone tomorrow? Ownership of land, home, businesses?"

The newspaper clipping showed Cathren that the radicals were gaining power much sooner than she could have imagined. It now scared her to turn her eyes to Stew's letter and what it held for her.

Dear Cathren and Kent,
We are managing to do quite well considering the circumstances we are living under. I have enclosed a newspaper clipping for you to read. I could have sent others, but this one says all. I know you are well read and have kept up with world events to know what accompanies this type of censorship.

There are still extreme shortages of food. Gangs and radicals are determined to gain control over the coming winter. The anti-government campaigning by radicals *is* blaming the present government for every one of society's ills.

I hope you are doing well and I am glad you are not here. What a statement! Taken out of context it would be a rude thing to say, but I am sincerely relieved you are not living here anymore, as much as I miss all of you. Some parts of the city are barely recognizable now. Gangs have become quite skilled at using explosives and other firepower to get their point across, in other words their way through fear.

I am afraid this letter appears to be quite depressing, but there is little to be cheerful about right now. Along with food shortages, medical facilities are doing with less too. There are a lot of injuries when fighting escalates and with the fighting there is always a shortage of medicine to treat victims of street trouble. I am truly sick of seeing amputees at every street corner I turn onto.

As for myself, I really can't complain. I have been extremely fortunate to continue making ends meet. My sister and I combining households was a relief in terms of finances.

She is still helping run the shop. This helps her have some extra funds for her children's clothing and other expenses. As for my job at the office, business is slow even as my hours are longer trying to keep it going with all the turmoil we have to cope with.

Our garden has helped us through the summer months and we have been able to store food for the winter months ahead. We even have bags of corn from a gain elevator and a small hand grinder to grind it into corn meal. We have also purchased several fifty-pound bags of potatoes from a farmer in the country. We have dehydrated vegetables. As for meat, it has become very expensive and nearly unaffordable. We have learned to make several meals from a single chicken by boiling it and making broth. We make chicken and noodles, chicken and rice, chicken and dumplings, and creamed chicken over biscuits all from one chicken. How's that for economizing?

We now have a piece of scenery that did not exist when you were still here, and that is outhouses. Yes, outhouses are in your old neighborhood. The lack of electricity at times has resulted in no water being pumped into houses for days. So out of necessity came the revival of the outhouse! We do not use them unless absolutely necessary. Luckily the smell has not reeked from them because they are not being used continuously.

I hope this letter gets through to you so you will know I am doing well and can still find a bit of humor in almost any situation when it comes to outhouses and chickens. A sense of humor helps to overcome the sadness of seeing children armless or without legs on a city corner. Please send my regards to the children. Take care. I hope to see you next summer. Tell Andrew to catch a fish for me!

Love always, Stew

Cathren was glad to see Stew was doing well under the poor circumstances that surrounded him, but she could read between the lines and could tell Stew was under extreme emotional stress. She was glad Stew stored food for the winter months ahead. She remembered Stew's bachelor lifestyle when he moved into a new upscale apartment complex as his income increased. He didn't have a dish, pot, or pan in his apartment for nearly a year until one of his girlfriends insisted on helping him equip his kitchen. When the relationship ended, so did Stew's culinary interests. Cathren decided in her next letter to him she would remind him of his pot and pan-free days and inform him that she would give about anything to see him cook a chicken then make several meals from it. She also planned to let him know she wanted a cooking demonstration of that feat on his next visit.

Kent walked in through the back door to ready himself for the meeting at the courthouse. Cathren decided to refrain from attending these meetings. She had enough defending herself before she left Ohio. She certainly did not want to start the same lifestyle here.

The sheriff, under the direction of a newly-formed state alert system, had organized those interested in setting up watches on roads leading into the county for the coming winter. The sheriff saw that the men got experience by setting posts several feet off the main roads so they could get used to watching and learn what to look for in the event there were raids in the county for food after cold weather set in.

The men were instructed not to take action under any circumstances. They were to show up for duty at their assigned posts unarmed until warranted. If problems were to occur, they were required to send a radio message and a runner to the next post for practice securing the entire county if needed in the future. All attendees were taught basic training for medical emergencies like CPR to care for a wounded soldier until medical help could be found.

Along with providing good training, the meetings kept rumors from running rampant and assisted the sheriff in delegating help. They also were able to find residents of the county who were in need of help. Most of the time, necessities could be traded for work on county farms, and in some situations local churches helped those in need.

It never failed to amaze Cathren how everyone seemed to know everyone else in the county, but considering the small population of the region it was understandable. Here individuals were important to their community. Things here were not perfect, but a person was clearly an individual, not a number. That had taken getting used to upon moving to the farm.

People in town knew the fate of Cathren's late husband, but most did not know they were divorced before his death. Some knew how she had been held at gunpoint and robbed. She had not told them, but one day Andrew told some friends, and the word spread fast. Marisa had been upset at Andrew for days after he told the story because her new friends from church asked too many questions to suit her. It was a sore point with her because she didn't want to dig up past feelings of her father's demise, but as time went on her friends held her in high-esteem because she had survived what they could only see on the nightly news.

When her friend was killed in Ohio and others were injured, Marisa's new friends were supportive. Slowly, she was able to let them know her feelings and how terribly it hurt when she received such news.

No one thought any less of Cathren because she did not attend the meetings with Kent. It was understood that Cathren had lived through enough violence before moving here, and they knew she was afraid of losing Kent.

But by staying away from the meetings, she did not know Seth had been attending them, too. Seth asked Susan not to tell her that he planned to do all he could to protect his family in their adopted Kentucky. They came as refugees and were welcomed. Seth wanted to let everyone know he could help contribute to the cause of keeping life safe in the region along with the other men.

Kent felt guilty because he had not told Cathren that Seth was attending meetings at the courthouse. He had asked Seth to please tell his mother because he did not feel it was fair to keep her in the dark. Kent was well aware Seth was simply trying to shield his mother from more pain than she had already experienced, but Kent let him know it would only be harder to let her know later, and if Seth did not tell her, he would.

Only two hours passed before Kent arrived home from the meeting. The courthouse had been full and all had left knowing there was nothing more to be done. The county was peaceful. Sheriffs from surrounding counties had been in attendance and reported the same. No one could see any cause for alarm; therefore the meeting adjourned early.

CHAPTER EIGHTEEN

Snow blanketed the ground shortly after the tobacco crop was sold. It was right before Christmas Eve. Christmas shopping was finished with some of the crop money. Each family member received a little to spend on gifts, for they all had worked in the field planting, cutting, stripping the tobacco, and helping on market day. Prices were low, but had to be accepted, and this put many farmers at task to make their mortgage payments through the winter.

Cathren's artificial tree had been a convenience by not leaving messy tree needles on the carpet as at her Ohio home in the past, but now it was a necessity. The woodstove could quickly dry a real Christmas tree to a fine kindling that could bring a home down in flames. Kent found it boxed in the barn loft, dusted the box, and set it outside the kitchen door to be brought in piece by piece as needed; thereby avoiding hay and straw that stubbornly clung to the bottom of the box from being strung across the kitchen floor.

Julianna's mother opted to let her remain on the farm for the holidays. She decided it was too risky for a trip to the city for Christmas, and she was right. Unusually cold temperatures gripped the nation through December and blackouts caused by the Left Wings and gangs were increasing. As expected, they increased their aggressive tactics in order to gain control over certain portions of the country. If they were successful, the United States would be broken soon.

Groups other than the International Left Wings were also determined to control the entire United States on their own. It was rumored that some wanted to have a military government, which would radically restrict rights of individuals through military rule. Others were known to desire a democracy type government without the federal government that drained the states' economies, thus forming new countries by combining certain states.

The gangs and Left Wings continued promoting anarchy with the outcome up for grabs. Many groups planned to be in control, ensuring a bloody winter in many areas of the country. Many of the least populated states which were virtually free of violence dreaded the outcome, for eventually the aggressors would be knocking at their doors too.

Snow continued to fall on the Appalachian foothills this December evening. Kent stoked the woodstove fire in response to the strong north wind that swirled drifting snow about the home and outbuildings on the farm. Andrew finished moving his belongings into his new bedroom and was still arranging it to his liking. Cathren relaxed by the warmth of the woodstove, leisurely leafing through one of her newly arrived seed catalogs, visualizing spring planting and jotting on scrap paper the varieties of crops she would plant. Kent spent most of the evening hanging the molding around the new bedroom. The kitchen flooring could be laid the next morning and dining furniture moved in after chores.

Marisa and Julianna took charge of the Christmas tree, decorating it with the joy of knowing once finished they could place their gifts for family and friends beneath its boughs. Seth stopped in to inspect the tree at the request of the excited girls, then left with a bucket of coal to use in the woodstove he installed in the small room they had recently built onto the mobile home. The new room had a cement floor and block wall four feet from floor level to avoid the chance of a fire engulfing the home.

The cacophonous ringing of the phone brought the homestead peacefulness to an end. Cathren placed the receiver next to her ear. By now she seemed to have a sixth sense for when the message at the other end was not one she wanted to hear.

"Hello?"

"Cathren, this is Martha. Are you watching the news?" Martha asked in a voice that commanded Cathren's concerned attention.

"No. Should we?" Cathren had made it a point not to disturb this evening with the depression the evening news could immediately place upon a person.

"There's a lot going on in the West. The Left Wings took over the California State Government this morning and disbanded the state legislature and even exiled the governor from his own state. According to the news, there is fighting from one end of the state to the other," Martha told Cathren. Martha was concerned about her brother who resided in the state. Her voice was full of alarm, for she had not been able to contact him for weeks. Phone calls were sporadic to the state and mail was not getting to many areas toward the West Coast.

Cathren informed Martha she wanted to turn the news on then immediately placed the phone back in its sedentary position.

"Kent, please come into the kitchen and watch the evening news. That was Martha on the phone." Cathren's tone of voice prompted his immediate response to her request. "I'll fix hot chocolate for everyone."

"Now all we need to do is wait to see which state falls next," Kent analyzed after Cathren informed him of the information Martha had passed on to her in combination with the news report. Kent sipped his hot chocolate. He turned the volume of the television down since the news simply reviewed what they just heard.

"How do you think all this will affect us?" Cathren asked Kent.

Kent sat motionless while considering her question. She probably meant how long it would be until border patrols around the state would require an increased force to be efficient through the winter if it was a harsh one in terms of trouble like California was experiencing.

"It has always been my opinion that the rest of the country was too dependent upon California as a food source, particularly the eastern portion of the country. If food can't be imported or if warehouses are not prepared to hold the East and Northeast through the winter, it is going to be tough all around." He was trying his best to avoid the real meaning of her question.

"Will you be leaving soon?" She struck her words adamantly.

"I don't know," Kent spoke the dreaded answer. "I really don't see anyone breaking their necks to get at the heart of farm country, with the exception of a few raids for goods and food," he answered her. "Most of these gangs wouldn't know what to do when they got here as far as holding farms for themselves. There's not a lot to offer as far as a play for power in regions like this, but certain freedoms could eventually be at risk."

"What do you mean by that?" The opinions he now communicated to her would give her a greater understanding of the risks he would be taking the next several months.

"I think if Kentucky takes a strong stand in the beginning when it comes to dealing with undesirables, so to speak, there will be less trouble in the long run." He spoke in a soft but adamant tone that quickly let her know he would defend their freedoms without any thought otherwise. He continued, "I believe the best move for the state would be to continue being a willing participant as a part of the United States, but at the same time push for radical changes on how much the federal government continues to dominate the nation and how much money it will be allowed to soak its people for. But at this point that view may not be realistic. Kentucky, out of a survival instinct and in the best interest of its citizens, may have to become a distinct country for a time, or part of a regional alliance with bordering states that are not hostile such as Ohio has become."

"Hostile? What do you mean, hostile?" Cathren knew his answer, but if he stated possible conditions again for her, she could keep abreast of the future of their home life.

"I mean states, such as Ohio, that are more heavily populated and have a lot of industry, are crucial strategically to the Left Wings. It is highly probable that states taken over by radicals and/or gangs will more than likely become hostile neighbors in the long run. That could be an immediate problem or one that could take several years to appear. States to the south, like Tennessee, will probably never pose a threat to Kentucky because culturally speaking they are compatible."

He ended with a sigh and shook his head. "I ask myself the same question a hundred times each day. How could this happen to the greatest nation on Earth? It breaks my heart. Now the country will be at the real test as to how strong it can still be, if it is still salvageable, and if the stranglehold of a runaway government that is used to being unaccountable for so long can finally control itself. We shall see, but I am ashamed to say that I doubt it."

"I don't care what happens anywhere else. We are here, and they are in California, a million miles away as far as I am concerned." Cathren turned, placing her hands at the nape of Kent's neck then methodically and smoothly rubbing the tension from his knotted muscles in his shoulders.

"Mmm. Don't stop," he begged. The motion of her hands moved to the round of his shoulders, then back inward to his spine, then lower to his back and then up again. "Can this be continued later when you and I are alone?"

"Oh, possibly. What do I get in exchange?"

"Now, Mrs. Freeman. What kind of mischief are you up to?"

"Oh, I don't know. I suppose whatever mischief you would like this evening."

"Well, keep that on hold until bedtime," Kent said, relishing the feeling inside him when she came on to him like she did after he put in a hard day of work. He knew her routine well enough now, and soon he would lie beside this woman he loved so. Tonight he would do little or no work so they could be alone. She planned to provide the entertainment to conclude their day together on their homestead.

CHAPTER NINETEEN

"Who could be at the door this hour of the night?" A dazed Cathren turned the bedside lamp on and placed her robe around her shoulders before starting down the staircase.

Bone-chilling temperatures of a heartless Arctic blast had introduced the New Year across the nation, and tonight was no different. Record breaking subzero temperatures grasped the hills of Kentucky. To Cathren, it seemed to be a bad omen and her very being shuddered at the thought. The knock at the back door had left her nerves on edge.

"Slow down a little. Let me answer it. Stay back near the steps in case there is trouble. It will give you time to get a gun and use it if necessary," Kent commanded her, in contrast to his usual soft question when he needed her to do something. This was the first time she heard this tone from his lips. It alarmed her, her heart raced. She did not hesitate to obey.

He paced slowly to the door and precisely turned the outdoor light on. Kent pulled the curtain back and looked out the window. He jerked open the door so hard that Cathren thought surely it would separate from its hinges. A man with his arm in a sling stood in the doorway. Kent had left the kitchen light off, so it was too dark for Cathren to tell who stood in her doorway.

"My word, man! You look like you are half frozen. Get in here." Kent helped the man into the house, as the figure looked unable to do so without help.

Cathren saw the tears before she saw the man beneath them. "Stew!" she cried out. She ran to help Kent walk him to the nearest chair.

"The heater in the car I'm driving went out about fifty miles back. I may be frostbitten. I can't ever remember being this cold. The car quit on me about two miles up the road. I had to walk the rest of the way." Stew barely managed to speak.

"I'll fix some hot chocolate to warm you. Get those wet clothes off before you get sick," Cathren ordered while quickly grabbing a saucepan to heat milk in.

"Come in here and sit next to the woodstove after you put this robe on," Kent told him.

"I'll set the hot chocolate on the end table nearest the woodstove." Cathren wanted to interrogate Stew with a million questions, particularly as to why he was here in the middle of this January night when he should be home, warm and sleeping in his own bed, but it was clear Stew was too exhausted and emotionally-drained to answer even the most simple of questions. Cathren and Kent would have to wait until tomorrow morning to get answers from their friend about his mysterious appearance at the door.

Silence surrounded the threesome for minutes. Kent added coal to the woodstove and made a cup of decaf. Stew sat on the couch near Cathren. The cat slid from behind Marisa's door, moved quietly across the room, and nestled in its corner behind the woodstove.

"I guess the two of you are wondering why I'm here in the middle of a night like this." Stew cracked a smile, much to Cathren's relief.

"What would make you think that?" Cathren unsuccessfully tried teasing back to break the tension in the room.

"Medicines," he answered.

"Medicines?" Cathren asked. "I thought you stocked well throughout the summer. Did someone break into your house and steal them?"

"Not exactly," he answered. "Food is getting more scarce back home. A group in our business community has formed an alliance of sorts. We're smuggling food and medicines back into the city when we are able to do so."

"Is it that bad?" Kent inquired.

"It's worse." Stew turned the focus of his eyes directly to Kent's. "The radical Left Wings and other factions, including what is left of the government, are putting the pressure on. Each is trying to make the other break, and people are caught in the middle. Nearly every road in and out of every major city is either controlled by someone or is bombed out. Food is scarce and children in the city aren't getting enough to eat."

"How are you getting food in?" Cathren asked.

"We're buying what we can in surrounding states and shipping it into Ohio."

"If the roads are so bad and are blocked off at many places, how are you getting food and medicine in?" Cathren asked again.

"We ship it across the Ohio River by boat before daybreak and store it on the Ohio side of the river before dawn. The next night we load the goods on canoes and run them up creeks off the Ohio where canoeing is possible to certain designated areas along the banks where we meet. Sometimes it has to be hauled by land for a few feet or a few miles until it goes back into a canoe or small fishing boat. I left home before this cold front came through. I hope it doesn't stay cold too long or the waterways will freeze over. Until now, we've been lucky this winter."

"Isn't it dangerous smuggling into the cities and suburbs?" Cathren asked.

Stew nodded her way, then smiled. "Yeah, but it sure as hell is a lot of fun! This is better than those pirating novels I was addicted to when I was a kid. I feel like a gunrunner on the high seas even if it is just the Ohio and its tributaries."

"Stew, for Pete's sake." Cathren stood and walked to him to embrace him. "You never cease to amaze me. You are selfless."

"Well, not exactly. I do make a little money doing this. We have been able to survive better than most through this catastrophe."

"Kent, would you wake Andrew and tell him to sleep on the couch for the rest of the night? I'll put clean sheets and blankets on Andrew's bed for Stew."

"We can talk more tomorrow. Stew needs the rest," Kent said.

Kent helped Andrew to the couch. "Hi, Stew," was all Andrew could muster before he fell back into a slumber.

Cathren followed Kent up the staircase. They could hear Stew showering before he went to bed. Cathren figured by his appearance that it had been days since he showered last. Half an hour later the house fell into a peaceful silence again.

Outside, the wind suddenly stilled and flurries ceased. In the distance, the occasional noise of a tree cracking under the combination pressure of ice and cold temperatures was all that dared break the silence in the deadly cold night. It sent an alarm throughout the world. Many cities in the nation were without power in this dead of winter. Families with young children huddled around inefficient fireplaces that were built purely for décor and not for practical use whatsoever. Many warmed themselves with kerosene heaters, and some just huddled without the benefit of any heat source other than the closeness of flesh.

The populace of some regions showed signs of scurvy and other ailments due to a lack of Vitamin C. Those in control were not letting essential vitamin-packed food get into the marketplaces where it was needed most.

Crops of citrus fruits simply rotted in fields and warehouses where they lay in California and Florida, as it was impossible to ship the produce to other parts of the country. Though many families had yard space enough to grow gardens to help them survive through the winter, they heeded not the warnings and went about life as if nothing would change for the worse. Americans had lost the art of the victory garden and the independence it could give them from the forces that now played with their very lives.

"Marisa, the radio station up town just announced there would be no school today because the roads are covered with snow. You can sleep in." Cathren gave Julianna and Andrew the same speech. Cathren was used to driving in snowy conditions back home during weather like this, but so much as an inch halted life here because winding hilly roads make it hazardous to wander out with a vehicle. Besides, temperatures usually did not stay cold long enough to let an ice storm's grip keep hold, so most drivers of this southern region were not experienced driving on ice and snow.

"Cat, Stew and I are going to tow his vehicle here. Keep Andrew off the lane until we pull it into the barn. I'm afraid we'll slide around as we pull it in." Kent always took safety precautions and planned ahead on farm work to avoid hastiness that could cause accidents. It was hard to keep from getting hurt doing farm work. Modern machinery took its toll on some farm families in accidents and Kent always made sure his would not be one of them.

Cathren began fixing breakfast for the household. She had to buy eggs this week because the chickens were not coping well with the cold weather and would not lay eggs. She placed the coffeepot on a trivet sitting on top the woodstove. Forty-five minutes later, the men were finished pulling Stew's car into the barn and were back in the house.

Kent started his daily chores by shoveling the ashes from the woodstove. He then hauled enough wood and coal in to fill the wooden box in the corner.

"Stew just left for the barn. Do you think the car problems are serious?" Cathren asked.

"I doubt it. We'll probably make a trip to town after the roads are cleared a little. Stew keeps that car on the Kentucky side of the Ohio River and uses it to drive around to make purchases to be shipped back to Ohio."

"Looks to me he could use a few days' rest before going back home." Cathren placed a plate of eggs, bacon, and toast on the table for Kent.

"I agree, but he wants to get some business taken care of as soon as possible so he can get back," Kent said as he picked up his fork and started on his breakfast. "If he had good sense he'd stay down here and forget about all the trouble going on up there."

"Stew was never one for using good sense, except when it comes to business. If you ask him to stay, don't count on yes for an answer," Cathren said after placing her plate on the table. Stew stepped out of his winter boots and placed his suitcase of clothing on the floor.

"Grab a plate off the stove and get yourself some breakfast before walking back into that cold air," Kent ordered.

"I didn't know I was so hungry until I stepped through the door and smelled breakfast. I don't believe I could walk out without a bite to eat," Stew told them as he filled his plate and sat down.

"How long can you stay?" Cathren asked.

"Probably just for the day. I will be driving to Knoxville after the car is running again to order shipments of food to be sent to one of the warehouses we rented in northern Kentucky." Stew paused to eat more of his breakfast. "I can do the negotiating, but that's about it since I broke my arm."

"How did that happen?" Cathren asked.

"Fell on ice in the driveway a few weeks back," he told her. "I haven't been able to do a lot of hauling since then."

"If you need a place to stay on the way home, just stop here," Kent told him.

"I may do just that very thing if it's this cold on the way home." Stew's face showed worry lines around his eyes and his forehead that accented heavily when he spoke. He smiled, then announced to the audience sitting at the table before him, "But

I'll probably try to go straight home if possible. My fiancée will be worried."

"Your fiancée?" Cathren squealed. "I can't believe it! Stew! Who's the lucky girl?"

"Sharon."

"Sharon, our Sharon from the office?"

"Sure enough. The wedding is set to take place two weeks from Saturday," Stew informed them.

"So you finally decided to hang up bachelor life. Good! You couldn't find a better person than Sharon. You have my blessing. I never would have dreamed of it before." Cathren hugged Stew. "Kent, do you have enough room for an extra person in the truck when you drive to town? I need to buy a wedding gift for the happy couple."

Andrew burst into the kitchen. "Hey, Stew. Want to make a snowman?"

"How many heads do you think it should have?" Stew asked his young friend. Andrew was growing into a clear image of his deceased father. Stew was happy and sad at the same time, knowing how pleased Nate would have been if he were still alive.

"How about three this time? I'll get carrots for the noses. Kent, can I use one of your hats?" Andrew asked.

"There's one you can use hanging just inside the coat closet," Kent answered. Julianna walked into the room clothed for playing in the snow, too.

"Dad, can you help me make a snowman? I don't want one with three heads, though," she asked while grabbing a piece of toast off the table and walking towards the back door.

"Yes, plum. I need to find another hat," Kent told her.

"Cathren, do you have a big straw hat? I want a snow woman."

"I'll get one from the attic. I'll lay it out the back door on the porch, when I find it," Cathren told her before she turned to the men and smiled. "You men need to get on the ball and make those snowmen fast. You have work to do."

Cathren turned the burner heat to simmer on the stove so the vegetable soup she just mixed together could cook slowly while she, Kent, and Stew were in town. She appointed Marisa babysitter and soup stirrer.

By afternoon, the January sun had shone brightly on the black pavement, making the trip to town less hazardous than a trip hours before would have been. Most of the snow turned to a miserable slush, ensuring that all vehicles on the road would be covered with a salt and mud mixture by the day's end.

On the square in town, Cathren went into one of the shops and purchased a robe and gown for Sharon. She then purchased a perfume at the drug store, one Sharon had always complimented Cathren on wearing. She then purchased gifts for the home and had them wrapped so Stew would not see them until he and Sharon could open them together.

"That was fast. I didn't expect you to be here this soon. Did they have all the parts you need for the car?" Cathren asked them as they climbed into the truck.

"Yes, we were lucky today," Kent said. "Would you like to walk to the restaurant and have some pie and coffee?"

"That's a good idea. I have a lot to tell you, and if we're in the restaurant I know the children won't hear what I have to say," Stew informed.

The three of them sat at the table nearest the window and ordered.

"How is the old neighborhood, Stew?" Cathren asked, though she was afraid to hear.

"We have the same neighbors as when you lived there. Now none of the children can attend public schools. It is not safe. The neighborhood has formed an educational co-op, meeting at the church a couple blocks away. Despite it all, when the students took their standardized test this fall they scored well."

"Have gangs bothered the neighborhood much?" she asked.

"Unfortunately, yes. A few hoodlums tried to terrorize a retired couple down the street." He turned to Cathren. "Mr. and Mrs. Wella. One of the neighbors saw the attempted breaking and entering then alerted the rest of us."

"Did everything turn out all right?"

"About five men got their guns and ran the gang off with an exchange of gunfire." Stew laughed. "You should have seen those guys run. They never expected to have anyone try to stop them. Doug shot one of them in the foot and the others had to drag their wounded friend over the pavement to get to their vehicle. Was that ever a sight to see!" Stewed chuckled.

Cathren asked, "Were any of the neighbors hurt?"

"Just one, but he was fine. It wasn't much."

"Well, I'm dying to know who was hurt. Come on, Stew." Cathren's excitement overcame her.

"I was shot in the arm, but it was a flesh wound. Then I fell and broke the same arm that was shot." Stew tried to put on a smile, but they could tell he was still shaken from the incident. "But everything turned out for the best because Sharon started bringing my work to the house each day while I convalesced, and that's when we really began to know one another. I realized I could not live without her, that I could not imagine not asking her to be my wife. I never felt that way about a woman."

Cathren sat with tears in her eyes. She had nearly lost Stew, too. Cathren started breaking down in the restaurant. Kent immediately changed the subject.

"Cat and I have plenty of garden seed. Would you like to take some back to Ohio? Have you started any tomato or pepper plants inside the house yet?" Kent asked. Stew saw why Kent changed the subject.

"No, but I will as soon as I arrive home. I don't think local nurseries will have many early plants this year because gangs see that utilities continue to be shut off. A greenhouse can't remain heated in the middle of a winter storm without electricity and gas," Stew told them. Kent left for the register to pay the bill.

"Each time you leave us, I am so afraid it will be the last time we'll ever see you alive. I have forgotten what it is like to live there since I have settled here. I seem to have blocked it out. Your being here and telling me about the conditions back home brings it all back. It is devastating," Cathren cried.

"Everyone lives from day to day and cope as best they can. It is where my work is, what's left of it, anyway. As long as I can eke out a living, I plan to stay. I won't let them run me out until I have no choice, and then I will go back to fight for what is right, any way possible. I can't have it any other way, Cathren. After Nate, I just could not live with myself if I didn't do whatever possible on my part to stop this madness. If you never see me again, Cat, please understand that I was doing what I wanted when I left this world. Never worry about me. I have found my peace with God after all I went through after Nate's death. I am doing what I have to do to help others."

Cathren nodded her understanding to Stew. Silence was the only language spoken as the truck Kent drove guided them through its well-known country path of a road to the farm that awaited their presence. The afternoon was filled with plenty for all to do until Stew's car repairs became final. Cathren packed a lunch for Stew's trip South and filled his thermos with steamy hot chocolate to keep away winter's chill in case the vehicle decided once again to break down in the cold.

Cathren did not leave the house to send Stew on his journey as the others did. She could only bear to witness the waves of good-bye from out a window through the dimming sun, which was filtered by the flurry of shimmering snowflakes fluttering about, deciding where to lay themselves for the night. Cathren felt as restless as the flurried snow all through the night.

"I slept in. Have the kids left for school already?" Kent asked.

"Yes, they have. You don't look well," Cathren told him, concerned because it was unusual for Kent to sleep in, especially with the commotion of all three students of the household getting ready each school morning.

"I feel a cold coming on. I need to get the hotbeds for seeds built. I have the lumber cut for them in the barn. I plan to use a plastic for green houses for the lids instead of glass, like I used on the other place."

"That reminds me, I need to send the last of my seed orders in today. I can't believe I want more pepper varieties." Cathren turned to answer the ringing phone.

"Thought I should call and check in to let everyone know I am well, and in Knoxville. It sure is nice to be able to use a phone when you need it. We haven't had phone service like this back home in a long while," Stew told her.

"I am so glad you called. Do you know how long you will be in Knoxville?" she asked.

"Not yet. I'll give you my number just in case you need to call me," he told her. He continued giving the information.

"Thanks. I won't keep you, but make sure you stay in touch. Bye now."

"Sure thing. Take care, Cat. Bye."

"Well, Stew sounds great." Cathren informed Kent.

"Cat. There's going to be a meeting in town tomorrow night at the courthouse. Our county volunteers may be traveling to the northern part of the state for practice maneuvers in a few days. If you want me to stay here, I will."

"When did you hear this?"

"I saw John when we were in town yesterday. He planned to visit here last evening, but I told him we would talk later today on the phone and not to bother driving all the way out here."

"I suppose Seth is going?" she asked, raising her chin and eyebrows to express her disapproval.

"Did Seth tell you he was attending the meetings?"

"No, I have my sources as far as those meetings are concerned, Mr. Freeman! I also know you promised not to say anything about Seth's plans until he mentioned it to me first. You should not have kept it from me."

"I am sorry. You're right. I felt he had more time to divulge this type of information to you than there is. He wants to do this but he is afraid of how you feel about his getting involved."

"You and Seth know how I feel about getting involved. I have no choice but to let both of you go because he needs you to be with him. You have to watch over him for me. I know there has been a lot of gang fighting near the Ohio River as of late. I also know that gangs have tried raiding inland from the Ohio River into Kentucky and crossing back over the Ohio with the loot."

"This group that has taken hold in Ohio has yet to grab onto any Kentucky soil. This training in the northern part of the state will never lead to any action, but will just be a precaution," Kent tried to reassure her.

"Sure. Right. Whatever. You know damn well that isn't so," she scolded.

Kent hung his head, unable to look into her eyes. "I fear you may be right."

Five days passed. Then Seth and Kent were not on the farm. A war-seasoned Kent left on a somber note while Seth left cheerfully on the adventure of a lifetime. Cathren never understood the appeal of a battle to young men. Susan appeared as enthused as Seth; her young husband leaving to defend their home was as romantic as any love story during wartime could be. Cathren could only feel sick at what might go wrong.

CHAPTER TWENTY

Seth and Stew crossed the Ohio River early in the day. Kent followed several yards behind in an identical aluminum jon boat. Winds still calm from the night, and a lazy drifting current made the trip across an easy one. All boats making the crossing were loaded with food and medicine. Stew stowed the wedding gifts from Cathren and Kent under a plastic tarp on the boat he captained. The coast had been cleared by guards posted several miles away in both directions along the river and along the tributary they would enter in moments.

Days earlier, the men had not known their paths might cross. The three knew it would be hard convincing Cathren otherwise the next time they spoke to her. When presented the opportunity to smuggle medicines and food into Ohio, Seth was more than eager to volunteer, though Kent told him it was not the wise thing to do. Kent could only follow and keep a watchful eye.

The current of the creek they winded into worked against them until they found the appointed area of hickory and oak trees lining the creek bank. From the landing on the bank, a trail led them to the edge of the remains of a cornfield where a tractor and wagon sat waiting. The unloading and loading began, and the woman on the tractor made five trips into the brown pole barn across the field. Stew pulled a motorcycle from the barn after the last load had been safely stored away.

"You have a safe trip home, Seth. Send my regards to your mother for me. Kent, I suppose you realize the next shipment will be at another location on the river. We change sites of delivery each time. I hope we can do this together again. This was a

216

great crew to work with," Stew told them, and without giving either a chance to respond, he turned his motorcycle and rode away.

Kent and Seth walked to water's edge and climbed into one of the jon boats. They made their way across the Ohio with the other boats but more carefully than they had crossed earlier, for it was later in the morning. The boats separated at the mouth of the creek. The sailors for the day pulled out fishing poles and pretended to fish until they reached the Kentucky shore.

The county group felt accomplished at having brought food and medicine into the territory now held behind a virtual iron curtain. It was now impossible to cross the main bridges connecting the two states without having all goods confiscated by the gangs. With the mission accomplished and another training exercise concluded for the day, Seth and Kent returned to their lodgings, ate their dinners, and slept peacefully through the night.

For another week, a line of boats crossed the Ohio at a different location for another delivery until colder temperatures set in and the banks began to freeze, making it too dangerous for the small aluminum boats to make the crossing. Seth and Kent were able to make another crossing together before subzero temperatures grasped onto the Ohio River Valley. Upon reaching the shore, they beheld the sight of Stew before them.

"How are things, Stew?" Seth greeted, always eager to hear news of home.

"Not so great. The fighting is severe in the cities right now. The federal government tried to send troops to restore order, but they didn't arrive. The gangs are putting up a lot of resistance, and are not giving an inch of territory," he informed them.

"Is your family safe?" Kent inquired.

"We're surviving so far. My nephew got into a scrape with some gang members the other day and was badly beaten, but he should be fine in a few weeks. They broke one of his legs for hell of it. Listen to me. I want the both of you to go back home now. You have done quite enough here. It is going to get bad through the next several weeks, and I may take Sharon, my sister, and her children across the river into Kentucky, too. Here is the address. You won't be hearing anything from us until late this spring, so don't come looking for us if all of Ohio's borders are cut off from the rest of the world. We will manage, and will be in contact, Lord willing. I will see you soon, hopefully," Stew told them. Much sadness was expressed in his voice.

"You know all of you are welcome on our place, don't you?" Kent asked.

"I know, but I put a little down payment on a place about fifty miles south of Maysville that we can go to. I don't want to leave my job, even if there isn't much of a job left to stay with. It is an income. I may be able to make some contact from northern Kentucky now and then." Stew reached into his pocket. "I forgot earlier. This is a letter from Sharon to Cathren. I need to go now. I'll be in touch. Take care on your trip home." Stew shook their hands, turned, and left them for the second time in days.

Kent and Seth loaded into the boats before heading across the Ohio River for the last time. Stormy skies alerted the water that in turn responded with white caps lapping harshly against the small boat hulls. It seemed an eternity to get to the other shore as the wind whipped across their faces and snow began to fall, stinging with the vengeance of winter's wrath. The freezing water's edge announced that the siege of Ohio was on. The county group of volunteers had two more days left of training after successfully patrolling their appointed area. All returned to the county a few pounds leaner than when they left three weeks earlier. During training, men and women alike worked from daylight to dark. Word had already been sent that all went well. Seth walked to the mobile home after delivering Sharon's letter to his mother. The crackling of hedge tree wood warmed the farmhouse while Andrew drilled Kent about the adventures. Andrew eagerly dreamed of when his time for duty would arrive.

March winds hurled around Cathren's head while she and Kent planted potato sets in the cold ground. Kent worked the soil twice to make the planting easier. The economy had not improved; therefore, the garden size increased dramatically, as most gardens throughout the county had.

Many Kentucky farmers planted extra produce crops to sell in the cities to the north if possible through the coming summer and fall months. All hoped getting across the river peacefully again would be possible soon. Farm communities smelled profit and planted from daylight till dusk. Without competition from the far southwest and fewer shipments of produce from foreign countries, farmers had good reason to believe their hard work would pay off.

Every bridge between Kentucky and Ohio had been barricaded for several weeks. The Left Wing radicals were increasing their arsenal with each day and did not hesitate to demonstrate a show of power along the Kentucky border.

Kentuckians protected their northern border along the entire river's edge and several miles deep into the state. Every precaution was made to keep the radicals and gangs from gaining any territory south of the Ohio River. Martial law existed for most of Ohio, but it was unsure at times who ruled. At this point, most of the population was willing to pledge their allegiance to anyone who could restore electricity and fill grocery stores with food.

Kent made no hesitation to get the early spring planting finished before he and Seth were called for duty again. The plan was for county volunteers to be placed farther from the river than the prior trip north, plans that comforted everyone in the county.

Southern leaders managed to maintain federal troops in the south by paying them for their duties since the federal government was for the most part unable to do so. Soldiers were glad to serve and receive pay to protect their country. States like Kentucky were relieved to have professionals do the job of protecting their borders. The military and states south of the Ohio and those wanting to protect their borders from the Left Wings in other states needed each other and worked well together.

Stew helped his family escape from Ohio in the nick of time. Orders had been given for anyone caught smuggling for the cause of freedom to be tried and hung immediately. Heat and electricity were non-existent for nearly a month, which was also a determining point of how much the family could stand. Stew made plans for each family member to carry on as usual. His sister's children would not be told of their planned escape until they found themselves on the way to crossing the river. No friends could be told.

Stew and Sharon left by separate means. Stew's sister took her children for an outing after working a few hours in the shop. The children still did not know the outing was a move across the river. They were going on a fishing trip, they were told. All this in secrecy, for if a family wished to move out of state now, it required approval from authorities. Even making a request could mean severe penalties, such as spending time in prison. Boats hid near the designated place. Stew waited for his sister until the car lights flashed from the barnyard in the distance. They were signaling all was well. They would meet in minutes beneath a cluster of locust trees on the slope nearing the creek. Stew managed to carry his nephew the final yard to the boat. He was not healing from the beating he had received from the gang members and needed medical attention urgently. The pain of making the trip had been gruesome for the young boy. Placing him in a comfortable position on the largest boat for the crossing proved to be a task.

Thunder had produced a cloud burst three hours earlier and continued its downpour until the earth could absorb no more and the fields held standing waters waiting to be shed into the nearest ditch or creek. The current was swift and muddy. Stew swore that no one with good sense would risk crossing the mighty Ohio River during the lightning storm that frightened the group. No one bothered to guard the river shores where Stew and his family crossed. Sharon had realized just three weeks earlier she and Stew would soon be parents. The child she carried truly finalized the decision to leave Ohio territory. Contacts Stew had made during his smuggling of food and medicine had proved invaluable. He was able to make up for business lost at home. They would be able to stay on the farm until they could return to Ohio at a future date and hopefully a better environment in which to live. Stew planned to go back as soon as the Left Wings were driven out of Ohio. Stew loved Ohio, and furthermore, life on a farm wasn't what he had in mind for his future.

Several hours lapsed before the family was able to cross the river and get to the home Stew had waiting for them. With each civil outbreak, Stew had stored more food and essentials there, so they wouldn't have to worry about those things. The old house was large and airy, too airy, and would have to be insulated to make it livable. Living quarters for both families in the farmhouse were private except for the large country kitchen that was shared, which gave Stew and Sharon privacy for the first time since they were married.

CHAPTER TWENTY-ONE

Cathren was following Kent into the house after the gardening tools had been placed in the shed when John Chaney arrived. Kent turned around to open the kitchen door, through which he had entered seconds earlier. He instinctively knew Sheriff Chaney would ask for him to serve shortly. When the visitor informed him of the expected news, Kent needed to make the dreaded trip into the other room to inform Cathren that he would be leaving. It seemed that as of late he and Cathren spent more time arguing than being civil to one another. Kent began wondering if she planned to stay in their relationship.

"Well, when are you to leave?" she bombarded as soon as he entered the kitchen.

"It will be in a few days. There are rumors of a gang buildup across the northern border. There may be an attack on the Kentucky side soon, at least it seems to appear that way. It is rumored the Left Wing radicals will attempt to spread their base and weaken the defense across the border." Kent grabbed a glass from the counter for a drink of water from the faucet.

"And?" she snapped.

"If there is an attack or any aggressive move, all volunteers will be asked to go to the northern border immediately to defend the state," he reluctantly told her, though his first instinct was to run from the hostility that grew thick in the room. Kent recalled feeling more comfortable in a war zone.

"If that happens, then there could be a war, so to speak," she commented.

"I hope not, but that's one of the possibilities. They are getting more opposition than they expected."

"What do you think they will do?"

"I think as long as Kentucky remains a free commonwealth it will be a threat to the Left Wings and the gang stronghold over the cities in the north. The more they control, the less threat there will be of a reinstatement of democracy in Ohio."

"Who will be able to rule over the gangs or so called Left Wings?"

"I don't even think they know. If they succeed in completely undermining the federal government, there will probably be several coups until the most dominate can survive and rule," he responded. "Seth is so ready to defend the cause of freedom back home that he would do anything if asked to do so. This trip will be more dangerous."

"And you plan to go and watch over him?"

"That was a silly question."

"Hope this is his last trip."

"That depends on whether he is the type to get his fill of whatever goes on and whether he can survey the situation properly to see if his service is of any use. He needs to be able to determine if taking a chance on losing his life would be futile in the long run. You cannot do that for him, and neither can I. I would like to but can't," Kent informed her.

"This sort of trouble could last for twenty, maybe thirty years or more. Some countries never stop the fighting. I guess we are no longer immune here in the States, are we?"

"I'm afraid not, Cat. Listen. I don't like this any better than you do. I don't like all the fighting going on between you and me. I don't like the thought of Seth going in the least, but he is going regardless. I did try to talk him out of volunteering for this. I told him his family had been through enough, but he wants to help squash what has been done to his country and his home state. He also wants revenge for his father's death. I cannot blame the kid. It is what it is, and our fighting over it is not going to change a single thing. I cannot do any more than I am doing to keep him safe. Besides, the tension between us is really upsetting the kids," he commented to her.

"I know, I know. I have decided to just turn all my frantic worrying over to God and let him take this from me. If I don't, it will drive me to the point where I cannot cope with anything well. Whatever happens, I need to be strong. I have let you down by being so snappy over something you have no control over, and I am sorry I have been taking it out on you." She walked to him and kissed him.

"I'm sorry, too. I don't want this arguing to continue to the point of divorce court. The future before us during the next several months and maybe years will be trying, and I need to be strong for you. I need to be your sounding board for whatever you're feeling. I have been so absorbed in thoughts of what is to come I have neglected us, and that is wrong. In fact, I think this would be a great time for all of us to leave the farm for a few days. The kids haven't had a break from our evening conversations and winter preparations. Let's pack up and take them to the Smoky Mountains for a bit, let them have some fun. We all need it," Kent told her.

"That is a wonderful idea! Let's not talk of any of this volunteer stuff while we're gone. But who will watch over the farm?" she asked.

"I will stop at Herb's and ask if he could feed the animals. And my new renters on my old place have been wonderful to work with. I can work out an arrangement to pay them for work on that place while I am gone from time to time. We can leave and not worry about anything going wrong," Kent assured her.

"Mom, did I hear right? Are we going on a trip?" Marisa yelled with glee.

"Have you been listening all the while?" Cathren asked, not too happy at Marisa's eavesdropping.

"You were so loud I couldn't help but hear," Marisa answered. "Can we go now?"

"How about tomorrow, just before daybreak? That will give us plenty of time to pack and make arrangements for someone to watch over the place while we are gone. How does that sound?" Kent asked.

"Oh, Kent. This is going to be a fun trip," Cathren told him. "But we need to be careful with our money."

"Not on this trip, Mrs. Freeman. I am pulling rank on this." He smiled. "Let's rent a cabin with enough bedrooms for all. And let the kids see all the sites possible."

Kent knew this could be their last chance to be together if the worst came knocking on their door in the coming months. The short trip revived the family spirit.

CHAPTER TWENTY-TWO

Stew could not resist the temptation of smuggling food into the Ohio territory, so his work continued, despite what could happen if he were caught. He knew the great need for the supplies he sent and loved the excitement of maneuvering around the Left Wings. The degree of danger increased with each trip across the river. He swore each would be his last, but there was always that sick child needing a certain medicine or that college student who had been caught behind the imaginary iron wall who needed to be reunited with loved ones in another state. The requests went on and on, and he did his best to fill them.

Many times Stew was rewarded quite handsomely for his heroic measures, while other trips were made out of his generosity. Remaining cautious, learning to smell danger, and being able to have the gut feeling to abort a mission saved his and other lives many times over.

The ability to read a stranger and to doubt when others were eager to trust led many to believe that Stew had the gift of early frontiersmen, that sense of knowing what was about to happen next. But even Stew knew one day his intuition would slip and his time would end, as it had for many others who had taken the same risks he took. Stew's capture and hanging would be a great prize for Left Wings. Stew's present paranoia, which he had good reason for, prompted him to set up a residence in a small hunting cabin along the Ohio River, filling it with personal effects and limited food supplies. He sometimes stayed there for several days, inviting guests who worked with him and keeping Sharon's location secret for her protection.

Guilt lingered in Stew's soul each time he left Sharon and the stress he knew she felt, but a child in need in Ohio now could be his own in the future. His trips were necessary, and a smuggling operation for a child needing food or medicine, no matter the risk, was one that could not be refused, no matter the danger.

Sharon heard the knock on the door and hurried to answer it.

"Oh my. Look at you. Oh, how I have missed you and your family," Sharon yelled with excitement. "Please come in. And bring your friend in. Any friend of Seth's is a friend of ours."

Sharon embraced Seth upon his entrance into the home.

"Stew was out most of the night. He made it back from another run across the river. He'll be glad to see you again. It's been weeks since he saw you last. Both of you please sit while I rouse him. I hope you can stay for breakfast." In her eagerness, Sharon had not given Seth the opportunity to introduce her to Kent.

Stew stepped into the front room to meet his visitors. Kent stood taken aback at how much Stew had aged since their last meeting. It was a clear indication of the strain of the life he had endured in the north before they escaped. Although Stew was genuinely glad to see his friends, it was hard for him to cover his somber mood. Kent had seen these same bearings on others who had served shortly before the fall of a country to regimes bent on killing thousands of humans to install communistic governments.

"Honey, this is Kent. Kent, my wife Sharon," Stew introduced the two.

"I am so pleased to meet you, Kent. I have heard such good things of you. How is my dear friend Cathren? I have missed her so," Sharon asked.

"She is doing well. She has been busy with spring planting."

"Stew tells me she is doing much better since she moved to Kentucky. Needless to say I was a bit taken back by her marriage so quickly after the move, but I can see her decision was the best that could have happened in her life," Sharon told him. "I am so glad you have been there for her. I worried and prayed for her and the children through their tragedies. I see after meeting you this morning that my prayers were answered. I am so happy for her. I hear she is quite the gardener now. I'm sure we are going to need her advice through the summer. I am so sorry to be rambling on so, but I am so eager to hear about her new life."

"That reminds me: Cathren ordered about twelve different varieties of tomato seeds. Hopefully Cat and I will be visiting soon. We'll bring more than you'll need for your garden," Kent told them, relieved to have found someone to dump plants on, for he knew Cathren would have at least two hundred plants for them to set out when the time came.

"I never thought of myself as a country gentleman and farmer, but I'm becoming accustomed to my fate. I will no doubt be one of the first back into the city and suburbs when times calm down," Stew said. "Seth, Kent, follow me into the kitchen for some coffee and I'll start on breakfast."

"We're ravished. I'll help," Seth told him.

"I'll be the head cook. Watch me demonstrate the new kitchen abilities I've mastered," Stew joked while Sharon smiled at listening to her husband's sense of humor that never left him despite the times. She then quickly followed them into the kitchen to orchestrate the meal.

"Stew, what is going on along the Ohio border?" Kent needed Stew's opinion to make an assessment of the danger they could face shortly.

A moment of contemplation on Stew's part was needed before he could answer. "I believe we can correctly speculate that the gangs and the Left Wings will probably launch an attack on this side of the river as soon as they think it is feasible. They are growing confident of a victory over us and I am afraid it could be so. They've drafted fifteen-year-old children into their campaign so they can have more bodies for a battlefront. It is unbelievable."

"Do they have the firepower to make that sort of move?" Kent asked.

"Now that is the million-dollar question with the million-dollar answer. I don't even know if the Left Wings do realize their potential or lack of it. They're being very secretive, and if there's an attack, it will probably be a surprise as to when and where. Their security has been extremely tight."

Kent gave his opinion, "I'm inclined to think that the Left Wings and gangs are cowards and will only pursue small border assaults similar to street gang warfare for turf control. That will be the extent of it."

"Whatever they plan, the coming spring and summer promise to be violent," Stew informed them.

Kent immediately sensed the tension in Sharon's movement and resolved to change the subject.

"I have seed potatoes in the truck if you want extras. Have you planted potatoes before?" Kent asked Stew and Sharon.

"Just a few last summer in the backyard," Stew answered. "I'll be glad to plant the extras you brought with you. The garden was plowed and disked last week. The family who owns the farm nearest this one made a trade for seeds I purchased on a trip south for working up the garden. They needed the seeds and I needed a large garden plowed. We have a lot of mouths to feed. It'll take hard work for all of us to make it through next winter."

"We could help plant them after breakfast," Seth told them.

Hearty mounds of home fries, bacon, eggs, biscuits, jams, and jellies soon graced the country table accented by beams of country sun light that mildly drifted through the south-facing windows of the kitchen. Stew had struck some good bargains in his travel through the south to create such a display of homemade fare.

"You have some great ground for a garden," Kent told Stew. "This should produce a bumper crop of whatever you plant."

"I'm glad to hear that because until this past summer I didn't really know or understand the difference between good and bad soil. And further, I never really cared. I bought several gardening books. I'm learning."

"You'll have a regular green thumb by fall if you listen to Kent," Seth told him. "How well you garden will surely mean whether you will eat or you won't."

"I'm willing to accept any advice on gardening from anyone who is willing to offer it. As soon as all this is over, I plan to never garden for my own food again. Not into it," Stew laughed.

Within three hours, the men had potatoes, peas, onions, and cold-tolerant crops in the ground. When they finished, Stew's sister, Anne, had lunch waiting for the hands. Her son limped into the kitchen.

"How are you feeling today?" Stew asked.

"My therapist says it shouldn't be long before I'll be able to do nearly everything I did before," the boy told them. "Stew bartered for my therapy. The therapist needed some equipment and Stew was able to locate and deliver it. She said if she or another therapist had not treated me, I could have been partially disabled for life."

The boy began assisting his mother by washing dishes.

"It'll be hard to get those two little ones back to town after living here," Stew told Anne. "They can't wait to go outside each morning, and if it's raining then they head straight for the barn."

"I can let them go outside without fear. It is a blessing to be here," Anne told them. "There's some fresh coffee if anyone would like a cup."

"We'll be leaving shortly. The rest of the volunteers from our county are off detail this morning, too. Most are doing some shopping for their families with a list for hard-to-find items," Seth told them, knowing he had such a list.

After taking leave of Stew and Sharon, Kent and Seth arrived at the motel room where the county volunteers were stationed by the Kentucky Militia. Tourism was bust for the year so hotels and motels were eager to rent their rooms at discount rates to groups of volunteers from throughout the state.

Upon their arrival to the motel, the two noticed a flurry of activity in the parking lot. Kent and Seth did not bother entering their room because their attentions were immediately drawn to the men around them.

"Why is everyone outside? What's going on?" Kent asked Sheriff Chaney. A transport bus arrived on the scene.

"Gangs and the Left Wings launched an attack about daybreak this morning just thirty miles east of here. The troops never expected an attack at the particular location and they're having trouble holding ground."

"Will we be assisting?" Seth asked in excitement.

"Not with fighting, but we'll help bring up munitions, food, and medicine just behind the front and see injured soldiers to safety. They're sending a bus to take us to the location in half an hour," the sheriff informed all.

Kent and Seth made a trip to their room and gathered accoutrements necessary for the day. Seth went about for an adventure while Kent absorbed himself entirely in seriousness. Seth reminded Kent of himself when he was a younger man, eager to change the tide of the times for the better of mankind. This worried Kent. Seth and the young volunteers from the county were just too eager to go, Kent thought. Kent knew they were good young volunteers with a lot of training from professionals with intentions of fighting for their freedoms and the freedoms of others. Kent could only pray that none of them would be hurt or killed in their eagerness to defend their freedoms, especially Seth.

"Everyone, load the bus," a rallying cry called forth.

Each volunteer stepped into the vehicle that in moments clamored to the destination, where it was met with a spectacle of fireworks that lacked celebration, as these works of fire were bombs in midair. There the signal of a battle in progress sat just yards from the location where their transportation had led them. They were in an area of fields and trees where cattle would normally graze lazily throughout the day. This place could be the dreaded ground where the dreams of mothers, fathers, daughters, and sons were destroyed with each breath that left a loved one for the last time in this sea of mortals. Kent shuddered at the thought.

The appearance of casualties on the ground caught the attention of the men from their home county just milliseconds before the burst of more blasts occurred against the sunlight. The scurrying of medics assisted those unable to lift themselves from the ground. The moans from beyond left the youngest of the county horrified at their introduction into warfare, the warfare and deaths now committed for the freedoms of others.

Seasoned veterans, sickened at the sight of the events in their homeland, burst forward to meet the needs of the moment. The others followed suit. It was too late to turn back history for the country that was engulfed in the flames of change. Each society since the creation of Earth has seen such change, turning the tide toward better, worse, or its end. The pitting of one American against another could not be helped, and the seasoned veterans patiently lifted one wounded soul after another into ambulances, beds of pickup trucks, and vans to be escorted to the nearest hospital. Young volunteers cried and sifted through bodies and blood in horror at the ghastly situation.

At nightfall members of the Left Wings and gangs could be seen quietly smuggling themselves back across the quiet waters of the Ohio. Landmines strategically placed well before daybreak that morning had helped give them plenty of time to slither back to the territory they held.

Another daybreak resulted in another invasion into Kentucky. The Ohio side boasted artillery and troops readying to cross on the hundreds of boats that lined the shore. The explosion of the first landmine shot by a Kentuckian, who had been drawn into the minefield, was the alarm calling the troops into battle mode. The Left Wings landed on Kentucky shores amid the confusion of the Kentuckians avoiding the landmines below their feet and the falling shells from the sky above. The Left Wings started with a clear advantage. With the arrival of the county volunteers, Kent saw Seth's enthusiasm fade, then turn to the survival instinct required to live through the day. Television and movies with their realistic approach on the screen could not prepare him for the sight of the real thing.

"I need y'all over here," a voice yelled from another direction. A bus climbed over the hill from the direction of gunfire. Men and women dressed in uniform tried to remove themselves from the vehicle, but all needed assistance. Kent covered his hands with latex gloves.

"Here, don't try to step down without some help," Kent yelled to the woman who struggled to exit the rear door of the bus.

"My arm is broken," she yelled to him.

"I can see that. Here, let me help you down from your side that isn't injured. I've been through all this before," Kent said, trying to comfort her.

"Overseas?" She asked. He nodded. She smiled through her pain.

"I would like to thank you for serving your country, ma'am," Kent told her while maintaining eye contact.

"I am honored to do so, sir," she cried. "Thank you."

Seth assisted another soldier climbing from the rear door.

"It will be at least half an hour before they get to us at the end of the bus. The severely injured are closer to the front. Thanks for the hand," the soldier told Seth.

"Can you tell me how the battle is going?" Seth asked.

"A lot of artillery has been launched from the Ohio side. A good many have been injured or lost their lives. It is just too hard to tell right now how many we have lost," a soldier responded.

"Who's winning?" Seth inquired.

"I honestly believe we are. The Left Wings were not aware of the buildup of forces just miles from here. Most of the Left Wings and gangs are without uniform or training. They're used to fighting on city streets during night hours and preying on defenseless citizens. They're not on city streets now, and there are no innocent bystanders to terrorize here, it's the real thing. They have no ally to run off to," the hurt soldier told him. Seth escorted still another soldier to the mobile clinic that sat waiting for minor injuries.

The steady stream of injured continued, but shouts of hurrah could be heard for a mile as reinforcements headed for the front. The mines in the surrounding fields were cleared and tanks now led the way for the troops. The Left Wings thought it would take days before their opponents could remove the landmines, but the job planting the mines had been done sloppily in a single night of nervousness. The planting places of the landmines were all too obvious. The Kentucky militia and the armed forces had only taken hours to clear them out.

The Kentuckians knew they did indeed have the firepower to see them through to victory. The afternoon dragged on. Each injured soldier in from the front held a captive audience with their stories that provided a new twist and angle, all with the news of ground recovered and Left Wings being shoved farther north and back across the river.

The evening enveloped the sky with its soft darkness and found itself illuminated cruelly with each bomb's glare that brightened the countryside. Glowing flares of light told the story of a slow retreat, and by early morning hours the flares and sounds came from the Ohio side of the river. Announcements over the airwaves confirmed what had been predicted by those watching the sky through the night. "The Star Spangled Banner" played loudly from speakers across the Ohio River. The American Flag flew bravely on Kentucky and Ohio land, though near the shore on the Ohio side. Kentucky was ecstatic at the victory over the Left Wings.

Ohio residents had been informed just days earlier that they no longer owned their homes and property, that the state had claimed eminent domain without compensation for the good of the people. The Left Wings were sure of future victories, but they had lost one battle, and those in Ohio who knew were jubilant. They flew their United States of America flags in joy.

All freedom fighting soldiers were accounted for, whether they had lost their lives or not. No prisoners were taken by the Left Wings. The volunteers were weary and ready for sleep each time they arrived at the motel. The same stories had been hashed and rehashed on the bus, and the enthusiasm of victory left them looking forward to a few hours of sleep and the work ahead each day.

Their next assignment arrived fast. As the Left Wings were across the river busy licking their wounds, the county volunteers loaded onto the bus. The day was quiet as Kentucky's militia loaded yesterday's prisoners of war, including gang members and Left Wing fighters, who were loaded onto heavily guarded buses. Seth walked with his new friends to receive their instructions for the day.

Seth watched a prisoner bus as it headed through the field toward the road when he recognized one of the prisoners, Jacob Bidewell from the university Seth attended in Ohio. He knew Jacob had been a radical socialist, ranting his ideas around campus, but Seth never dreamed it would come to this. Jacob turned his head toward Seth in recognition. Seth smiled, but Jacob only glared back with deep hatred and flipped both his hands with middle fingers upward in response to Seth's smile and for all Kentucky to see. Seth then realized Jacob was now his enemy, though they were casual acquaintances and had been on friendly terms when Seth departed from Ohio. Disgust for Bidewell shot through Seth's heart. He now saw Bidewell as one of many who worked to collapse Seth's world. He was too ashamed to relay to the volunteers that an old friend was now his enemy. Seth hoped Jacob's face would be the only enemy face he would recognize from here forward.

The moment the bus of heavily guarded prisoners turned onto the paved road, a formation of aircraft dominated the sky and the attention of all. Were the Left Wings retaliating? Seconds later, explosions could be heard across the river. Announcements informed them that Left Wing warehouses containing artillery were in the process of being blown to pieces. Shouts of jubilee filled the air. The enemy had received a serious blow, and it would be a good while before they had any thoughts of launching an attack on Kentucky again.

Crews of volunteers cleaned the battle area with a team of professionals that arrived to locate and remove the remaining landmines. Every precaution was taken. Close to evening, little evidence was left of what had taken place the past days. When off duty, Seth and his friends celebrated the victory with a few cold beers

Their eyes had beheld a rude awakening and none were eagerly anticipating the sight of more death and injuries. They had enough stories to take home with them for the rest of their lives as far as they were concerned. A true hatred for their enemy became engraved in their conscience. It was war in the true sense. They planned to win the war with all their hearts and lives, if need be.

CHAPTER TWENTY-THREE

Kent parked the truck and walked into the Kentucky home he and Cathren shared with their children. The smell of bread baking surrounded him. The large pot on the stove simmered and a burst of steam that hid the pot's contents escaped when Kent removed the lid. Soup made from the garden bounty appeared to have already simmered for the hours needed to make any chilly day stand at bay. Kent knew Cathren had received word that all was well with the volunteers and they were on the way home. Kent was glad to be where Cathren's strengths, her love of her family, her kindness toward others, and her faith in God were on display in the home they made together. Kent had missed this kitchen as much as any place on Earth during his absence the past weeks.

"I called Stew time and again to see how you were. He didn't know your location," Cathren spoke from the kitchen table where she sat.

"Is Stew's family all right?" Kent asked, bending to his knees to lay his head in Cathren's lap. Cathren softly soothed his head with her right hand.

"It remained quiet near their home during the entire episode. I need to place a call through to let him know everything went well and tell him you and Seth arrived home safely.

"Quiet here, too?" he asked her.

"Yes, nearly everyone stayed at their phones and televisions the past several days. Everyone I know has been home for the most part.

Here, I'll dial Stew's number and you talk," she told him.

"Hello, Stew?" Kent asked.

"Yes. Kent? Are you calling from home?"

"Yes, we arrived a bit ago. How are you?"

Stew responded, "We're fine. I am assuming you and Seth came out of this unscathed?"

"You assume right. We remained behind the lines the entire time and mostly assisted those hurt and did clean up detail," Kent told him.

"There're rumors of another buildup across the river and another skirmish in a few days," Stew told him.

"Didn't a good part of their munitions get destroyed in the air raid?" Kent asked in a disturbed tone.

"Some of it did, but a certain munitions factory in Ohio is more interested in money than lives or their own country. They need business, and the Left Wings are giving it to them. This factory is giving gangs and the Left Wings a toehold in the cities that will be increasingly harder to break if they aren't defeated soon," Stew told him.

"The federal government's credibility continues to decline, especially with this last financial crisis to deal with. The only thing that can defend the states from the tyranny of the Left Wings and gangs are the states themselves. The states will have to finance their own armies outside the federal government," Kent commented to Stew.

"Some states are seriously considering stopping any taxes from going to the federal government at this point. They are rationalizing it by saying that they can spend tax dollars better than the feds can, and I am inclined to agree with them," Stew said.

241

"The news had reported rumors that there might be a military coup in Washington if things do not shape up soon. The government is still sitting on its high horse, spending money they don't have. Can you believe it?" Kent said sarcastically.

"They still don't want to see it, do they? They're losing control of large chunks of the country to gangs and the Left Wings every day," Stew answered.

"You are right about that," Kent agreed. "Listen, keep in touch, and if anything else happens the next few days, give us a call."

"Will do. Send Cathren a hello from all of us. Take care," Stew told him.

Kent placed the phone on the counter and turned the radio on. With events heating up throughout the country, radio talk shows would be announcing information needing to be spread across the nation. Conversations on talk shows would give the pulse of the people.

Kent drove to the other farm to start work where he had left it. Each time he left, work continued to accumulate no matter how hard he prepared for his time away. Work could never be caught up on a homestead.

Seth had fallen behind on his schoolwork. He was granted leave by the school administration for volunteer duty on the condition he tested well and was able keep abreast with class assignments. He began studying the hour he arrived home.

Herb and Martha drove to the farm that evening to hear what news the internet had to offer, for they were not computer savvy and had to watch the evening news on the television. The news media played up the ever-crippling actions of the federal government for the day's top news story. Nearly every person in every home in the country had a discussion on how badly the situation was dealt with from coast to coast.

Kent closed his evening by listening to the airwaves from the small radio next to their bed, but slumber caught him before the nightly heated debates began. Cathren listened to the daily bombardment of callers distressed at civil unrest across the country dashed with pleas for sanity on the streets.

One anonymous caller claiming to represent the Left Wings told listeners the streets would be safe again when the Left Wings ruled the nation. Another caller asked at what cost would the streets be safe again? The caller claimed the Left Wings were another name for communism, anarchy, Hitler, and Stalin rolled into one horror story. The caller detested the Left Wings' influence over so many young people and the Hitler-like worship followers had for some of their leaders. Still others decided it was time for states to rule their own territory, that at this point the federal government had no more power over the people than the Queen of England.

Some declared states should be able to set their own tariffs with foreign countries and keep their own armed forces, including nuclear arms to prevent invasions. Since the federal government had sold nuclear arms race capabilities to foreign governments during the past several years, anyway, why not to its own states? This led to the debate of which state would control which nuclear armaments already in existence and how the Air Force, Navy, Marines, Army, CIA, etc. should be split. The federal government could not meet the payroll of the armed forces as it was, many complained.

A sense of normalcy calmed the Freeman home the next morning with the usual readying for the school bus and feeding of animals in the barn. The morning news declared a safe zone had been established across the Ohio River that extended several miles north into Ohio territory. The forces had constructed a base of operations across the Ohio River in the area regained from the gangs and Left Wings. Food, medicine, and other necessities, along with armaments, were shipped and stored on the base with plans to spread the base farther north several miles each day. It would now be up to the people of Ohio to decide who would rule over them.

In hopes of restoring the government, the base planned to welcome all towns and cities to join them. It was reported the gangs and Left Wings were preparing for a long battle to keep their hold over the cities in Ohio and would split into smaller sections if they had to rule over smaller areas with a heavy fist until they could spread their power again. By afternoon, Kent and Seth received the call for their return to duty in two days and to their relief, their assignment base was located just minutes from Stew and Sharon's Kentucky home. Upon hearing the news, Cathren packed jars of different jams and jellies she had preserved along with other canned goods. Kent boxed several jars of kraut and knew enough still remained to last two more winters.

Seth attended classes until the time of his departure, when he packed his books for the trip with the confidence and patience of his instructors, as many of them were also from the north, having friends and family who remained behind enemy lines, too. The plowing of the fields required Kent's attention from the break of day until dark in order to get the job done before duty called him. Susan and

Cathren cooked stews and soups that could be frozen and placed in coolers for the men to take with them. Kent packed his old camp stove and pans in order to heat the food their wives sent. He remembered his granite coffeepot for the trip. Calls to and from the Freeman home frequented throughout the evening. The county volunteers planned to be more organized for the coming call of duty.

Susan announced she would also accompany the group to the Ohio River border, after noting to Seth it was a free country and motels to the north were still open to the public. The threesome departed shortly after Julianna, Marisa, and Andrew stepped onto the school bus.

Hours later, Stew greeted his friends at the front door and bid them to enter. He was pleased to announce he had been able to cross the river during daylight hours with the assistance of the forces committed to freeing Ohio from the hold of the Left Wings and gangs.

With this note of optimism also came the downfall. Stew's connections inside Ohio gave him photographs of the destruction throughout the cities under control of the Left Wings. Photos of what had once been shopping malls revealed merely twisted rubble, concrete, and mass steel beams. Turn of the century buildings in many downtown areas of cities were reduced to skeletons. Now only one's mind and old pictures could represent their former architectural splendor. Many of the modern structures of steel and concrete that towered over cities proved to be much harder for the Left Wings to destroy in the fighting. They now stood windowless, or as if chunks had been pulled from their sides with bits of concrete and steel girders sticking out here and there.

Destruction of buildings also caused the downfall of the state government facilities that would normally handle everyday affairs, such as the licensing bureau for vehicles. The Left Wings had planned to use the computerized system to their advantage to track car owners, but it was in shambles. This left law enforcement, for who was in control at any given moment, a serious disadvantage dealing with stolen vehicles and finding out who had financial responsibility for wrecks throughout the state. Many cars were driven unlicensed.

As federal and state tax revenues continued to decline, highway crews responsible for litter control, grass mowing, and other upkeep ceased. Grass along the highways and median strips remained uncut from the past year and small trees found their roots along roadsides.

Funding for paving and patchwork of roads no longer existed. Potholes restricted the proper flow of traffic, instigating traffic jams lasting for hours on main roads and highways. In many parts of cities, traffic lights were sabotaged by gangs, yet another irritant to travelers on roadways. Some lights still remained untouched, but with electricity out so often the lights uselessly dangled in intersections only as reminders of the order they once kept.

After the state's welfare system collapsed under the financial stress, along with unemployment services and Social Security services, offices for these agencies sat empty, if not bombed out by irate former recipients because government funds no longer existed to send monthly allotments.

Many in the agricultural community that had grown used to collecting thousands of dollars in subsidies each year now had to depend on their own ingenuity to farm again. The lucky ones in this new society were those who never depended on government handouts in the first place. Naysayers of the social-program society now saw the results of their predictions come to light. These very naysayers had predicted that a catastrophe of this magnitude would soon result if drastic measures were not taken to straighten the immoral society the nation had become. Many had fled the cities at the birth of their predictions when gangs started their takeovers. Like Cathren and her small family, they were surviving now by their wits and bare hands. The formerly scorned prophets of doom for detesting any form of tax increases during the latter years of the nation were now the survivors of their great society's self-destruction.

The banking industry came to an abrupt halt. Few financial institutions were able to survive with a bankrupt government to deal with. Sophisticated financial institutions were being weeded out daily, leading to further societal rumblings, for the government could no longer bail out the these institutions, thus causing millions of individuals to lose their savings. All the while, fortification near the Ohio River continued to build and spread each day, preparing for the final assault that would drive the Left Wings out of Ohio and lessen the threat of another invasion into Kentucky.

The armed forces from the Kentucky side now controlled an area of twenty square miles across the river into the Ohio Territory. Reinforcements arrived daily. Temperatures rose each day, ensuring easier working conditions for the volunteers. Sporadic outbreaks of tuberculosis, C. diff, MRSA, and hepatitis haunted Ohio's cities and now seemed to be of epidemic proportions. Most city sewage waste plants could not function because of outages and lack of funding, which led to a stench that rose with the warming seasonal temperatures. Death could be found everywhere.

"Kent," Seth said, catching Kent's attention after reading their instructions for the day. "We've been assigned to load a barge with supplies on the river. They want it done by late afternoon so it can cross before nightfall. They provided buses, but we were told we can drive the truck to the location."

"Load up. We'll get a head start. Do the rest know the orders?" Kent asked.

"I believe so. Some have already left the parking lot, and others are on the bus," Seth informed him.

He and Kent left and within twenty minutes were walking toward the barge anchored and waiting on the banks of the Ohio.

"May I have your attention?" A person in charge asked. "If anyone would like to cross the river on the barge this afternoon to unload on the other side, you may assist. Help will be appreciated but not required. There is the possibility of an attack, so we are unable to promise safety on the other side of the river. Supplies being loaded today are food rations and medical supplies. We can be finished before dark."

Seth turned to Kent and the other men. "I would like to go to the other bank. Maybe I will see someone from home."

"I would like to go, too," responded another young volunteer, Jason Collins, and the others nodded in agreement. All were willing to help the

248

cause since it was duty that called them. The crew loaded the barge twice as quickly as expected and the barge headed toward its port by noon.

The crew stood silent and apprehensive on the deck as they docked, realizing there was that small chance the shaky silence could end at any time, interrupted by mortar fire. The shredded building at a thirty-yard distance from the northern shore was evidence the enclosed compound was still at risk.

Seth went about trying to find information about friends back home while others took time to look about the surroundings and talk to soldiers on duty about the conditions just miles from where they stood. One of the men working in the mess hall informed Seth of a bulletin board with messages to read. Seth investigated to see if there was information from home. There wasn't. He asked the reception clerk on duty if he had extra paper and a pen so he could leave a message in case someone he knew came into the building to read the message board. Seth no longer knew which of his friends were dead or alive in his old community.

"Did you find any information about friends in Ohio?" Kent asked him when they met on the barge for the trip back across the river.

"No. Not that I expected to, but you just never know. There are a lot of messages just saying, 'hey, I am so-and-so, still alive and well' from many, but none I recognized. It's just scary having to do that, I mean read a bulletin board to see who is still living back home." Seth was haunted at having stood on Ohio land, unable to travel there as he pleased.

"Son, I know it's hard to come here, especially with all the memories you left. I lost my father when I was about your age too." Kent patted Seth on the shoulder. He could see that Seth was hurting on the inside as they stood on the barge that departed from the Ohio shore and headed for the secure side of the river.

"You're back sooner than I expected," Susan said with a sigh of relief in her voice. "There was increased fighting east on the Atlantic coast and most of Congress has fled Washington. I was worried the entire time you were gone, I was afraid the trouble would spread here, too."

"No, all was quiet on this front, anyway," Kent smiled and told her.

"Stew says he'll keep dinner warm for you two, but it looks like we will be there in time after all. Cathren called earlier. A storm hit and a few trees were blown down. The kids were on the way home from school when a tree fell in front of the school bus. Julianna is still pretty upset. Cathren thought it would be a good idea for you to try and call her," Susan informed him.

"Will do. I will call right away then I need to clean up a little before we go to Stew's for dinner. I could eat a bear after all the work we did today," he told them.

Kent spent the evening informing Stew the information he had absorbed while on the other side of the river. "Hepatitis and Tuberculosis has broken out in the cities, due to unsanitary conditions. Rumor has it that many people have died from different viruses, and others are suffering terribly. Those at the compound are being careful who they let enter from the Ohio side. They already place relief supplies several yards outside the compound for pickup with no human contact. I can't say that I blame them."

"I had planned to try and get into the city where my job is, but in light of what you heard today, I will stay put. Is there still heavy fighting in the streets back home?" Stew asked.

"There doesn't seem to be. It sounds like the people are doing their best to survive from day to day now. I saw pictures of men seining a park pond for fish in your hometown. People are desperate," Kent informed them. "They say the Great Miami River is lined with people fishing each day, though at times raw sewage floats down river."

Sharon replied. "My father would not let me put my big toe in the Great Miami when I was a child. It was beginning to clear before all this and fishing enthusiasts were beginning to gather along its banks again. What a shame."

"Before industrialization, the Great Miami was one of the best fishing spots around. Maybe it can be that way again someday," Stew told them. He turned to Seth and Kent. "Are you to going help load the barge again tomorrow?"

"That's the plan. Would you like to come along?" Kent asked. Stew looked to Sharon.

"Why don't you go along, Stew? You could use some time away from here," Sharon told him. "Your work across the river has nearly halted. Go find out firsthand what is likely to happen the coming weeks."

"If you don't mind, I believe I will go along in the morning." Stew's eyes brightened.

"Meet us where we're staying at five a.m. The bus leaves around five-thirty. Speaking of five-thirty, I need to go back to the motel to get plenty of rest for tomorrow. What about you?" Kent asked Seth and Susan.

"I'm ready to turn in. I plan to wake earlier than the two of you and cook on the camp stove." Susan let them know. "I have been so tired these past couple weeks."

CHAPTER TWENTY-FOUR

Shattering glass broke Cathren's dream of her family safe and together under the shade of a tree next to the lake. The crash of thunder and a downpour of rain sent them climbing into the boat under its canopy and cuddy cabin. She woke from her dream and threw off her covers.

Thunder outside turned into crashing of glass and lights flickered, stirring Cathren into full survival mode. She pulled the fully loaded .44 Magnum from Kent's nightstand, the stand that sat locked during daylight hours and that she unlocked upon laying her head on her pillow each night he was not home.

Covered only by Kent's t-shirt, Cathren caught her breath, and her brave consciousness took over where fear lurked half a second earlier. The instinct of her womanhood to protect her family caused her to slip quietly down the staircase.

With each step downward, Cathren knew any mistake on her part could mean the death of her and her children. She prayed that she was really dreaming, but another crash inside the farmhouse told her differently. Someone invaded her home three hours before daylight would appear. She could hear strong whispers, one female the other male. Cathren had to assume they were armed and it was her against the two inside and probably more outside waiting for the events to end favorably for the intruders.

Cathren's mind had prepared her for this moment thousands of times, but nothing compared to the ultimate moment of truth she was about to face within feet of where she now stood.

The two intruders had been clever enough to only turn the utility room light on and to leave the door only slightly ajar, enough to keep most of the living area on the first floor darkened to camouflage where they were in the home.

Cathren's right foot landed on the first floor with the .44 Magnum in front of her body. She tried not to shake but found it impossible. She could only go forward. There would be no other choice until her home was rid of the vermin inside. Cathren slid to Andrew's bedroom door, where he lay fast asleep. Getting to the girls' room was an altogether different problem. She would have to cross the living area to peek inside their bedroom door, and she knew it creaked loudly upon opening. Since she had not heard the creaking of the girls' bedroom door, she felt comfortable assuming they were still sleeping and were unharmed. It amazed her what kids could sleep through.

Cathren heard motion from the den. Whispers revealed the location of the invaders. Cathren had no choice but to go forward to confront them. She could lose her life, she knew that. She also knew that if there was gunfire and she was killed instantly, the invaders were likely leave before discovering children in the household. She crept into the den.

She had listened well. The invaders were indeed two, male and female. She looked forward. The male opened the door to the outside from the den, stepping over the threshold, female in tow with sacks full of stolen goods. The female turned to her partner to hand over some of the goods she was unable to carry and turned to grab one last full sack lying near her feet. She lifted the sack and saw movement just feet away. She dropped all goods and went for the gun in her holster. Bullets flared loudly from one side of the room to the other.

Cathren fell to the floor. Blood dripped from her body.

"Damn," a feminine voice yelled out. "my fucking shoulder got shot. I'll be a son-of-a-bitch. Help me!"

"You've got to help yourself. Get out here now and help me carry all this shit. You're not hurt that bad. Get the hell out here. We got to meet the rest up the road, and don't forget the last sack, or you'll pay dearly," the male responded.

"Fuck you," she yelled back, "I got the damn sack. Right behind you, you sorry bastard. We'll see who pays when we get back to the warehouse."

"Well, that's three hours away, so shut the fuck up and get the hell out of here" he yelled.

The two made it to the truck waiting in the drive, spinning tires out the lane. Cathren lay unmoving on the floor. Cold air shuttled itself through the house, hitting Cathren hard and caused her to wake.

"Mom, oh my God! Mom. Please, Mom. Please, Mom, move, do something. Please God, please don't let my Mommy die," Marisa yelled.

"What's wrong with Mom, is she bleeding?" Andrew asked.

"Andrew, go dial 911 now. Tell them Mom is hurt, that we heard gunshots," Marisa demanded of him.

"I'm scared," cried Julianna.

"I know but can you help me Julianna?" Marisa asked.

"Yes," Julianna whimpered.

"I need some clean towels and all the bandages you can find from the bathroom. I think Mom hit her head when she fell, so I need some ice from the refrigerator, too. I have to stop the bleeding on her arm, so bring the bandages first."

"I called 911, and they are on the way," Andrew told them.

"Marisa?" a weakened Cathren asked.

"Mom, you are alive," Marisa said to her.

"Yes, honey, I am. Andrew and Julianna?" she asked.

"Andrew just called for help and Julianna is getting bandages. We're fine, Mom. Help is on the way."

"Help me up," Cathren told her.

"You need to stay there, Mom," Marisa told her.

"I have to check on Herb and Martha." Cathren pulled herself to her knees, then became upright, gun in hand, staggering to the keys for the vehicles hanging on the wall. Cathren reached into the gun safe on the far wall of the kitchen after decoding the lock. She removed Kent's shotgun from the safe.

"Kids, sit in the kitchen until help arrives. I have to get to Herb and Martha's now. When help gets here, tell them what happened and tell them I am armed since the intruders mentioned they had others elsewhere around here, too." Cathren ran out the door to the van sitting in the drive.

"Mom, don't leave us," Marisa begged.

"You will be okay, Marisa. They are not going to come back here twice. I injured one of them severely. She may not live to tell it by all the blood she left. Just sit tight until I get back. I have to go."

Cathren staggered and climbed into her van and shortly the back tires sent loose gravel in every direction. Cathren turned off the guiding lights of the van, letting available light from the moon, her memory and wits steer the van from the paved, one-lane road into the hay field. She steered the van across to the small creek to one side of the orchard on the south side of the home, parking behind Martha's blackberry vines. Cathren gasped at the sight of the house across the orchard. All lights were on. The elderly couple never lit the house through the night. Not until five-thirty a.m. each morning would there be light in the home, and it was usually the kitchen light. Cathren's hunch had been right. Opening the door, she pulled the keys from the ignition putting them beneath the van behind the front tire. She double-checked to make sure she had enough shotgun shells to defend herself and the couple inside the home. She placed the .44 Magnum in the holster hanging from her right side and covered the short trek across the yard to look into a window mostly covered by a snowball bush.

Herb and Martha sat in the dining room, each tied to a dining chair with rope and duct tape. Cathren began to shake uncontrollably for what she would have to do and she crept back into the orchard to a small drop-off leading to the secret place of her childhood. She entered the garden shed. She moved away straw on the wooden floor revealing a latched entrance.

Martha had told her stories of how the door led down to a tunnel to the old farmhouse, where a former owner hid slaves until they could make their way north across the Ohio River to freedom. Only once was Cathren allowed to enter the tunnel

257

leading to the place in front of the hutch in the dining room where the old brown braided rug covered a hatch at the other end. Cathren made her way past the entrance of the tunnel toward the dining room.

The rug moved next to Herb's legs. The silent joy of seeing Cathren climb from the entrance of the tunnel made him smile. Cathren quietly closed the door to the dining room and latched it from the inside with the antique lock. She removed the hunting knife from the sheaf hanging from her left hip to cut through the rope and duct tape that had held the couple hostage. Herb quickly helped Martha into the passage to safety. Cathren followed. Herb grabbed onto the rug, pulling it as best he could back into its former position over the trapdoor leading to the tunnel for their freedom, all the while listening to the intruders tearing through his home.

The threesome slowly made their way to the tunnel's end, then up and out across the yard to the van waiting in the hayfield just yards away.

"Both of you go ahead and get in the van while I take the key off the ground where I hid it. We have to get out of here before that bunch leaves the house and sees the van out here," Cathren told them.

"Cathren, you're bleeding. Did you cut yourself in the tunnel some way?" Martha asked her.

"No, they came to our house first. I have a gunshot wound that needs tending to," Cathren told them.

"Blessed Jesus was with us tonight," Martha told her.

"I hear sirens and see lights. How is that?" Herb asked.

"The kids called for help. I told them I was going to your place. We need to tell them we are safe so they can go in your house and arrest that bunch," Cathren said to them.

"Then you are going straight to the hospital to get that wound taken care of. We'll stay with the children while you are away," Martha told her.

"Thank you, Martha. I don't know how much blood I've lost. I'm getting weak. There is the ambulance in my lane. Thank you, Lord. Oh my God, look at me. Covered in blood and dressed only in this long t-shirt of Kent's," Cathren stopped the van and said no more.

CHAPTER TWENTY-FIVE

Susan nudged Seth when the alarm clock sounded at four-thirty. Susan managed to find the light switch to the bathroom and sleepily washed her face with cold tap water that startled her into wakening. She pulled her nightgown over her head and replaced it with a t-shirt, then slipped her jeans over her legs and hips.

She opened the entrance door and walked across the sidewalk to the back of Kent's pickup to lower the tailgate. She pulled the camp stove toward her, raised the lid, primed the tank, turned the knob, and lit a match. She grabbed the iron skillet sitting behind the camp stove. She placed the skillet on it. She pulled the cooler from the truck bed, removed the bacon, and placed it in the now heated skillet that sizzled and popped when the cold meat landed on the hot iron.

Susan leaned against the outside panel of the truck bed, trying to stay awake until the first cup of fresh coffee could be poured. The smell of bacon frying in the morning usually helped Susan look forward to the coming events of a day, but today it only served to nauseate her. She could not hold food in her stomach; after the meal, Susan made a mad dash to the bathroom and vomited her breakfast into the commode, all the while attributing the nausea to her nerves.

Seth finished breakfast while Susan went back to their room to rest. Soon Kent, Seth, and Stew were on their way to help unload medical supplies and food on Ohio ground. Seth wanted to go to Ohio.

"Anyone volunteering to ride to the other side of the river to unload again today?" The man in charge asked the men as they came aboard the barge. Now another chance to unload a vessel was here. Soon the barge was unloaded on the Ohio side of the river.

"Kent, I plan to stick around the compound for an hour or two and have a late lunch here. You and Seth are welcome to stay if you like. One of the officers I am friends with will take us back to the other shore later," Stew told them.

"I would like that," Seth told them.

"Enjoy the trip, Seth," Kent told him. He could tell the crossing of the river had lifted Seth's spirits, and knowing the Left Wings had been pushed back a good way helped, too. "I'm going to fish the rest of the day on one of the creeks on the Kentucky side. I will see you this evening at the motel. Got to go before the barge leaves me. Bye."

"Stew, you have friends everywhere," Seth told him as they walked around the compound. He was always amazed at what Stew could come up with at a moment's notice. The men working on

261

detail spoke freely to Seth about the events in the cities of Ohio as he and Stew approached one of the buildings of the compound. "I'm going to see if any messages were left since yesterday."

"I will be in to meet you there shortly. I have a little business to attend to while I'm here," Stew responded. He strode away, but had gotten just feet from Seth when the thunderous, deafening sound of bombs made their ears throb with pain and the ground shook beneath them.

Stew could not see Seth through the dust-filled compound and found himself falling to his knees, partly from the vibration beneath his feet and partly from fear. In an instant, he realized the compound was under attack and he must find Seth and his way to the river shore.

Seth tried running to Stew as planes flew overhead. The sky was littered with Left Wing fighters who parachuted onto the grounds of the compound. Bombers flew around above, strategically shredding storage warehouses.

Vehicles and tanks surrounded the enclave as if they were formed from the smoke itself. They were not filled with allies, but Left Wing fighters.

"Stew-w-w!" Seth yelled through the dust, but his cry fell unheard amid the confusion. Seth managed to lift himself off the ground and began running. He ran to the mess hall in hopes of finding Stew. Stew glanced in the direction where the dust and smoke cleared, his eyes caught sight of a visibly shaken young man, and upon closer examination realized it was Seth.

"Seth!" Stew shouted. "Head for the river."

"I can't. I have to stay and help," Seth said, as he stumbled over chunks of strewn bricks, wood, and a few bodies that could possibly have no life in them anymore, braced himself with each explosion around him, his adrenaline rushing as he had never felt before.

A crash from the front gate showed more of the Left Wings invading, beheading each person confronting them. Blood flowed along the ground, creating its own miniature creeks from maimed bodies in all directions.

"There's nothing we can do here," Stew yelled to him. He would probably stay if it were just himself, but now he had Nate's son in his care and he had to get him to safety. The compound already had begun to return the fire within seconds of the assault.

Seth's fellow troops fought bravely as some of the Left Wings abandoned then changed their side of allegiance and fell into helping those at the compound. Stew led Seth toward the riverbank through the fighting.

"We will no longer fight for the Left Wings," many of the Ohio natives yelled to the crowd. "We are free, free, free to fight for freedom. Death to the Left Wings," they yelled, stripping themselves of the uniforms they had been forced to wear for the invaders they chose not to serve when the option came to them.

"I've got to get you out of here, Seth. I will never be able to face your mother if I don't. I was a fool to think it was finally safe here. I let my hopes get in the way of reality," Stew yelled to him through the noise of another volley of firepower.

"Shouldn't we go back and help? Stew, I don't want to leave them. I am going back," Seth screamed through the noise.

"There is nothing we can do here. I have to get across that river, and you need to help me do that. Now! We would only be in the way. My friend in command had already told me to get out of here at all costs if there is trouble. I can get medical supplies across the river to him when others can't, and besides, he said untrained personnel would only be in the way. This attack is a complete surprise. No civilians would have been allowed on the grounds if anyone had dreamed the Left Wings had this much firepower in the area. If I go down, you need to get me across to medical attention," Stew said as he tried to get Seth to the riverbank.

"I don't want to go. I am needed here. Stew, I will go across to see you safe on the other side, but I am coming right back. I can't abandon the men here."

"Okay," Stew answered, hoping the fighting would be over by the time they arrived on the other shore.

He led Seth over an embankment to a canoe hidden under brush. His friend kept it there in case an emergency like this one should occur. Stew worked rapidly, pulling the canoe into the water deep enough to float without dragging bottom in concert with Seth pulling two life jackets from underneath the seats and grabbing one of the paddles that slid into the water.

"I don't hear any more shelling," Stew remarked.

"I hope it is over," Seth responded a millisecond before a thundering crash. Stew felt another crash ring through his brain, so loud was the thunder. It caused his body to jolt so hard it was not obvious to him whether he had been shot. His body fell into the muddy shoreline.

"Seth, Seth. Where are you? Answer me!" Stew screamed through the smoke. Stew stretched his arms forward on the ground, then pulled his own body to the end of the canoe where Seth had stood just moments ago, with no response from the young man. Stew's hands felt the wet, warm, soft flesh of another human being, Seth.

A river breeze cleared the confusion of smoke and dust. Stew tore the shirt off his back for use as a bandage to wrap around the wound that bled a river of red freely onto the ground next to Seth's forehead. Stew refused his basic instinct to check and see if Seth still had a pulse that would tell whether he still was a part of the living on this Earth. Stew could not conceive of Nate's son's death.

Stew dragged the limp body to the canoe, tilting the edge over far enough to pull Seth's torso into the hull of the craft. It was not until then Stew found Seth bleeding profusely from his right leg. Stew gasped aloud at the sight of Seth's shredded leg, where bloody bone lay shattered in every direction.

Stew worked fast to cut off the circulation to the injury. Stew centered Seth's limp body in the canoe so they would not tip, still not having mustered the courage to feel the young man's pulse. He pushed the canoe into the current, paddling furiously toward the other shore. Across the river would be help because the shelling would have alerted a need for medical attention. To Stew, the river seemed ten miles wide, and he was only able to paddle a snail's pace though he used every ounce of strength working toward safety and help.

Stew successfully paddled a hundred yards from the shore when another volley of fire echoed along the riverbanks. A shell plunged into the river so close to the canoe Stew felt they would not stay afloat, but to his astonishment the canoe was not hit, and it still headed for the Kentucky shoreline.

Stew's cries were heard before the landing, where they were met by soldiers with arms who radioed without pause for help. Stew instructed the soldiers to move and carry the canoe onto the shore instead of moving Seth more than necessary. Stew heard sounds of sirens growing louder by the second, seconds that seemed to have converted into hours by the time paramedics met them on the scene.

"I'm not getting a pulse," the woman shouted above the screams of Stew's hysterics.

"Here, get him on the stretcher fast where we can get working on him. On the double!" Another paramedic yelled.

"I've got something!" yelled the woman who hadn't felt a pulse seconds earlier. "It's not much, but it is something."

"Radio a chopper. This one needs care fast. He's not going to make it unless he gets to a trauma unit," one of the men shouted. "He's losing too much blood."

"Are you a relative of this young man?" one of the paramedics asked Stew.

"He's my son," Stew lied. He would do anything to keep Seth alive during this awful moment of his life, even if it meant signing a lie to permit surgery. The paramedics on hand did not doubt Stew's word after witnessing his reaction when a pulse could not be felt the first time. A man motioned Stew to get into his four-wheel drive truck to follow the ambulance to a small town hospital in order to stabilize Seth and to meet the chopper that would fly them to a larger hospital with a trauma unit approximately seventy miles to the south.

"Hello, Sharon?" Stew asked over the emergency telephone. "Listen, we got caught in a bad situation at the compound across the river. You need to call or go to the motel and find Susan and Kent. Get them in the car and drive straight to the hospital. I've got to go. Seth's in bad shape. They are flying him to the hospital we talked about the other day, as soon as the chopper lands. I'm going to give the phone to someone here who will give you the directions." Stew handed the phone to the hand that stretched out to him. Stew said thank you without even a thought or glance. Stew ran to Seth upon the arrival to the first hospital.

"What's taking so long?" Stew's frantic voice asked.

"It has only been a few minutes, sir. You son's condition is stabilizing, but he is still unconscious," someone told Stew.

"He is going to be fine. There is no doubt in my mind," Stew answered, but the silence from the others told a different story. Their eyes displayed the horrors of mass tortures and killings the staff had been coping with the past couple years.

"The people standing on the shore thought the canoe had a trolling motor attached and running. They never witnessed anyone canoe so fast. You are a brave man to cross that river during trouble like that. You and your boy are lucky to be alive," one of staff told him. "You're also lucky to have made it here before anyone else. The parking lot is filled with ambulances at this very moment, and the hall there is filled with those injured during the fight. More choppers are on the way, too."

The chopper landed. Stew made it to the other hospital with Seth, but the repeating of history crushed Stew. Sharon, Susan, and Kent could get no response from him after finding him in a catatonic state as he sat in the waiting room next to the surgery wing.

Kent stood at attention, praying unceasingly, at the entrance of the elevator, waiting to be there for Cathren as she would exit it.

"Are you the family of Seth Billiter?" Kent heard from the waiting room. He turned away from the elevator door and walked through the archway to the others. Kent was unaware of the changing lights behind the numbers above the elevator door.

"Seth's condition is more stable than when he arrived, but he is in intensive care due to the extensive injuries. He was conscious before surgery, and he did speak with us. He was in a great deal of pain when he woke, but he took it all quite well," the surgeon told them. "I am sorry that I was unable to brief you before surgery. He's not out of the woods yet. The next few hours are crucial."

"What about his leg?" Stew asked.

"I am sorry. There was nothing we could do. We had to amputate from the knee down. The explosion shredded the lower part of the limb. He is truly lucky he has lived up to this moment, and now we wait." The doctor could not finish his sentence for the moan at the entrance of the waiting room. Cathren stood in the doorway having heard every word of the conversation.

"When can we see him?" she asked, not acknowledging anyone else in the room. "When they get him settled in his room?"

"He will be in an intensive care unit for a good while due to the extent of the injuries sustained. He is a lucky young man to have pulled through this. You'll have limited visits. He will not be aware of much for several days, so it would be best to let him rest as much as possible. Just be there for him. He needs the support of all of you now," the surgeon informed them. "The staff will take you where he'll be staying, and I will be in to check on him through the night. This will be a busy one, as many have been recently. I'll be staying on the premises."

"Stew, why don't you get Sharon to a hotel so she can rest," Kent told him. "You have done so much for us today. You saved Seth's life, and we are so grateful. He wouldn't be alive were it not for your quick thinking and ability to get him across the river as fast as you did."

Cathren approached Stew and embraced him. Stew stood unresponsive once more. He blamed himself for Seth's fate at the compound.

"Stew, I could really use the rest. Could you take me to the motel now? Besides, we need to find the nearest motel and get a room for the others, too. Someone will need to stay here, and it can be done in shifts through the night. Cathren and Susan are going to stay most of the night. Kent, would you follow us and try to get a room next to ours?" Sharon convinced him, though she was not really that tired, but wanted to get Stew away so he could pull himself together. Kent nodded, understanding Sharon's need for support on this request. Susan followed the nurse to Seth's room.

"My leg, it hurts," Seth groaned.

"It is going to be all right. I'm here with you," Susan whispered softly. "Your mother has already left for the nurses' station to tell them you need something for the pain."

"Stew?" Seth asked. "Is Stew all right? Is he alive? I can't remember anything past running from the compound. Did I go back to help them? I just can't remember right now."

"Stew and Sharon went to a motel around the corner from the hospital. He'll be here first thing in the morning to see you. You made it, and Stew is fine."

"My leg?" Seth moaned.

"It's going to be all right. Get some rest, and we will talk when you wake. You're going to make it. The doctors said you will pull through just fine," Susan whispered, covering him when he shivered. Susan rose to walk to the entrance of Seth's room where Cathren stood. "He just woke and muttered a few words to me. He was coherent. Why don't you go to the motel and get some rest now that Seth seems to be doing better? I'll take a break when you get back."

"I don't really want to leave, but you are right. If all of us stay here at one time, we'll be worn to a frazzle," Cathren spoke softly.

"Good. Our things need to be removed from the motel where we stayed near the river," Susan told her.

"Kent spoke with the men, and they had already packed your belongings. They're going to drop them at the motel we are staying in so you'll have something to wear," Cathren told her. "I'll be back soon. Love you."

"My leg!" Seth shouted.

"I know, I know." Susan grabbed onto his hand. "Shhh. The nurse is coming in the room this very second with something more to relieve the pain."

"Thank you," Susan told her after the nurse administered the medication.

"Mrs. Billiter, why don't you sit in the recliner and try to get some rest? Here is a blanket to lay over you. I'll be in every few minutes to check on your husband. It's going to be a rough night. Sleep for you will do some good."

Susan did not recall what woke her, the beam of morning sunlight shining on her face or the doctors' conversation with Seth. Tears of pain rolled down his face in mourning for the loss of his limb. The doctor told him the entire story.

"Good morning, Mr. Billiter," Seth's nurse greeted, going about her work and talking with Seth about the nature of his injury and the therapy that would begin when he was better. Susan sat helplessly next to his bed.

"I am not going to live like this. Never, never," Seth screamed to them.

"What are you proposing to do in place of living?" Susan reluctantly argued. It frightened her to hear such words from him.

"Whatever it takes! I can't live like this," Seth continued.

"We are so lucky you are still with us. Please don't talk that way. Just don't say that again. Please," Susan begged.

"You are not the one lying here in this bed mangled, left an invalid," he rudely told her.

"You have to live on. We can conquer this. Other people cope with much worse!" Susan snapped back.

"That is them. Not me!" he spoke through pain.

"You are scaring me with this sort of talk," Susan told him.

"My life is ruined, I can't live through this. An invalid. I would rather not live. Why did I live through that?"

"Because God wants you here with us. Me and this child of yours I am carrying," she scolded. "I've been nauseated for two weeks. When you left yesterday, I took a pregnancy test. It was positive. I only confirmed what my heart already knew."

Seth cried at the news, "I am so sorry. How can I be a good parent like this? I didn't mean to hurt you. I will not leave you." Although he was not really sincere about the apology, he felt a need to protect Susan after the news she just informed him of.

"We can work this out. Nothing is different between the two of us, and nothing will ever change," she told him.

"How can you still love me when I am lying here like this?" he sadly asked her. "How am I going to provide for a family?"

"That is the most foolish talk. I won't hear any more of it. We have someone else to think of now, someone we have created together from our love for each other. We have much to live for. I want you to get some rest now. Your mother and Kent will be here soon to stay with you for a few hours so I can get some rest at the motel." Susan kissed his cheek, but he was oblivious to the softness of her lips as he was already asleep from the pain medication.

Glimmers of sun shining in from the edges of the drapes in the motel room nudged Cathren's eyes open from the nightmare. Not until she found herself in unfamiliar surroundings did she know her nightmare to be a stark reality. She saw the outline of Kent sitting in the shadows in the opposite corner of the room, dressed for the day and reading the morning paper.

According to the paper, the Left Wings had dealt a hard blow and had left a great deal of damage in their path. Twenty men were killed and dozens of others injured, many hanging onto life like Seth. Kent feared the Left Wings' grip over the area would have become tighter if they had been able to win the compound.

Although the compound had sustained heavy damage, it was not lost. A wave of reinforcements launched a heavy assault on the Left Wings, driving them back to their position prior to the battle. Nevertheless, it had been costly for both sides.

"How long have you been awake?" Cathren asked.

"About an hour. The day just broke. I called the hospital. Seth's condition improved more than expected through the night. His nurse said he was sleeping soundly and Susan slept well on the recliner in the room," Kent told her.

"Does he know?"

"Yes, he knows. It was best we were not there when he was told. According to the nurse, Susan helped him handle the news and keep him calm. The nurse didn't know how Susan did it, but she told me she had never seen anyone face an amputation as bravely as he handled it after the initial shock of finding out and talking it over with Susan."

"I need to get to the hospital to give Susan a break," Cathren said, her forehead pounding in pain as she stood. "I need to check on the kids this morning. Herb and Martha are taking them to their farm for chores this morning."

"I'll turn the shower on for you. We'll get a bite to eat before we go to his room. You will need strength, both physically and emotionally today," Kent softly spoke with kindness.

"I am laying rules down here and now. There will be no more volunteering on your part in this fight against the Left Wings, gangs, or any other group that comes to light for the rest of our lives, Mr. Freeman. My family has sacrificed enough," Cathren commanded.

"Let's talk about this later," Kent told her.

"I am upset, and the more the better. This is enough, and I mean it. No more! We are going to get straightened around, go back home, and let the rest of the world go to hell for all I care." Cathren slammed the bathroom door behind her and was no less calm when she exited the motel room twenty minutes later. She found Stew standing next to his car.

"Cat, I am so sorry I let this happen," Stew apologized.

"Let's get one thing straight, Stew. You did not let anything happen. Seth was dead set on getting in this fight, and if it were not for you and Kent watching after him, he would have already been buried. I could never blame you for this. I am just thankful you were there. You risked your own life for my son. Stew, you are the greatest friend any family could possibly have." Cathren turned to Kent. "I don't feel like having breakfast now. Could we go to the hospital?"

Kent nodded a yes.

"How are you feeling?" Cathren asked upon entering Seth's room.

"I am a little better. Did you buy a newspaper this morning?" he asked his mother.

274

"Kent has one with him in the waiting room. Are you up to reading?" Cathren asked.

"Maybe just an article or two. I want to know what happened yesterday," Seth told her, his face contorted with a twitch of pain. "I heard there were battles all along the river yesterday."

"I guess you went through quite a time from what Kent has read in the paper. I haven't had time to read it yet," Cathren told him. "Susan, how are you doing?"

"Just a little nauseated. Do you mind if I leave now?" she asked Seth.

"I want you to get some rest, and I mean all day. Don't come back until this evening." He smiled to her, but inside his heart was broken as he felt no other could be broken. He could not help but ask over and over in his mind how he would be able to take care of his wife and child. He no longer felt like the man he had grown into the past few years, but a dependent child again. The past twenty-four hours devastated life and haunted his soul. As far as he was concerned, his life was ruined.

Cathren could only feel sympathy and love for her son, but she had already decided from that very moment on she would not let her pity show or treat him differently than prior to the accident. The news of this was one of the hardest things she would ever have to bear. She would rather be the one in the hospital bed, not her child.

"Mr. Billiter," a nurse announced when he walked into the room. "I will be your nurse for the next several hours."

"Are there other people at this hospital with injuries from the same incident I was caught in?" Seth asked.

"A few. Most are in hospitals closer to the northern border of the state. You are one mighty lucky person to have made it through as well as you did," the nurse told him. "You will be up and out of here in no time. With all the medical technology today, you will be able to lead a normal life. You have a long life ahead of you. Don't let this one bad thing ruin it for you and your family. Too many people let one bad thing in their lives ruin the rest. Don't let that happen to you. Just keep praying; God can see you through this and turn something just horrible around into something good. I know you don't believe it this very moment, but just wait and see. Everyone is special regardless of what physical condition they find themselves in. You are a fighter, I can tell, so fight!"

Seth did not pursue the conversation with the nurse. He absorbed what advice was given, but the loss of his limb was still too unbearable to comprehend.

CHAPTER TWENTY-SIX

September nights cooled the Kentucky earth while signs of fall crept in. Once again squash vines of the garden lay yellowed and withered. Horseweeds towered where Cathren and Kent had neglected to mow despite their intentions before Seth's injury. The freezers were nearly full again, and every canning jar available on the farm was sealed and stored with food for the winter months ahead.

Plenty of rain had fallen throughout August encouraging a late planting of fall crops for winter storage. Much of the bumper crop had been dried in a dehydrator in the farm kitchen that in turn was stored in canning jars using oxygen absorbers to extend storage for years ahead.

Once green potato plants were now brown dry stems. The furrowed mounds gave away the tubers' hiding place. Kent wanted to wait a few more days before digging the potatoes and storing them in the root cellar.

Late cabbage was already planted and doing well, along with other hardy crops like kale that would not reach their peak of flavor until a heavy frost. Tender fall lettuce waited to be picked. Greens were planted that favored cool temperatures. Julianna and Andrew's pumpkin patch yielded plenty of jack-o-lanterns for themselves and for selling at the farmers' market in town on Saturdays.

Susan spent the better part of the summer driving Seth to therapy, which had curtailed their preparation for winter. Seth's emotional roller coaster stalled in a deep depression, but was slowly coming around while his desire to live revived. The college he attended the past winter offered him a part-time job performing deskwork. He would have to eventually obtain a degree to support his family.

Susan and Seth talked of moving their mobile home closer to the campus where he was employed instead of commuting such a distance each day. Seth adapted to his new limb and tossed a baseball with Andrew as he became physically able.

"What do you think about driving to Lexington to visit bookstores before winter sets in rather than ordering all of our winter reading online?" Kent asked Cathren. He was already contemplating winter evenings by the woodstove with a good book to read.

Cathren replied, "I would like that since the leaves are changing."

"We could take the kids for a drive to Natural Bridge from there and spend the night at a bed-and-breakfast," Kent told her. "By the way, one of the volunteers from town called this morning."

"What's going on now?" she asked.

"Same old stuff. Don't worry. The most I plan to do is attend the meetings in the area to keep up on the latest unless trouble starts around here. I don't think that's going to happen. Kentucky has done well protecting its lands and people. I think the Left Wings will weaken through the winter. It will pass, just as communism in many countries has. Too many Americans have a taste for freedom. We lost a lot of freedoms in the past to big government. I believe the country has learned a lot, but there is more to learn before it'll be strong again. It'll just have to be strong differently this time. Our freedoms will be won again, but it will cost more lives before it is completely regained."

"I know. I will never regret my decision to bring the children here. It has been good for us, as if

God had intended for us to be here during this time. I see now that all the sorrow we have had to bear these past years has molded us into better people. I am thankful for what we have," she told him.

"I'm curious to see how events will turn since several states have formed their own independent governments and plan to refuse tax payments to the federal government. This demise in the fabric of our society may be a blessing for some regions of the country," Kent reflected.

"Maybe, maybe not. It is scary to think of what is happening. Maybe in the long run there will just be a decentralization of the once powerful federal government. It is quite a shame our country had to learn this lesson the hard way; it came to an abusive federal government, its domination of our rights and confiscation of our hard-earned monies in order to support bloated bureaucracies. Just look at what it has cost our family," Cathren told him. "Do you suppose Kentucky and some of its bordering neighbors will combine and refuse further drain of tax dollars from being sent to Washington down the road?"

"Possibly. When we ran the British out of the country during the American Revolution, King George was soaking the Americans for a small amount compared to what Washington has been soaking us for. I guess they never thought they could get the boot, too. You know this country has always been a great nation. Now it needs straightening around a great deal and with a change of priorities. Maybe it is time for a change as far as who is running things on this continent. Who says the change has to be for the worse? I believe all this trouble these past years has caused much soul-searching on the part of thinking Americans, and this country will become greater than it ever has been. American blood has always been spent for freedom, like Seth's was the day he was injured in that battle on the Ohio. He served his Constitution well. It will work out for the best in the long run. Just wait and see. Smell the free air outside. By God's will, we are still free to come and go, speak, and worship as we please in Kentucky. That is not coincidence, but fate! Time will let our part of the country set the tone for renewal. I am optimistic." Kent spoke with emotion.

CHAPTER TWENTY-SEVEN

"Kent! Stew's on the phone," Cathren told him. "Sharon just delivered baby number four last evening. It's a boy. Finally! Three girls then a boy!"

"Send them my congratulations," Kent told her, exiting the door to feed the livestock and to watch the lane for Andrew and Julianna to get off the bus.

It was hard for him to believe these two little ones were nearly grown. He wanted to finish his chores before Marisa and her new husband stopped in shortly to discuss remodeling a farmhouse that sat on some acreage they recently purchased. Marisa was rarely seen on the farm since she obtained her nursing degree and was working long hours trying to get her household in order before starting a family.

"How's it going in the old neighborhood?" Cathren was curious to know as she went back to her phone conversation.

"Pretty well so far. We still haven't completely unpacked yet. The garage is full of furniture needing to be moved into the house, but that can wait," Stew answered. "When are you going to visit?"

"Oh?" Cathren was surprised by the question. "It has been so many years now. A trip back to Ohio would be hard, with all the memories of what we have been through. I just don't know, Stew."

"I think you will be pleasantly surprised by what you will find when you get here. Give it a thought. The fear of coming back here is worse than the reality, believe me. I have been there and know firsthand," Stew told her.

"I suppose you're right. Kent has wanted to go north to see my old stomping grounds. He thinks it would be good for me, and besides, we are dying to meet that new baby," she answered.

"It is much different here. It just is not the same place we left. Crime is scarce, there is little pollution in the rivers, and the bombed buildings are nearly cleaned up. You will hardly know the place, and most of all you don't have to be afraid here anymore. The regional battles where the Left Wings still aggravate are not affecting us here. Even with the federal government not regaining its full force as before, most of the country is flourishing. Never mind that stuff. Come on up and see for yourself."

"We will discuss it, I promise. Send my love to Sharon and the new baby, will you?" She asked.

"You know I will, Cat. See you soon," he said softly, ending the conversation.

The entire country slowed its fast pace and an inner peace took hold, but not without a price. Several million lay in graveyards, having lost their lives in fighting the war or diseases. Sadly, a few had taken their own lives, unable to cope without the government to take care of them. Others had been unable to face the loss of their fortunes. The strong survived with ever more enthusiasm for the future.

Stew had been able to get into Ohio to do business the past four years. The renewal of the free market system led Stew to be a wealthy man and a legend as a hero who put his life on the line over and over for the welfare of others during the siege of Ohio.

The Shawnee tribal groups purchased tracts of land along the White Water, Great Miami, and Little Miami Rivers and once more became caretakers of the land. Industry thrived, working for a better and cleaner Ohio, while also creating a tourist industry along its riverbanks. Clear creeks and rivers leading into the Ohio and its lakes, once boasted some of the best fishing in the world. They were once more regaining their titles. The woods and forests once again provided the hunter with ample deer, grouse, turkey, and other wildlife to hunt. A new, greater respect for the land and rights of the landowner emerged. The Left Wings, along with all other political power-hungry snakes, were no longer welcome. Leaders in the world came to see how this new group of Americans once again claimed victory through their Constitution.

The Great Miami River was once more navigable by canoe. Visitors from all over the world canoed its waters and traveled its banks on horseback. Europeans flocked to the region for a sight of the new frontier. Suburban chemical lawns of years past now stood converted into stylish gardens of grape arbors, fruit trees, and roses. These very yards lent themselves to being tourist attractions of sorts when tourists looked in wonder at the ingenuity of these Ohio Buckeyes and their independence earned the past few years.

Alternative sources for energy flourished. Energy moguls of the past now had to compete in a different marketplace for public appeal. The populace swore to never fall prey to the blackouts of past years again. Each new invention resulted in lessened dependence on fossil fuels and catapulted its inventor into stardom overnight. Hollywood and sports heroes no longer held that monopoly. Real heroes like Stew and others who were valuable assets to the country now became the people looked upon for advice and leadership.

The small family grocer and hardware store regained its former status in communities. Farmers' markets flourished year round because technological advances in hydroponics and self-heating greenhouses that boasted fresh vegetables in January helped create an income for many thousands of Ohio's people.

Through necessity, the family farm became diverse as never before. Fish hatcheries flourished throughout the region. Hatcheries were needed to restock rivers and creeks in the region for the ever-growing sport fishing industry. Specialty crop farms such as herb farms, organic farms raising organic meats without use of antibiotics or growth hormones, and organic fruit and vegetable farms grew to be profitable on a smaller scale than the mega farms of the past that required massive doses of chemicals that poisoned aquifers across the nation.

Education changed along with everything else. New practices could no longer allow the consolidated messes created prior by the state. Communities no longer tolerated consolidated school districts that sometimes covered up to a hundred square miles in rural areas that ultimately diminished the quality of education. Parents depended on few public funds to educate their children, and those who could not afford to educate their young received vouchers or a tax credit to do so.

Landfills were a thing of the past. Technology created to sort through waste and reclaimed useful trash was widespread. Not even a tennis shoe was discarded. What refuse was termed unusable was burned in high-efficiency incinerators and converted to electricity.

Crime was now dealt with swiftly and with harsh punishment. No longer would a murderer who committed the crime beyond a shadow of doubt be allowed to appeal the courts over and over, but received just punishment swiftly and harshly. Hardened criminals such as child molesters were never let out to prey on children again. Years of litigation and long jail terms for such offenders became a thing of the past, as they were hung publicly for their crimes. Safe streets came with a cost to criminals. Hanging murderers outside courthouses and left for all to see proved to be effective with former street gang members. Habitual lawbreaking decreased substantially because public whippings and other humiliating, harsh punishments deterred youths and adults from risking a life of crime. Cruel as many of the deterrents seemed, they worked, making the streets of cities safe at any hour.

Cathren's stomach churned as Kent drove onto the bridge that crossed the Ohio River. Just a few years ago, she had been positive she could never set foot on Ohio soil again. The political climate, though calmed, still intimidated her. She could not imagine the region as a safe place to live, but Kent insisted they make the trip to see Stew and Sharon's new addition to the family.

Kent told her she needed to face old fears and put them to rest. He had tried to tell her the past was the past, to let go, but occasionally Cathren still experienced nightmares. Marisa and Seth had visited their home state the year before and had assured her that it was safe to come back. Cathren still doubted it could be true.

Stew was finished preparing dinner when the doorbell rang. Sharon rested on the couch after attending to the new infant in the bassinet next to her. Nate, their infant son, slept peacefully after his feeding. Stew crossed the room to answer the door.

"Welcome home," Stew said then hugged Cathren. Kent remained behind her. Cathren's feelings overwhelmed her, and she stood still as a pillar, unable to move. "Well, just don't stand there. Get in here and see my son."

Cathren stood teary eyed, unable to step into her old home for several seconds. The memories and emotions made her light-headed before she regained her composure. "Where is he?" Cathren asked.

"Follow me." He led them to the bassinet. "It is so good to have you visiting. We'll spend tomorrow looking at the changes in the area."

"This is truly the strangest feeling, to be here again." Cathren was visibly nervous.

"We have a room ready for you," Sharon told them.

"We can't do that, we plan to stay at a motel," Kent told them.

"No way!" Stew told them. "You have opened your home to me so many times through the good and the bad. Let me return the favor."

Kent looked to Cathren. At first, she did not know if she would be able to walk into this house with all its memories, but her fears were unfounded.

"Sure. We'll stay," Cathren told them.

"Dinner is simmering," Stew told them. "Let's go for a walk through the neighborhood before it gets too late. Some of your old friends are still here and are looking forward to seeing you."

Kent felt like a puppy on a leash for the next three days while he watched her come to terms with her troubled past. He supported her while they drove from location to location, and finally to where Nate had been gunned down so many years ago.

Evidence of the war was disappearing. A new pride taking hold in the region was obvious to Cathren. Kent began to think Cathren would not want to go back to his beloved Kentucky when she saw it was safe to live in Ohio again. He decided they could live where she wanted.

"Kent, the alarm went off several minutes ago. Didn't you hear it?" Cathren asked.

"No." Kent sat up. "What do you have planned for today?"

"I'm getting homesick. Would it be okay if we left for home today?" She asked.

Kent asked, "Would you like to look for a place to live here again? We have lived near my home all these years. If you want to be here again, that will be no problem on my part."

"No, silly! Our home is where we found each other. This was another life. I don't belong here anymore. I miss our home," she told him.

"That lifts a burden from my shoulders. All these years you have been a refugee, and I know I caught your love on the rebound from all the hurt you experienced here. Sometimes I wondered if we moved too fast into our marriage. I ask myself at times if you had enough time to heal on your own. But now I see that was foolish thinking."

"Oh, Kent. I have no regrets about staying in Kentucky and our marriage. Don't you see? You and Kentucky breathed life back into my very

287

being. There was a blast of a sound in my heart to leave Ohio, a tantara! There hasn't been a day since I left Ohio that I didn't walk out the door in the morning to pick up a handful of Kentucky soil to smell its freedom and hospitality. You and Kentucky harbored me and let me grow into the woman I needed to be. Don't ever forget that, Mr. Freeman."

Kent's eyes were filled with tears of joy.

"Then let us go home," he told her.

Author Catherine Taylor lives on rural acreage in southwest Ohio. She enjoys gardening, writing, camping, hiking, researching her family history and cooking for family and friends.

Cover by thecoverartisan.com

Back cover author photo by Jack Crowe. St. Mary's Glacier, Colorado.

www.ingramcontent.com/pod-product-compliance
Lightning Source LLC
Chambersburg PA
CBHW060522260626
47161CB00003B/733